"DON'T MOVE,"
JIM WHISPERED.

"Just let me look at you for a moment."

Moonlight filtered through the open window, bathing Joanne in its silvery sheen. She lay quietly and watched as Jim's eyes caressed the gentle curves of her naked body. Her breathing quickened beneath his probing gaze, and she shivered.

Slipping off his jacket, Jim draped it over her. "You're getting cold now."

She smiled up at him, her voice thick with desire. "Then you must warm me."

Quickly he shed his clothes and lay beside her, his strong warm flesh sending waves of liquid fire through her.

Joanne closed her eyes. This man was what she'd been yearning for all her life, and now he was here, with her, as close as a man and woman could be. So why could her heart not believe he would stay?

WELCOME TO...

SUPERROMANCES

A sensational series of modern love stories
from Worldwide Library.

Written by masters of the genre, these longer,
sensual and dramatic novels are truly in keeping
with today's changing life-styles. Full of intriguing
conflicts, the heartaches and delights of true love,
SUPERROMANCES are absorbing stories—
satisfying and sophisticated reading that lovers
of romance fiction have long been waiting for.

SUPERROMANCES
Contemporary love stories for the woman of today!

LOVE'S STORMY HEIGHTS

JACQUELINE LOUIS

A SUPERROMANCE FROM
W RLDWIDE

TORONTO · NEW YORK · LONDON · PARIS
AMSTERDAM · STOCKHOLM · HAMBURG
ATHENS · MILAN · TOKYO · SYDNEY

Published October 1983

First printing August 1983

ISBN 0-373-70084-9

Printed in Canada

CHAPTER ONE

He was a tall man, broad shouldered, powerful, and he seemed to dominate the room, not only with his size but with his voice, his grin, his laughter. Joanne Patton stood across the room watching him. She asked herself whether she thought him attractive and decided she didn't. This was clearly a minority opinion. The man she watched was encircled by women who were struggling to get in closer to him, women who gazed at him adoringly as they vied for his attention.

Scottie appeared at her elbow. He had left her a few minutes before in search of drinks and information. He handed her the martini she had asked for.

"I've found out which one our man is." For some reason, instead of speaking out, Scottie leaned close enough to whisper. He motioned toward the tall man surrounded by women whom Joanne had been watching. "That's Bryant over there."

"Yes, I know." Joanne spoke in her normal voice. She dropped her eyes to her drink and took a sip. "I heard someone address him by name while you were gone."

They stood silently for the next few minutes, gazing across at the man they'd come here to meet. They were in the lavish home of Penelope Palmer, who was throwing this party to introduce her close friend James Anthony Bryant to the elite of San Francisco. Joanne's brother Dominic, who had climbed in the Swiss Alps with Bryant and knew him well, had wangled an invitation for them.

Scottie lowered his glass and faced Joanne with a resolute air. "Well, time's a-wasting. Let's walk across now and introduce ourselves."

Joanne felt a momentary quickening of her pulse. Her eyes narrowed on the tall powerful-looking man across the room, then dropped again to her drink. "No, Scottie, I don't want to. At least not yet."

"But, Joanne, honey—"

"Please, Scott, I just don't want to." Why she felt so coldly certain of this, Joanne wasn't sure. But she knew it would take a major earthquake to make her change her mind.

A surprised look flashed through Scottie's blue eyes, but he dropped the subject and said no more.

Relieved to have the matter settled, Joanne glanced around curiously. The large room they were in was crowded with people. Most stood in small groups of three or four, talking and drinking. Penelope Palmer, their hostess, stood near the entry, greeting guests as they arrived.

Joanne sipped her martini, regretting that she had come. She and Scottie had had tickets to a concert that night, and she'd really looked forward to attending. But her brother had phoned that afternoon to tell her that tonight was her best chance to meet James Bryant, and the lure of meeting him had proved too strong. She'd given the concert tickets to a friend, and she and Scottie had come here instead. Now the man she'd been dying to meet stood less than thirty feet away—all she had to do was walk across the room to meet him—and her feet felt like lead. There was no way she could persuade herself to approach him.

After she'd slowly and casually surveyed the room, Joanne felt her eyes irresistibly drawn back to James Bryant. She sipped her drink and over the rim of her glass stared at him. He had short, curly brown hair, which gleamed with a reddish tint in the artificial light. Thick brows curved over heavily lashed dark eyes. His broad face, which was constantly breaking into an infectious amused grin, was sprinkled lightly with freckles. He looked somewhat younger than the thirty-four years she knew him to be. Watching him, Joanne felt a sudden, unexpected shiver run down her spine. She quickly dropped her gaze, again sipping her drink.

It was the last Friday in October. The night before a friend of hers from the Alpine Club had phoned. During the course of their conversation Hope had mentioned that James Anthony Bryant, the millionaire businessman and dedicated mountaineer, was in San Francisco finalizing arrangements for his expedition to climb Dhaulagiri in the Himalayas, the sixth highest peak in the world and one of the most treacherous. The expedition was scheduled to leave for Nepal in February.

The moment Joanne heard this, her pulse had begun to race and she'd scarcely heard another word Hope said. Two years before, when notice of Bryant's planned expedition had first been posted on the board of the Alpine Club, she had immediately sent in an application for a spot on the team. A month later she'd received an acknowledgment of her application with the message that she'd be contacted soon if she was found acceptable. Obviously she had not been found acceptable, since she'd never heard from anyone again. A second application had met the same fate. Now, with the departure date only a few months off, James Bryant, head of the expedition, was here in San Francisco making final arrangements.

"I suppose he has all his climbers?" Joanne asked suddenly, after Hope's conversation had already gone on to something new

"Who?"

"Bryant, on the expedition to Dhaulagiri."

"No, from what I heard he hasn't. He's still one or two short."

That was all it took. Joanne was so excited she couldn't sleep all night, and first thing in the

morning she had phoned her brother Dominic in
Los Angeles.

"Dom, Joanne. You remember James Bryant, of course. Well, he's in San Francisco now
to—"

Dominic broke in, laughing. "Hey, don't say
hello or anything. How are you, anyway? Yes, I
remember James Bryant, and now he's in San
Francisco. Go on."

"Well, he's here to finalize arrangements for
an expedition to Dhaulagiri, and from what I've
heard he's still one or two climbers short. Oh,
Dom, I've got to join that expedition. It's what
I've wanted all my life, you know that. Can't
you please fly up here to see Bryant and do what
you can to get me on?"

Her brother laughed again, not so heartily
this time. "Hey, hold on a minute, Joanne,
please. Yes, I know you've always dreamed of
someday climbing in the Himalayas, but why
not phone Bryant directly instead of coming to
me? If you made application—"

Joanne groaned softly, her fingers tensely
curling the telephone wire. "Dom, I did, two
years ago, the very day I first read of the expedition. When that application was ignored—"

"Maybe it got lost in the mail and was never
received."

Joanne gave a short laugh. "Don't I just wish
it. I received an acknowledgment, so Bryant got
it all right, but as soon as he checked it more
closely and saw that J.M. Patton was female,

that ended that. About ten months later I sent in a second application, again I received an acknowledgment, again that was that. I'm not going to make it without your help, Dom. Please, *please* drop everything and fly up to see what you can do.''

It was her brother's turn to groan. ''Joanne, honey, I wish I could, but I'm absolutely snowed under right now. Besides that, if I tried to intercede for you, it might do you more harm than good. Some people are more flexible than others, more easily influenced. Bryant's a great guy, but in many ways he's about as flexible as a bar of steel. Remember how dad used to run his expeditions? With him, it was democracy in action, each of us had his say-so, and dad automatically delegated as much authority as possible. Well, Bryant doesn't work that way. There are two ways to run things, and Bryant's way is at the other extreme from dad's, completely autocratic. On any team he's organized, he's been the undisputed boss. He organizes and runs things exactly the way he wants it and takes no back talk from anyone. Believe me, Joanne, I know. And when I think of that, it seems to me that you don't even belong on his team. After years of climbing with dad and me, you wouldn't enjoy yourself. You'd be very apt to hate it. So why don't you just forget Bryant and wait for the next expedition?''

Joanne drew in a long deep breath trying to calm herself. ''Because,'' she answered slowly, "there's no telling when the next American expedition will be formed, and time is getting away from me—in another month I'll be twenty-six. Going through college and then law school, I've already let slide all the years I can spare. The moment I read about this expedition, I *knew* it was the one I'd been waiting for all my life, ever since I was twelve and you and dad and the others went to Everest, and dad wouldn't let me go because I was too young. Well, I *was* too young then, but I'm not anymore, and one way or another I'm going to make it onto Bryant's team, either with your help or without it."

"All right, honey," Dom said, "I'll do what I can. I just don't see how I can free myself to fly up, but I'll do my best to make arrangements for you to meet him. Once you have, once you've been exposed to the guy and see what he's like, maybe you'll change your mind and let this one go. There will be others, you know."

Yes, but this is the one I want, Joanne thought. "Thanks, Dom, you're a sweetheart. Let me know how it's going."

"Will do. Talk to you later."

They had said their goodbyes and hung up.

By afternoon Dom had phoned back to tell her about Penelope Palmer's party, being held in honor of Bryant, and had given her instructions as to where to pick up an invitation. Everything had gone smoothly and now here she was, across the room from where James Bryant stood surrounded by fawning adoring women.

Joanne gazed unhappily at him again, wondering why she couldn't work up the nerve to cross the room and meet him.

It wasn't like her to suffer a sudden attack of shyness. She wrinkled her mouth, upset with herself. It wasn't shyness, though; it was.... She couldn't pin down what it was. She knew only that with every moment she stood watching Bryant, she became more sure that she did not wish to meet him. No doubt it was partly what Dom had told her about how autocratic Bryant was. Staring across at him now, Joanne could easily believe every word her brother had said. Despite Bryant's constant grin and deep amused laugh, there was an arrogant gleam in his eyes, a defiant tilt to his head that Joanne didn't like. Quite possibly her brother had been right. Maybe she would hate being part of a team of which Bryant was the head. To give up all thoughts of trying to join his expedition was to turn her back on a very real dream, and it hurt to do this, hurt so much it brought the sting of tears to her eyes, but there it was. No way was she going to walk across the room to meet that man.

Scottie took hold of her elbow. Again he leaned close enough to whisper. "Ready now, honey? Come on, before this place gets even more crowded, let's go over and introduce ourselves."

In a sudden fury, more at herself than at anyone else, Joanne pulled her arm free. "Please, Scottie, I still don't want to!"

Scottie's light blue eyes flashed with an even deeper surprise, but the smile that followed almost at once was genuine. "But, honey, why not? That *is* why we came here, you know."

Fighting down a sudden anxiety that she couldn't understand or control, Joanne answered quickly, "Scottie, please, I just don't want to, that's all."

He released her elbow and straightened up, his smile fading away but his pleasant expression holding no hint of reproach.

Joanne had been keeping fairly steady company with Scott Rowland for more than a year now, and not once in all their months together had she seen him lose his composure or act even momentarily irritated. She'd assumed when they first began dating that in time this facade would slip, and she'd get a glimpse of a less composed person, but in time she had realized that the sweetness and patience were genuine, that Scottie was the most reasonable human being she had ever known. Nothing seemed to annoy or disturb him. In their year of closeness she had grown to admire, respect and trust him, which all seemed to add up to love. Of this last point Joanne was never quite sure. As terribly fond as she was of Scottie, it sometimes seemed to her that something was missing. Scottie had never pressed her for physical intimacy. At the end of their evenings together, when he put his arms around her to kiss her good-night, she enjoyed it, except his embraces always felt more comforting than exciting.

But surely that was the way it should be, she often argued with herself. The last thing she wanted was to become physically infatuated with some man, ruled by her body's chemistry instead of her mind and her heart, and for almost a year now her mind and heart had told her that Scott Rowland was as nearly perfect a man as she was ever likely to find. Still, she didn't seem quite able to silence that childish voice inside that cried out for excitement, that craved a touch that would send chills through her. At this thought Joanne shook her head in annoyance. Women who went chasing after excitement and thrills brought nothing but trouble upon themselves. Any woman lucky enough to have found a man like Scottie would be a complete idiot not to love and cherish him. She certainly wasn't an idiot and she did love and cherish him.

As she finished her drink, Scottie reached for her glass, smiling. "Want another?"

"Yes, thank you." She wished they'd gone to the concert instead of coming here.

He left her side, maneuvering through the crowd. The room rang with speech and laughter, and the air was turning hazy with cigarette smoke. Joanne noticed a door leading out onto a veranda. She'd go outside for a breath of fresh air. Scottie would know to look for her there.

She began pushing her way forward, smiling

at those she passed. She felt overly warm and decidedly unhappy. Ever since Hope's phone call the evening before, she'd felt a tremendous excitement. It hurt now to give that excitement up. But she'd seen enough of James Anthony Bryant to know that she did not wish to put herself under his leadership, did not want to become part of his team.

Suddenly she felt a man's hand on her back, pressing lightly. The touch sent an odd thrill through her. Her eyes lifted and circled around, and she found herself staring up at the man she had just been thinking about. Though his hand pressed her back as he tried to pass her, his eyes weren't on her. They were directed over her shoulder at someone else. Bryant was grinning. He laughed. He started to push on past her, but then, as though abruptly aware that he had touched someone in passing he glanced down and his eyes rested on Joanne's face.

"Hi... sorry," he said in his full deep voice, a voice edged with laughter.

As he spoke, he still didn't seem to see her, then suddenly their eyes met. A riot of feeling rushed through Joanne. She felt tense and cold. Acknowledging his apology with a tight little smile, she moved on by.

Out on the veranda she stood by the waist-high railing, leaning against it, gazing out. She was five feet seven inches tall and slender of build. Despite years of strenuous mountaineering, she was deceptively nonathletic in appearance, her femininity asserting itself in subtle delicate curves. While her skin was very fair, her hair was a deep gleaming black. When she felt unhappy, as she did now, the dark shadows in her violet blue eyes made them appear as black as her hair. The eyes of almost every man lit up with interest on first meeting her, but this interest was usually killed rather quickly by the reserved disinterested coolness in her manner and voice. Joanne was not overly enamoured with men and felt there were other pursuits far more entertaining than indulging in a string of shallow flirtations. So far in her life she had never been seriously in love, though now she was quite sure that she did love Scottie, not in a bell-ringing, earth-moving way but in a mature responsible fashion. She did not intend to marry for several years yet, so whether or not she loved Scottie enough to marry him was not a pressing matter. Her work as a lawyer was of great importance to her, and her avocation, mountain climbing, her deepest passion.

As she stood on the veranda of Penelope Palmer's home, Joanne felt distressed. It was a cool fall night, bright and clear, with a three-quarter moon overhead. She was warmly dressed, and there was no reason for her to feel chilled. Nevertheless Joanne felt cold and she hugged herself. James Bryant had disturbed her. He was the type of man she most disliked. All her life she had been attracted to a far different type of man, quiet, pleasant men like

Scottie. Scott read a lot, wrote poetry, worked as an accountant, contributed both time and money to social causes in which he believed. He wasn't very tall, less than an inch taller than Joanne, and was slender and fair. He had blond hair, light blue eyes and a soft complexion. Joanne tried to concentrate on Scottie and push away the lingering image of big, grinning, extraverted James Bryant, whose hand touching her back had infuriated her, all the while sending that odd thrill through her.

Gazing up at the moon, Joanne suddenly sighed. She had wanted so much to join Bryant's expedition. It hurt now to give up all hope.

"So here you are." Scottie smiled, walking up beside her. He handed her a drink. "Maybe after we finish these, we can go back inside and meet the man we came here to meet."

"Maybe," Joanne agreed, though in her heart she knew better. She would leave this party without ever approaching or speaking to Mr. James Anthony Bryant.

THEY WERE IN THE FOYER, saying good-night to their hostess, thanking her for the lovely time they had had. Joanne had her evening wrap over her shoulders. She had worn a calf-length cocktail dress, a faint-gray-on-black rayon dress she had bought with high hopes earlier that day, right after Dominic's call. The dress flowed beautifully over her slender form. She had drawn her black hair tightly back from her face, hoping this would make her look hard, strong, energetic. Joanne sighed. All for naught. She was leaving without ever approaching Bryant.

"Thank you so much, Mrs. Palmer, for inviting us." Joanne smiled, shaking the woman's hand.

"Call me Penny, for heaven's sake, dear," Penelope said. She laughed. She was a divorcée in her early thirties, heavily made up yet attractive in a hothouse flower way. She squeezed Joanne's hand. "After all, we're all friends here. I've known your brother Dominic for years and simply adore him. I'm so sorry he couldn't make it here himself tonight to renew acquaintance with Jim. But give him my love."

"Thank you, I will."

Scottie took hold of her elbow and they started out. Joanne felt a heavy weight of depression sink through her. I really bombed out, she thought. Had she made a mistake? She hadn't reasoned out her decision not to approach James Bryant; she had simply followed her instincts. Surely it was time, anyway, that she gave up on silly adolescent dreams of climbing mountains and began to deal with the real world, whatever that was, wherever it was. She sighed again.

The butler pulled open the front door for them, solemnly bowing, and they stepped through. She was a slight bit ahead of Scottie. Suddenly a man came striding up from behind, clasped her arm and stopped her progress.

Glancing quickly around, Joanne saw it was the man she hadn't been able to get off her mind all evening, James Bryant.

With an odd little smile, Bryant thrust a card into her hand. "Here, Miss Patton. Call me tomorrow, please."

"But—"

"No buts. Just call me, please." Bryant tossed a polite smile at Scottie and let go of Joanne's arm. With a farewell nod, he said, "Please do as I've asked and phone."

Joanne smiled nervously to acknowledge these parting words, but she was too startled and unsure to indicate whether or not she would comply with the request.

AT ONE THE FOLLOWING AFTERNOON Joanne finally made up her mind: she *would* call. No matter what her reaction to Bryant had been, if she let this opportunity slip by she might never get another. She might live the rest of her life without ever having a second chance to make her most cherished dream come true. It could be years before another American expedition to the Himalayas was organized, and who knew what responsibilities she would have by then. Now she was free and unencumbered. She could easily go—if only she could make it onto the team. Dom had undoubtedly contacted Bryant yesterday, but Bryant must have some interest in signing her on or he wouldn't have insisted she phone.

Joanne sipped down some water, spoke several times to the air to make sure her voice was steady, then dialed. She felt calm and in control.

On the third ring the phone was picked up. A man's voice said, "Hello, James Bryant here."

"This is Joanne Patton. You asked me to call."

"Yes, Miss Patton. Your brother Dom phoned me yesterday and told me of your wish to join the expedition I'm organizing. He told me you'd introduce yourself to me at the party last night, but apparently you preferred not to. It wasn't until you were leaving that I ran across someone who knew you and could point you out to me. I'm sorry about the abrupt way I gave you my card, but you seemed to be in a hurry to leave."

"Yes," Joanne murmured. "I understand and I'm glad you did."

"Well, good. If you're still interested in joining us, when would you like to come over to discuss it? I'll be free around four this afternoon if you'd like to come then."

"Well, I—" Joanne hesitated. She had a three-o'clock appointment with a client referred to her by Ted Myers, in the law firm where she was employed, but she could almost certainly advance it an hour; the man had wanted to come in earlier. "All right, four is fine, thank you. Where shall I come?"

"I'm at the Hilton at Fisherman's Wharf."

He gave her a suite number. "I'll be looking forward to seeing you at four."

"And I you," Joanne murmured, then wondered if she really meant it.

A few hours later she was seated beside Bryant on a sofa in the living room of his suite.

"We'll be flying out of here in mid-February next year," Bryant explained to her. "Over the past two years, since the expedition was first conceived, I've signed up twenty climbers. My thought was that, with the inevitable falloff, I would not go with fewer than sixteen. We had sixteen firm until a couple of weeks ago when circumstances forced two others to drop out, leaving us with only fourteen, two under the minimum originally set. This is why I sent out the emergency call to all the clubs nationwide for a last-minute sign-up. Although we could go with fourteen, I'd rather it be sixteen. Better too many than too few, right?"

Bryant grinned. His grin was so warm and personal it was like a caress, as though he'd reached out to stroke her skin.

Joanne fought down a blush, smiling. "Right. That's why I felt so excited when my friend phoned to tell me of the memo she'd seen. For years I've wanted to go on a climb in the Himalayas more than anything in this world."

Bryant's grin died away. His dark green eyes gazed intently at her for a moment, then he rose. There'd been a knock on the door, and he walked over to answer it. "In that case, why didn't you send in an application?" he asked over his shoulder in his deep pleasant voice.

Joanne laughed. Her excitement of the previous day was back. To have her greatest dream almost within her grasp now—she could hardly believe it. "I did," she answered quickly. "Believe me, I did. Not just one application. When the first was ignored, I sent in a second. And never heard on either one."

"Oh?" Bryant pulled the suite door open and a waiter entered carrying a tray, which he set on a sideboard. Bryant tipped him and he left. "How do you take your coffee?" he asked Joanne.

"Black, please. No sugar."

Bryant poured them each a cup. He walked back, handed Joanne hers, and seated himself. Again his narrow eyes fastened intently on her. "Well, apparently my secretary, who was screening the applications, set yours aside as undeserving of any follow-through."

Joanne sipped the steaming coffee, drew herself inwardly together and raised her eyes to face Bryant directly. "Why?" she asked bluntly. "I'm an experienced climber, I answered every question asked, I sent in the applications with extremely serious intent. So why wasn't I deserving of any follow-through?"

Bryant's gaze met hers without wavering. A smile began pulling on the corners of his lips. He shrugged, then murmured, "You tell me."

Joanne could feel herself stiffen. Bryant was playing with her. His arrogant little smile showed clearly enough that to him this was all just a joke. Why had he asked her here for this discussion when, judging from his smile, he had not the slightest intention of allowing her to join the expedition?

"Well, if I had to hazard a guess," Joanne responded, in a thin tight voice, "I would say it was because your secretary saw that I was a woman and knew you wanted only men."

Bryant's eyes, glittering with sparks of amusement, met hers over the rim of his cup. As he lowered his cup, he said, "I would assume you are right."

"So—had you given her that directive?" Joanne asked. "Men only, women need not apply."

Bryant grinned. He put down his coffee cup on the low table before them and rose. "No, I had not. However, my secretary has been with me for years and knows me pretty well. I did not have to tell her how I felt. She knew how I felt. And that's why there was no follow-through on your application."

Joanne felt a cold fury sweep through her. She leaned forward, slapped her coffee cup down on the table and stood up. "And you still feel that way: men only, women go away."

Bryant was striding across the room. He glanced back to nod at her.

"Then why did you give me your card last

night and ask me to come here?'' she demanded. ''You knew it would be a complete waste of time.''

Bryant picked up a paper from the desk against the far wall. As he swung back around, he smiled across at her, a smile so warm and personal that again Joanne felt it was like a caress, an unwelcome touching. ''Possibly a waste of time for you, Miss Patton, but certainly not for me. I climbed with your brother Dom a few years ago and have always been fond of him. I looked forward to meeting you. When he phoned to suggest we get together, I was delighted. That's why I gave you my card and asked you to phone, in order to have the pleasure of talking with you.''

She could feel despair overwhelm her rising anger. As Bryant walked back to seat himself, she sank back down on the sofa. Picking up her cup, she sipped the coffee.

The hot strong brew rekindled a flicker of hope within her. She faced Bryant directly again, trying to speak as calmly and matter-of-factly as possible, to keep any servile entreaty out of her voice, expression or eyes.

''Look, Mr. Bryant, believe it or not, I can understand your position, even though I feel that such prejudice against women is unfounded. I'd be ready to bet my life that I have at least as much experience as any male climber my age. I started climbing with my father and brother when I was only six, and until my father's death four years ago we spent almost every weekend and every summer vacation climbing.'' Joanne paused momentarily, then dared to add, ''And from the time I started, my father repeatedly claimed that I had a greater flair for it than either he or my brother. He said I had the greatest natural aptitude for climbing of anyone he'd ever seen.''

Bryant's green eyes danced. ''Miss Patton, one of the deep regrets of my life is that I never had the chance to meet your father. He was one of my boyhood idols, and for years my fondest dream was that someday I'd be fortunate enough to climb with him. From that stand-point, I can't tell you how I envy you. How-ever—'' the twinkle in Bryant's eyes became even more pronounced ''—when it comes to his comments on you as a climber, I have to reserve judgment. Men have been known, you know, to be less than fully objective when it comes to their children, especially their daughters. It could be that your father was just a slight bit partial to you.''

Joanne's face burned. She felt so tightly coiled inside she hurt. ''All right, you may be right. But did you ask Dom? Or did your secre-tary, before tossing my applications out, bother to contact any of the references I gave? I'm not the first woman climber, you know. Women have always played an active role in mountain-eering. There have been any number of expert female climbers. In 1975 an all-women expedition from Japan successfully placed a woman, Junko Tabei, on the summit of Mount Everest, one of the few peaks in the world, Mr. Bryant, that I understand you have not yet attained yourself.''

Bryant burst out laughing. ''So why don't you follow their example—form an all-women expedition yourself and have a go at Everest or Dhaulagiri or whatever Himalayan peak most attracts you?''

''Sure, why don't I?'' Joanne responded bitterly. It took years of planning and endless hours of work to mount an expedition. Bryant knew that. Financing had to be arranged, supplies acquired, climbers recruited, permits obtained—it wasn't something easily accomplished. Someday she might do just what Bryant had facetiously suggested, but the last few years, going through college and then law school while working part-time, she hadn't had the time or energy to devote to such an enterprise. Now that she'd passed the bar and gone to work for Coghill and Myers, she still had very little extra time. It might easily be several years before she could seriously consider the possibility. Meanwhile, why should she be shut entirely out of climbing? She could take a few months off next spring. Why shouldn't she have the same break that male climbers had and be allowed to join an expedition that someone else had organized? Bryant needed two additional climbers. Why couldn't she be one?

Bryant picked up the sheet of green paper he had brought back from the desk across the room and handed it to her, smiling. "Possibly this will interest you, Joanne." It was the first time he'd called her by her first name. "It's notice of an all-women team being formed for a summer of Alpine climbing next year."

"Thank you, I've seen it," Joanne answered coolly.

"And you're not interested?"

"No, I'm not." As she saw the instant, satiric gleam light up Bryant's eyes, she went on to explain, "For three consecutive summers when I was in high school, when my brother was in college and working and not free to join us, my father and I climbed everywhere through the Alps. I loved every minute of it, but now I want to go on to something else. I want to fulfill my dream of climbing in the Himalayas." Joanne put her coffee cup down, steeled herself and turned to gaze directly, steadily at her host. "So will you allow me to join your team of climbers?"

Bryant's narrow, dark green eyes gazed steadily back at her. He shook his head. "I'm sorry, Joanne, but no."

"For any reason apart from the fact I'm a woman?"

This brought a smile of amusement to Bryant's face, its warmth once again reaching out to envelop Joanne. "Isn't that reason enough?" he countered softly. "I'm not about to risk the life or limbs of such a lovely young woman on a mountain as treacherous as Dhaulagiri, the Mountain of Storms.''

Joanne felt a sharp pain run down her right arm, she was holding herself so tensely. Her violet blue eyes reflected scorn. ''Yet you'll sign up male climbers and risk injury to them.''

Bryant shrugged. Although his smile had died away, a warm glow still suffused his face. ''Men are expendable. Beautiful young women aren't. For the life of me I can't even imagine why you want to go.''

It took all the energy Joanne could gather to stay seated and continue the calm rational discussion they were having. ''Why can't I have the same motivation men have? I want to climb the highest mountains there are simply because they are there.''

Shaking his head, Bryant broke into a soft, sad little laugh. As he rose to his feet, Joanne stood up, too. ''There's no way I can get you to change your mind?'' she asked.

He picked up the green sheet Joanne had put on the coffee table and walked across the room to replace it on the desk top. He shook his head as he walked, then muttered, ''No, no way.''

Joanne watched him as he moved. She wanted to feel angry, and did, but to her distress she also felt suddenly close to tears. She watched Bryant swing around from the desk and walk back toward her through a hot stinging mist. He came to a stop a few feet from her, his beautifully set narrow eyes gazing thoughtfully at her. Joanne hurriedly blinked her tears back and pulled herself tautly up to her full height. Shoulders back, chin up, she stared imperiously across at him.

"Well, it's abundantly clear I wasted my time coming here. You had your mind made up before I ever arrived. Obviously this is all just a big joke to you. That being the case, I'll say goodbye and leave now." She thrust out her hand.

Instead of looking chastised, Bryant laughed softly. His broad, lightly freckled face broke into another warm grin, his curly, reddish brown hair gleaming in the afternoon light. He stepped closer and took the hand she held out in both of his. Joanne felt an immediate, unwelcome shiver of pleasure at the strength and warmth of his two hands holding hers. Her eyes glared defiantly at him, denying the enjoyment she felt at his touch.

"It may seem a waste of time to you, but I've enjoyed every minute of it." Bryant's dark green eyes gazed intently into hers. "If you'd get over this foolish notion that there's something romantic about freezing one's tail off scrambling up forbidding walls of ice and snow, we could part friends."

Joanne snatched her hand back in immediate fury. "If it's such a foolish notion, why have you spent years organizing this team so that you can do it?"

When he didn't answer apart from a shrug, Joanne hurried on, suddenly feeling compelled to explain, aching to grab onto one more chance to change his mind.

"To me there's nothing foolish at all about climbing, Mr. Bryant. I love it. The happiest moment of my life happened five years ago, the year before my father fell ill, the last time he and my brother and I went climbing together. We were climbing in the Andes, near the Chile-Argentina border, where there are numerous unscaled peaks, where legend says it takes a sturdy man to survive. A few days after we got there, we struck out from our base camp to challenge a peak that the maps said had never been scaled. After an exhausting struggle, as we neared the summit, my father climbed down past me and insisted I lead. As far as we could discover, I was the first person in the world ever to stand on top of that peak. I can't tell you what a marvelous feeling it was. As exhausted as I was, I almost burst with happiness."

"Congratulations," Bryant said. "I'm impressed. But with an achievement like that behind you, one that is bound to make at least a footnote in mountaineering history, why don't you quit now and rest on your laurels? What else makes sense?"

Joanne had been momentarily lost in the past, but as Bryant said this, she snapped back to the present. She was furious. If he truly believed what he was saying he'd quit mountaineering himself. Why should she be expected to turn her back on climbing when he was still going at it with no hint that he was about to retire to rest on *his* laurels? Seething with anger, Joanne stepped past him, eager to leave.

"Climbing is in my blood, Mr. Bryant, just as it is in yours, I'm sure. I'm like my father—I'll be planning another expedition even as I lie on my deathbed. Obviously we have nothing more to say. Goodbye, Mr. Bryant."

She walked rapidly toward the door, shoulders back, head high. She could feel Bryant swing into step behind, could hear his quick stride following hers. He sped up his steps, reached the door as she did and reached around her to pull it open. After she stepped out into the hall, Joanne glanced angrily around, only to feel a sudden becalming of her heart at the thoughtful expression on Bryant's face.

His expression—sober, thoughtful, almost soft—sent a wild new hope spiraling through her. Her anger melted instantly away. Trying desperately to keep any hint of reproach out of her voice, she asked, "Mr. Bryant, please, in consideration of the fact that I did as you asked, phoned and came over, and also because you do know and are friends with my brother, won't you at least level with me and tell me straight out in unambiguous terms, why you won't sign me on? In all truth, I know I'm a good enough climber, stronger than I look, tough and experienced. When you wouldn't even check out my references, it must have been something more than doubt about my endurance or skills. Won't you please tell me what it is? Surely I'm entitled to a little honesty at least, if nothing else.''

Bryant's dark green eyes, sober and thoughtful, met Joanne's. His gaze slowly drew away and traveled down her face, over her slender form, then slowly rose again. There was nothing flirtatious or suggestive in his slow thoughtful appraisal of her. At last his eyes returned to meet hers.

''There is always some question about any climber's skill and endurance.'' Bryant spoke softly, but there was a steely edge to his voice. ''Mine or anyone else's, but especially when it comes to a rather slender, almost frail-looking young woman. However, as you say, it wasn't only that. One reason I wanted to talk to you today was to get a better idea of what you look like, how attractive you are. Last night I got only a swift first impression, but unfortunately that impression held up today, two- or three-fold. You are an exceptionally beautiful young woman, Miss Patton, as I'm sure you're aware, and that works against you. Add an enticing young woman to a team of more than a dozen men and that adds up to only two things: tension and trouble. An even more serious consideration is that I know most of the men who've signed with me, and at least three of them would quit me on the spot if word got out that I'd signed a woman. That may be unfair—I'll even admit it is unfair—but there it is. I have to deal with reality, Miss Patton, and the reality is that the world is still full of men who believe women have no place scaling a rugged mountainside. I'm sorry, but there it is.''

Joanne felt herself tremble. She didn't doubt that Bryant had at last told her the truth, and how the truth hurt! Tears stung her eyes, and she frantically blinked them back. There was obviously no point in staying. She held out her hand.

"Well, thank you, Mr. Bryant, for your time and trouble and for—especially for leveling with me." As her voice died away, Joanne unconsciously thrust up her chin, regaining complete control. No more trembling, no more tears. Later, when she was home and alone, she'd deal more fully with the disappointment and the hurt.

Bryant took the hand she offered, then he brought up his other hand to enfold hers in both of his. He gazed even more thoughtfully at her. "However, there is one condition on which I might sign you on," Bryant murmured softly after a moment, almost as though speaking to himself, his eyes wandering off.

Joanne's heart soared so swiftly it almost burst. Her mouth went dry. "And what condition is that?"

His eyes circled around to catch on her face. Frowning, he said, "Preliminary plans call for a base camp to be established at nineteen thousand, three hundred feet. If it was agreed that once we'd arrived there and set up camp, you would remain in the base camp supervising supplies, handling logistical details, etc., because of my friendship for Dom and my desire to accommodate you, I'd be willing to risk the flak and sign you onto the team on those terms.''

"Well—'' Joanne's heart pounded wildly. Her mind raced, too, thoughts tumbling frantically over one another. If she was forced to abide by these terms, Bryant's offer didn't interest her at all. If she was stuck in the base camp while the other climbers took off to assault the summit, she would die of frustration. At the same time, if she accepted the offer, she would at least have a fingernail hold on the expedition. Other climbers might become ill or be injured. She might be able to work on Bryant, get him to change his mind. Wasn't a fragile hold better than no hold at all? "Well, I—''

"Never mind,'' Bryant broke in, his voice brusque for the very first time, "I withdraw the offer.''

Joanne's eyes flashed. "But—''

"No buts. The offer is withdrawn.'' The corners of his lips curled in scorn. "I could tell from your expression exactly what was going on in your head, and I'm not about to sign on someone determined ahead of time to break the agreement she'd made, someone whose entire thrust would be to undermine my authority. At quite a risk of trouble to myself, I was ready to do you a favor, put my head on the block for you, and all you could think of was how fast you might be able to chop it off. That kind of grateful associate I don't need. It was a pleasure meeting you, Miss Patton. You can tell your brother I'm glad he phoned to suggest this discussion, but now that we've covered everything I won't detain you any longer. Good day, Miss Patton.''

With a curt nod, James Bryant stepped back into his suite and closed the door.

CHAPTER TWO

JOANNE TOOK A DEEP BREATH and completed the dialing. As she listened to the rings, she forced herself to continue breathing slowly and deeply. On the fourth ring the receiver was lifted.

"James Bryant here."

"Mr. Bryant, this is Joanne Patton." It was Tuesday, three days after their Saturday meeting. "How are you?"

There was a slight pause before his deep voice said, "I'm fine, Miss Patton. And you?"

"Fine, thank you. The reason I'm phoning— something has come up, and I wondered if I could make an appointment to see you again?"

"For what purpose, Miss Patton?"

Joanne's throat felt so dry she reached for the glass of water on her desk and quickly downed some. It was a little after four in the afternoon and she was phoning, from her cubicle office at work. "Because of what I've said...something has come up. I'd really appreciate it if you'd see me again."

There was an even more marked pause this time before Bryant responded. "As much as I'd enjoy seeing you, Miss Patton, I'm an extremely busy man these days, as I'm sure you can understand, so I doubt if I could schedule you in. However, I have a few minutes right now if you'd care to tell me what it is that's come up.''

Joanne's hand tightened on the receiver. She'd been afraid of this and really did not want to discuss the matter with him over the phone. But better over the phone than not at all. She took another quick sip of water and plunged in.

"Well, as you possibly know, Mr. Bryant, I'm a lawyer, currently associated with the firm of Coghill and Myers here in San Francisco, and yesterday afternoon I happened to get into a discussion with Ted—Mr. Myers—about my very strong wish to join your expedition. He reminded me that it is now against the law to discriminate in employment on the basis of race, color, religion, national origin or sex. Any private employer who employs fifteen or more persons—"

"So I have only fourteen climbers, and that number includes myself," Bryant said impatiently. "Miss Patton, forget it. This call has no other importance than nuisance value, and if that's all you have to say, I'll hang up now."

"No, wait, Mr. Bryant, please." Again Joanne reached for her glass and hastily took a swallow of water. "I did not phone simply to annoy you, I give you my word. What I'm saying has validity, Mr. Bryant, whether you wish to acknowledge it or not. I know you have only fourteen climbers at present, but I also happen to know you are trying very hard to line up two more. That would put your number at over fifteen."

"Fifteen *volunteers*, Miss Patton, not employees. And tell me where the law stipulates that a man can't choose freely his companions on a vacation outing. You're barking up the wrong tree and I suggest you forget it."

"And I suggest you listen to me," Joanne answered curtly, her anger rising. "Ted—Mr. Myers—has been a successful and prominent attorney for twenty years and knows the law inside and out. I told him exactly what the situation was, and he sees several angles that excite him, for we would admittedly be pushing the application of the law into new frontiers. Consider this, Mr. Bryant. As president of your own firm, Bryant Tools, you have held two parallel positions for the last few years: on the one hand, you managed your company, on the other hand you organized this expedition."

"In my spare time, I assure you," Bryant snapped. "And how I use my spare time is no one's business but my own."

"While your secretary, according to your own admission, screened applications and responded to them?" Joanne said, her heart pounding so hard by now, so excitedly, that she felt faint. "With your secretary so actively involved, that brings in the legal question as to whether the discrimination laws don't apply here to you in your position as president of Bryant Tools, where you employ not just a handful of people but thousands. In addition—"

"Enough of this bull!" Bryant cut in, his deep voice cold with fury. "I've heard that women were petty and vindictive, but this is too much. Good day, Miss Patton."

"Just one more thing," Joanne said hurriedly, trying to avert his hanging up, "one more angle you ought to consider. One of the sponsors of your expedition happens to be a tax-exempt foundation, and for a nonprofit tax-exempt foundation to underwrite expenses for a project in which open sexual discrimination is being practiced makes for several interesting legal questions. For example—"

"So sue me!" Bryant said, and slammed his phone down.

Joanne felt embarrassed as she found herself holding a dead receiver. Her heart still raced, she felt excited, but she didn't feel proud of herself. Was she valiantly attempting to tear down barriers unfairly erected against women, or thwarted in her desire to participate in a challenging climb, was she simply being petty and vindictive, as Bryant had claimed? A little of both, she had to admit, weighted on the side of personal frustration. But Ted Myers had been immediately intrigued, anxious to study the ramifications of Bryant's prejudicial hiring policies, with the thought that possibly they could undertake legal action that would push nondiscriminatory law into virgin territory. The thought of initiating such a drastic step against James Bryant was not an appealing prospect to Joanne, but she couldn't turn her back on her dream. If she did, she knew she would regret it for the rest of her life. Pushing back her chair, she stood up to go and talk to Ted again.

"MR. BRYANT WILL SEE YOU now."

"Thank you." Joanne set aside the magazine she'd been reading, rose to her feet and crossed over to step through the open door. She had flown to Seattle and come to the home offices of the Bryant Tool Company at Ted Myers's urging. When she'd phoned from her hotel room and asked for an appointment with the head of the personnel department, she'd been taken aback to be told that Sidney Bryant would see her that morning. Sidney must be a relative of James's, she reasoned, but how close? Father? Brother? Cousin? She wished that the man's name had been Smith or Johnson instead.

As she stepped into Sidney Bryant's office, Joanne walked with an easy stride that would not betray her nervousness. The office she entered was spacious and expensively but not lavishly furnished. As the man seated behind the large executive desk rose to greet her, Joanne felt a slight, unnerving shock. The resemblance between James and this man was marked. Sidney too was a tall broad-shouldered man, with a lightly freckled, pleasant face. But Joanne, walking forward to meet him with a self-conscious smile, couldn't decide what age he was. He looked rather old to be James Bryant's brother, yet she wasn't sure he was old enough to be his father.

"Good day, Miss Patton. Have a seat please." Sidney Bryant motioned her toward a chair in front of his desk, smiling. As he seated himself, he asked, "To what do I owe this pleasure?"

Joanne smiled back. She was glad she'd decided to dress as she had, in a conservative, light gray suit, yet the instant gleam in the older man's eyes made her feel pretty despite the severity of her clothes. She said, smiling, "I'm afraid you won't think it much of a pleasure once you know why I'm here."

The man's narrow green eyes, so like the younger Bryant's, began to twinkle a little less brightly, though he held easily onto his smile. "I'm sure that no matter how unwelcome the message, I'll still enjoy having met the messenger," he remarked gallantly.

Joanne's smile broadened. What an attractive charming man he was! An odd feeling zigzagged through her, a sudden awareness that if she hadn't met James Bryant under such inauspicious circumstances, if he hadn't had such an obvious, frightening power to smash her dreams, she would have found him handsome and charming, too.

"Mr. Bryant, just a few days ago, in San Francisco, I had the opportunity to meet and talk with the head of this firm, James Bryant, and you two share a very marked resemblance, which makes me wonder—"

"I'm his uncle," Sidney said, leaning back in his chair, smiling with even greater friendliness. "I'm Jim's father's ne'er-do-well younger brother. So you talked with Jim just a few days ago, did you? Has that perchance anything to do with your visit here today?"

Joanne briefly outlined what had happened: Bryant had refused to consider her for a position on his team, and the refusal had been based solely on her sex. "He did not dissemble on this in the least," she said firmly. "When I asked him if the reason was because I was female, his response was, and I quote: 'Isn't that reason enough?' A very clear-cut case of sexual discrimination."

Sidney's attractive face was no longer smiling. He sat with his hands clasped together under his chin, a thoughtful look in his eyes. He did not seem to feel threatened; rather he appeared more interested than angry. "So?" he prodded Joanne as momentarily she said nothing more.

Joanne leaned slightly forward, feeling a spurt of triumph. At least Sidney Bryant, unlike his stubborn nephew, knew enough to pay attention, knew that he couldn't do away with all problems simply by refusing to listen. "Well, Mr. Bryant, as I'm sure you know, the amended Civil Rights Act makes such sexual discrimination illegal. When I mentioned this to your nephew, he quickly dismissed my comments, claiming that this was not an employment situation and therefore the law didn't apply. But Mr. Theodore Myers, a respected San Francisco attorney with whom I am associated, took a far different view. We've learned that the Himalayan expedition under question is being financed principally by the Grey Foundation and—"

"Jim's putting up about thirty percent of the money out of his own pocket," Sidney threw in. He spoke in an informative tone, not an argumentative one, as his face was gripped in an ever more thoughtful frown.

"Right," Joanne agreed quickly. "When we phoned the Grey Foundation and spoke with the man most familiar with this, that's what we were told. But it also became clear, according to the figures we were given, that the foundation is putting up about a third, or thirty-three percent of the money, which means the foundation becomes the principal employer. Now the foundation has a regular paid staff of over twenty people, which means they fall under the jurisdiction of Title VII of the amended Civil Rights Act. In effect your nephew becomes an employee of theirs, and the foundation itself could be considered guilty of illegal discrimination through James, and for this reason we are in the process of seeking an injunction to prevent the foundation from going through with its plans to finance the expedition until a court hearing can determine whether the discrimination that is occurring is in effect illegal. Such an injunction, if successfully obtained, might cause problems with the foundation's tax-exempt status. This is what I've come here to discuss with you.''

As she finished, Joanne leaned back in her chair again, feeling suddenly exhausted. She had scarcely slept the night before and had caught an early flight that morning. The strain seemed to be catching up with her abruptly. Where moments before she had felt triumphant, now she felt deep stirrings of embarrassment tinged with shame. She wished she could excuse herself and go phone Ted Myers.

Ted had surprised her by taking such a strong interest in all of this. She knew it was partly because he was very fond of her, but it was also because to him it presented an interesting legal problem. Ted seemed to savor this simply as a delightful puzzle, though of course he did want Joanne to get on the team, too. Thinking of this, Joanne felt not only tired but thoroughly dispirited; there was a sudden rotten taste in her mouth. If going on a Himalayan climb weren't the deepest, most compelling dream of her life, she wouldn't be here now.

Sidney Bryant sat silently watching her for several moments, and then he asked, in the same soft reasonable voice with which he had addressed her earlier, ''All right, so the alternative is? Obviously you had some alternative to this course of action in mind or you wouldn't have come here to discuss it. You want my nephew to be forced to rescind his decision and allow you to join the expedition, is that it?''

Hearing it phrased so badly, Joanne felt her cheeks warm. She could understand the pride and reticence that caused so many people discriminated against from fighting back, forcing their way into where they weren't wanted. She fought against her blush, reminding herself that *she* wasn't the one in the wrong, James Bryant was.

Thrusting her chin up, Joanne said, in as calm and full a voice as she could manage, ''Yes, that's what I want. If I'm signed up to join the expedition, an opportunity I'm fully qualified for, then we will of course drop any notion of taking legal action. We seek no redress other than the nullification of the discriminatory action taken.''

''Of course.'' Sidney Bryant rose, sporting the civil smile of a gentleman. He glanced at the watch he wore. ''It's almost twelve now, Miss Patton, and I wonder if you could give me until two this afternoon to check this out? We have a cafeteria in the building if you'd care to go have lunch. How would that suit you?''

Tired and worried, Joanne rose. She felt her knees tremble but did her best to mask her nervous state. She had followed Ted Myers's instructions to the letter but wouldn't know until two whether or not she had won. She would go have lunch, phone Ted and return at the specified time.

"Thank you, Mr. Bryant. You've been most courteous, which I deeply appreciate. I'll see you at two."

IT WAS A FEW MINUTES AFTER TWO that afternoon when Sidney Bryant appeared in the open doorway of his office and waved for Joanne, who sat in the outer office, to come in. The young secretary who had been there that morning was nowhere in sight. No doubt she was still at lunch.

"Come in, Miss Patton, please." Sidney Bryant's broad face looked gray and strained, but his voice and manner were not unfriendly. After Joanne entered the office, he added, "I've talked to Jim a couple of times since our little chat this morning. He's on the phone right now and wishes to speak to you." He escorted her to the desk and handed her the phone.

Joanne was furious at herself for feeling so shaky. As she spoke into the receiver, she did her best to keep her voice steady. "Yes, Mr. Bryant? This is Miss Patton."

The deep voice that came stabbing over the wire was icy with anger. "All right, Miss Patton, it seems you've won. I've been forced to take you, regardless of my feelings in the matter, but I just want to tell you this. I'll wring you out of the operation and toss you aside before we ever get higher than the base camp. Mark my words, you can count on them. Good day, Miss Patton." The phone was slammed down in her ear.

As her trembling hand lowered the receiver, Joanne noticed that Sidney Bryant stood less than two feet away. He was gazing steadily at her, a compassionate look in his eyes. "Congratulations, Miss Patton," he murmured. "Let's hope you don't live to regret your victory."

"Thank you. I hope not." Joanne managed to turn herself around and begin the long walk out of the office. At the door she glanced back. "Thank you again, Mr. Bryant. You've been very kind." Tears flooded her eyes, and she wanted to say something more but couldn't think what. After a goodbye wave, she turned and stepped through the open door. So she'd won. But how high a price would she have to pay?

SCOTTIE PICKED HER UP at the airport when she flew back from Seattle early the following morning. When she told him that her stratagem had worked and she was now a member of the expedition, his face broke into a broad smile.

"Darling, I'm so pleased. I know how happy you must be." He reached across and gave her hand an affectionate squeeze.

"Yes, thank you, I am," Joanne murmured, wishing she felt half as happy for herself as Scottie seemed to be. The truth was she didn't feel happy at all; she felt tired and worried. As Scottie straightened up behind the wheel again, still smiling delightedly, Joanne studied his profile. Scottie claimed to love her. He had asked her several times to marry him, yet he seemed genuinely pleased at her news. If he really, truly loved her—loved her with any depth of passion at all—wouldn't he object at least a little to her success at becoming part of Bryant's Himalayan expedition? She'd be leaving the country for several months and would be exposing herself to a considerable amount of risk. She would also be the only woman climber on a fifteen- or sixteen-member team. Didn't any of that worry Scottie?

"I'll be gone about four months, you know," Joanne murmured. "Think you'll miss me?"

Scottie's eyes flew around in surprise. "Why, of course I'll miss you. You know I will. But I know how much this means to you, and it would be the height of selfishness if I tried to intervene or to throw any kind of damper on your plans. What kind of a chauvinist pig do you take me for?" He gave her hand another gentle squeeze.

Joanne tensed, feeling instantly annoyed with herself that she did. What a foul mood she was in! She leaned back against the car seat, closing her eyes. *Couldn't you be selfish just once in your life, Scottie,* she thought rather irritably. Suddenly she visualized an entirely different scene: Scottie swinging the car off the road, slamming to a stop, grabbing her into his arms and ordering her to stop this foolishness and stay home where she belonged, here with him. Then he would hold her even closer and begin pressing passionate kisses all over her face and throat until she began to tremble and thrill to his caresses as she had never done before. He wouldn't ask her not to go, he would tell her in no uncertain terms that she couldn't go, and as he held her and passionately kissed her, she would know that the last thing she wanted to do was leave. All she wanted from life was to be held forever in his arms while his fierce, hot, demanding kisses sent fiery thrills racing wildly through her.

Thinking this, Joanne felt the corners of her mouth curl into a smile, and she began to feel a little less tired and snappish. Crazy thought. Scottie would never act that way, and if he tried—if he ever so lost control that he tried, which he never would—she wouldn't put up with it. It was childish of her not to be entirely pleased and grateful at the friendly accepting way he'd reacted. Still, the scene with the passionate lover telling her she couldn't go lingered in her mind.... But no, that wasn't the kind of lover she wanted. She would resent having any man tell her what she could or could not do, and no sensible woman wanted to be dominated by her body, either. She preferred to stay firmly, calmly in control, Joanne reminded herself, and immediately she felt happier.

IT WAS FRIDAY, the day after her early-morning return from Seattle. She had spent the morning in court, and when she got back to the office

after lunch, Ellie, the receptionist, told her that
Mr. Coghill wished to see her. This caused a
slight tension in Joanne but nothing serious. She
had started to work part-time for Coghill and
Myers during her second year of law school and
had worked there ever since. She felt liked, appreciated and secure in her job. During her time
there, she had worked almost exclusively with
Ted Myers, a man she admired. She rarely saw
or talked with Leonard Coghill, though of
course they knew each other by sight, and he
always greeted her in friendly fashion.

There could scarcely have been two men more
dissimilar than Ted Myers and Leonard Coghill.
Where Ted was short, bright, energetic, driven
by intellectual curiosity, a passionate active
liberal, Leonard Coghill was tall, heavyset,
paunchy, slow and ponderous in thought and
speech, an ultraconservative. Though he was the
same age as Ted, midforties, he looked a genera-
tion older. Joanne hadn't seen enough of him to
like or dislike him, though from the beginning
she'd been delighted that it was Ted she worked
with and not Leonard. To be summoned to his
office was such an unheard-of occurrence that
she couldn't keep from feeling slightly nervous.
She'd been in Leonard's office only twice before,
when she'd been interviewed by him before being
hired, and when he'd called her in to congratulate her after she'd passed the bar and become a
full-fledged associate. She couldn't imagine
what Leonard wanted with her now.

The door to his office stood open, so she walked in. Leonard sat behind his massive desk. A man was seated in a chair opposite him. The visitor rose and swung around, and Joanne saw in shock that it was James Bryant.

She had forgotten how big he was, how tall, broad shouldered and physically powerful. She had also forgotten the reddish tint of his curly brown hair and the way his eyes lit up when he smiled. At the sight of him her heart all but stopped.

"Oh, Joanne, I'm glad you're back," Leonard said. He waved toward his visitor. "Mr. Bryant dropped by to see you, and when he found you hadn't returned from lunch yet, I invited him in to chat with me. He tells me you're now formally a member of his expedition to the Himalayas next spring."

"Y—yes," Joanne stuttered, her throat almost too dry to speak. Her heart was now racing wildly. Bryant stood watching her, smiling, as she walked unsteadily forward. When she was within a few feet of him, she could see that his smile held more derision than friendliness. There was a deep cold fury in his narrow green eyes.

"Hello, Joanne. It's pleasant seeing you again."

"Thank you, Mr. Bryant." After a slight hesitation she put out her hand. As Bryant took it, his eyes fastened intently on hers. Joanne felt her knees go weak. "This is a surprise," she added, in a voice that to her ears didn't sound quite steady.

"I thought it would be." Bryant gave her hand a hard squeeze, then dropped it.

Leonard Coghill leaned his heavy body across his desk and thrust out his own hand. "Well, it's been a very great pleasure meeting and talking with you, Mr. Bryant."

After the two men shook hands, Leonard straightened up again, his thin lips parting in a smile. "Well, you be good to our girl, hear? Make sure you return her in one piece. I'm not too happy to know she's going, but then she's been working hard for us and deserves the time off." He rocked back on his heels, crossing his hands over his paunch. "This is a very bright young woman, Mr. Bryant. She has a brilliant career in front of her, an outstanding career, so don't let anything happen to her. But I know you won't. Now run along, run along. I know you must have a million things to discuss. Again, it was my pleasure meeting you, Mr. Bryant, and I'll be talking with you again soon, Joanne."

"Yes. Thank you." As Joanne turned around to leave, she was acutely aware of Bryant's powerful presence at her side. After they'd left Leonard's office and were walking down the hall, she glanced around and said, "Well—you wanted to talk to me, Mr. Bryant? What about?"

Bryant's eyes flashed with satiric amusement. "You can't even guess, Miss Patton? That doesn't seem to fit in with Mr. Coghill's description of you as a very bright young woman.''

Joanne's cheeks flushed with embarrassment. She said no more. At the end of the hall she led the way into her small cramped cubicle. She stepped in behind her desk and motioned for Bryant to seat himself on one of the two chairs in front of it.

"Very spacious indeed," Bryant remarked dryly, glancing around the crowded area. Bookcases lined two walls. The large scratched desk, half buried beneath stacked papers, briefs, books and baskets, took up more than half the floor space, leaving room for little else.

"Yes, it is very small," Joanne conceded. "There's a larger room down the hall, nicely furnished, which I use when I have clients in. If you'd rather go there—"

She left the sentence hanging and eyed the man standing in front of her desk. During the last few moments she had regained her composure and no longer felt threatened. Bryant didn't like what she'd done, but there was no going back now. Instead she must steel herself for the fact that he would try to make her as uncomfortable as possible. Only time would tell whether he could make good on his threat to wring her out of the operation and cast her aside.

"This is fine," Bryant said. Instead of seating himself, he walked over to the outside wall and stood for a moment gazing out the window down at the parking lot below. Joanne watched with renewed nervousness and mounting irritation. After a minute she'd had enough.

"Look, Mr. Bryant," she remarked in annoyance, "I'm a very busy woman and if you have something to say to me, please say it. Otherwise I'd appreciate it if you'd do your sight-seeing elsewhere. I really must get back to work."

He ignored her for a moment, then swung around, gazing intently at her. "What would your esteemed employer Mr. Coghill think if he knew how you'd manipulated your way into the trip?" he asked bluntly.

Joanne blinked, then answered truthfully, "He wouldn't like it. At best he would feel it was presumptuous and unbecoming of me... 'unladylike.' At worst he would feel my behavior was unethical."

Bryant's lips curled disdainfully. "He wouldn't approve of the way you used legal blackmail to get your way?"

Joanne felt her arm muscles twitch with tension, but she kept her expression coolly under control as she returned Bryant's gaze. "No, he wouldn't."

"And if I were to tell him—?"

"Go ahead."

"You're not afraid it might cost you your job?"

In dismay, Joanne became aware of a stinging mist in her eyes. Not trusting herself to speak right then, she shrugged in answer.

"You don't care?" Bryant's tone was scornful. "You don't mind being fired for a cause, don't mind having the sticker, 'unethical lawyer,' slapped on your brow?"

To Joanne's relief, her eyes cleared, and she felt able once more to use her voice. She rose to her feet, calm and in control.

"Look, Mr. Bryant, you asked me if I might lose my job, and I'm honest enough to admit that yes, I might. That does not make what I did unethical, nor did I indulge in blackmail. Let me remind you that you were the one who would be breaking the law, not I. I merely went to your home office to discuss the situation with your personnel manager, who I knew would be more familiar with the antidiscrimination laws than you are. I had the full backing of Ted Myers, who is also my employer. In fact, it was Ted who, for the most part, planned the strategy I used. Therefore I quite possibly would not suffer even a reprimand were you to go to Mr. Coghill and lodge your complaint. Ted Myers, whom I admire and respect, was behind me all the way. Leonard Coghill I don't really know. He and Mr. Myers are often at odds, and this is one of the things about which they would be in total disagreement. As to which one would carry the day, whether I'd be fired or not, I can't truthfully say. But if you wish to go complain to Mr. Coghill, go ahead. In any case, please be so kind as to leave my office so I can get back to work."

Out of breath, emotionally spent, Joanne dropped back into her chair, lowered her eyes and pulled a brief over in front of her. Her fingers trembled as she did so. Once again her eyes seemed misted. In a fury at herself, at the bullying man standing over by the window, at life itself, Joanne opened the brief on her desk and stared down at it, trying to see the words, trying to get her mind on it. She had been compelled by a dream, and she would never regret her actions—at least she fervently hoped not.

Bryant stepped away from the window and walked to the front of the desk. There he stood staring down at her. Joanne felt as if his eyes were piercing into her. Finally she flicked her eyes up to meet his.

She felt jolted by the soft little smile on his lightly freckled, handsome face. "I haven't the least interest in informing on you," he said softly. "I want you to have a job to come back to after I've successfully wrung you out. You're not only too beautiful to waste on the icy slopes of Dhaulagiri, I now hear you're also too brainy, with too brilliant a future in front of you. And that makes me more determined than ever that you'll be miles away when we launch the final assault on the mountain of storms. Good day, Miss Patton." He straightened up, turned away and in two strides was gone.

CHAPTER THREE

JOANNE'S TWENTY-SIXTH BIRTHDAY fell on a Tuesday late in November. At three o'clock the following morning her phone rang. As she groggily reached for it, Joanne became aware of the steady splashing against her bedroom window and realized that it was raining even harder than it had been when she and Scottie had returned home a few hours earlier.

Her birthday celebration with Scottie had been fun in one way, painful in another. They'd had a marvelous French dinner at the Blue Fox, then afterward, as they'd sipped their coffee, he'd given her, or tried to give her, a birthday gift: a lovely diamond-and-ruby pin.

As she'd opened the jeweler's box and caught sight of the pin, her heart had plummeted. One look and she could tell that the pin must have cost Scottie several thousand dollars. Slowly Joanne closed the box. Her eyes caught on Scottie's light blue ones.

"Scottie, it's beautiful, one of the most beautiful pieces of jewelry I've ever seen, and you were incredibly sweet and generous to buy it for me, but—" She picked up the box and extended it toward him, "I really can't accept it. It's far too expensive."

"But, Joanne—"

"No, Scottie, please." With a smile, she pressed the small velvet box into Scottie's hand.

"Joanne, you're sure?"

"Absolutely sure."

"But—"

"No buts, please."

Scottie frowned. "It wasn't meant as a bribe, only as a token of my love."

"I know, but I still can't accept it. Thank you anyway."

With a sigh Scottie slipped the box into the inside pocket of his jacket. His blue eyes met Joanne's and his lips curved into a soft pained smile. "Well, this tells it all, doesn't it? What I really wanted to give you, as I'm sure you know, was an engagement ring. I figured you wouldn't accept that, so I chose this instead. When you won't even accept this—" Scottie looked away for a moment. When he turned to face her again, he was smiling warmly. "Okay, message received and accepted. While you're fond of me, I'm sure, you're not in love with me and are pretty sure you never will be. Does that about sum it up?"

Joanne felt a catch in her throat, but she nodded her response. "Yes, it does, I'm afraid."

"Could I ask you this—have you met someone else?"

Joanne experienced an odd sensation of tightening within her, but she answered quickly. "Oh, no, it's not that. It's just—well, I do care for you, so much, but—"

"But not enough to even consider marrying me?"

Joanne sighed, her eyes meeting his straight on. "I'm afraid not. Scottie, I'm sorry."

He smiled across at her, as though to ease her feelings of distress. "Well, if you haven't yet met anyone else, can we at least continue seeing each other, as friends, I mean, until you leave for your climb?"

"Yes, of course! Though I will be awfully busy." Joanne reached across and squeezed his hand. "I *am* your friend, Scottie, just as I know you are mine."

Scottie's expression reflected both warmth and pain. He rose, leaned across the table to press a kiss on her cheek, then picked up his wineglass, extending it in a toast. "So here's to our friendship. May it afford us both joy and long endure."

Joanne clicked her glass to his, feeling deeply relieved and happy. "Amen to that."

After Scottie drove her home, they sat for a few minutes in his car, talking. Joanne learned to her dismay that everything wasn't quite as settled as she'd thought. As Scottie held her hand he asked her if she minded that he had not yet entirely relinquished hope, despite what she'd said.

"Oh, Scottie, no!" Joanne protested.

With a light laugh he leaned close and kissed her cheek. Drawing back, he grinned. "Joanne, yes. As long as there's no one else—I don't mean I'll press you ever again, or try to influence you with expensive gifts, but as long as your heart is free, who can tell what the future might bring? Once you've gone on this Himalayan climb, maybe you'll get mountaineering out of your blood once and for all and will be ready to settle down. Then maybe you'll look at me with different eyes, and I'll be the lucky man you decide to settle down with. Stranger things have happened, you know."

Joanne's eyes caught his. "It's not going to happen, Scottie. Please don't nourish any hope that it will. *Please.*"

Scottie laughed. "All right, whatever you say. Good night, sweetheart." Again he pressed a light kiss on her cheek.

They had agreed that he needn't walk her inside as he had drawn up in the only available space, a no-parking zone, and risked having his car ticketed if he left it.

Joanne climbed out, threw him a kiss, swung around and went inside.

After reaching her apartment, she'd gone straight to bed and had fallen quickly to sleep, only to be awakened by the phone a few hours later. Had Scottie had an accident driving home?

"Hello," Joanne murmured sleepily into the receiver. Scottie was an excellent driver. Surely this wouldn't be him. But who else could it possibly be? Maybe it was simply a wrong number.

"Good morning, Joanne. This is James Bryant. Throw on some jogging clothes, and I'll be over to pick you up in fifteen minutes."

"*What?*"

Joanne woke abruptly. She rose to a sitting position, switched on the bedside lamp and immediately tugged on the blankets to wrap them around her shoulders. It was cold. Rain pounded like thunder against the windowpane. "It's the middle of the night. Are you crazy?"

Bryant laughed. There was something steely in the sound. "Not as crazy as you are. You heard what I said. Throw on some jogging clothes and I'll be there to pick you up in fifteen minutes." He hung up.

Joanne sat glaring at the dead receiver she held. She plunked it down, switched the light off and crawled back under the covers. A crank call by an angry crank, she told herself. Surely Bryant didn't mean what he'd said. Even if he did, so what? Her apartment door was locked and bolted. Let him pound on it all he wished. There was no way he could get in—and no way, if she stayed snugly in bed, that she could prove to him she had the mental determination, the moral strength and physical stamina to be part of the expedition.

Joanne took a deep breath, reached out to turn the light back on and threw herself out of bed.

She dressed quickly and hurried out to her kitchen to fix herself hot chocolate. With every passing minute she felt less upset, more keyed up and excited. Though she'd been too busy finishing college and law school the last few years to do much climbing, she hadn't let her physical condition deteriorate. She'd been a runner since early adolescence, before jogging had become as popular as it was now. All through college and law school she'd run to and from campus, and to and from the Coghill and Myers offices. She still ran to work and back. She had yet to own a car and might never buy one. Early in the fall she'd entered a marathon and had finished the twenty-six miles in fine style, the third woman across the finish line. As she sipped her hot chocolate now, Joanne smiled to herself. If Bryant thought he could scare her away with a little predawn in-the-rain running, he was out of his mind.

She finished her chocolate, pulled her rain-coat off its hanger in the front closet, plopped her rain hat on her head, tying it under her chin, and leaned against the back of the armchair, waiting.

She hadn't long to wait. True to his word, Bryant rang her bell at just about fifteen minutes after his call. Joanne stepped out into the hall and closed the door. Immediately she was aware of an aura of raw power she had come to associate with him.

"Ready?" Bryant asked skeptically.

"Ready," Joanne snapped, and strode off ahead of him toward the stairs.

Outside, the cold fall rain came lashing down. Bryant stopped by a dark blue Mercedes parked at the curb. He pulled off the heavy raincoat he wore, pulled open the back door of his car and tossed the wet coat onto the floor. "Let's have yours, too. No need for a coat in a light mist like this. It will hamper your running."

"Right," Joanne agreed, ripping off her coat and tossing it into the car.

Bryant had on a long-sleeved, gray sweat shirt with loose, gray sweat pants. As the sweat shirt dampened, the material clung to his broad shoulders and powerful upper arms. As Joanne noticed this, she felt a sudden quickening of all her senses, and a warm flush radiated from somewhere deep within her.

"All set?" Bryant asked, his narrow green eyes gleaming with amusement.

Instantly the sensation passed. Joanne nodded her head in furious affirmation.

With a laugh, Bryant swung around and began jogging up the wet sidewalk. Joanne followed. The rain sliced coldly against her face. Within minutes her light blue jogging suit was soaked through. She felt weighted down by it. Bryant reached the cross street, glanced each way, then went on across without breaking stride. In the few seconds it took Joanne to reach the corner behind him, a car appeared, and she had to wait. Visibility was so poor that

Bryant disappeared into the rainstorm. The moment the car had passed, Joanne spurted ahead, determined to catch up. No way would she let that man think he had lost her to fatigue this early.

At the next corner, Bryant swung to his left and began running up a hill. Half of San Francisco was hills, and it hadn't taken Bryant long to reach one. Joanne ran behind, breathing hard but steadily, adjusted now to the feel of the heavily clinging suit. She was no longer the least bit cold, and the water streaming down her face felt good. She ran at a steady rhythm, twenty or so feet behind, enjoying the movement, breathing in the fresh invigorating smell of the cold fall rain.

Up one hill, down the next. Reaching a corner, Bryant would swing right one time, left the next. Joanne followed. Before too long, she felt a slight painful stitch in each side, her thighs began to ache and she felt a splashing nausea in her stomach. Still it felt good to be running, even in the darkness and rain. Ahead of her she could detect no sign of weakening in Bryant, no faltering in his rhythm. Her confidence grew, her sureness that she could keep up with him, stride for stride. Biting back a smile, she assured herself for what must have been the tenth time that he would tire before she did. Even if her body gave out, which she didn't think would happen, she would continue running on sheer willpower, as she had at one point in the marathon before getting her second wind. Though Bryant never glanced back to check on her, she was sure he listened for her steps and was aware that she was still there, following him.

Another hill, the steepest one yet. For half a second Joanne faltered, thought about stopping—not for good, just long enough to catch her breath, to ease the painful stitch in her right side—but with a sudden upsurge of energy she continued on. If Bryant could make it, so could she. Biting her lip, she jogged up the incline, sheer determination forcing her weary body, to take one step after another.

Fortunately what goes up must come down, and soon they were on the far side heading downhill. Joanne had caught her second wind and was breathing easily again. Her mind took off, reliving previous climbs she'd been on. Suddenly she could see her father's weathered face before her, and she felt inundated with love, remembering all the wonderful times they had had together. A smile broke out along her lips. At the bottom of the hill Bryant stood waiting, facing up toward her. She ran down beside him, feeling warm and triumphant.

"How you doing?" Bryant asked, his hair and face streaming water. He used a wet forearm to wipe some of the water from his eyes, then smiled down at her. Joanne's insides jumped nervously. They stood under a streetlight and could see each other with ease.

"I'm doing just fine." She grinned up at him to prove it.

To her surprise—and chagrin—he threw an arm around her shoulders and gave her a quick hug. "Good for you. What do you say we find an all-night café and warm ourselves with some coffee?"

Joanne felt a sudden surge of even greater triumph. "Oh, I don't think so. I think I'll just run on home. Goodbye." She swung around, glanced quickly each way and plunged into the street.

Not at all to her surprise, she heard Bryant's steps following her. After she'd climbed onto the far curb, she stopped long enough to call over her shoulder, "Are you following me?"

Bryant caught up and stood grinning down at her, his green eyes dancing. After catching his breath, he said, "I'm afraid so. The truth is I haven't the slightest idea where we are."

Joanne laughed. She'd suspected as much. She'd paid strict attention to each change in direction he'd made and was reasonably sure she knew the way home. "So be my guest." Swinging around, she began running forward again.

It was Bryant's turn now to follow behind. Joanne's face broke into repeated smiles as she ran. The rain was letting up a bit, and even though it was still an hour or more until daybreak, the sky seemed lighter. Joanne led them back to her apartment building, without a single wrong turn.

She came to a stop beside his car, then leaned forward gasping for breath, waiting for Bryant to catch up. After reaching her side, he, too, bent over, struggling for breath.

"My raincoat, please," Joanne gasped. Bryant laughed. He dug his key out, opened the car door and grabbed the coat, which he handed to her. Joanne threw it over her arm and broke into a quick jog down the sidewalk, then up the walk into the building.

"It's been fun," Bryant yelled after her. "Thank you, Joanne."

"You bet. Any time," she called back.

AT TEN-THIRTY THAT MORNING Bryant phoned. "Just wanted to make sure you didn't come down with pneumonia," he said. "Obviously you did make it into work."

"Obviously. But I'm terribly busy right now, talking with a client on the other line, so if you'll please excuse me—"

"Of course." Obligingly he hung up.

He phoned her again the following morning. "Still no pneumonia, I see," he greeted her cheerily.

"Not even a sniffle. And you?"

"Oh, I'm fine, too."

"I'm sorry, but I'll have to put you on hold," she said. "My other phone's ringing."

"Don't bother. I'll just say goodbye."

Joanne listened to the sound of the disconnecting click.

It was two weeks before she heard from him again. This time the call came at 3:20 in the morning.

"Hello, Joanne. Bryant here. Please put on your jogging clothes again, and I'll be there in fifteen minutes."

This time after she'd dressed, Joanne went downstairs and out onto the sidewalk to wait, curious as to why he had chosen this particular night to schedule another run. It wasn't raining. As soon as she stepped out of the apartment building, she knew why. The fog was so thick she could see scarcely a foot in front of her face. Anger surged through her as she moved cautiously forward. If they tried running in pea soup like this, they'd trip over each other.

She stood on the sidewalk shivering, wishing she'd waited inside. Even better, she should have told Bryant to forget it and stayed in bed. As a hand took hold of her arm, her heart stopped and she jumped a foot.

Bryant laughed. "Relax. It's me. I'm parked half a block down. Come along." His hand still clasping her arm, he led her down the sidewalk to his car.

Once they were snugly inside, he drew away from the curb. Joanne felt relieved to find they weren't going running after all. But he'd told her to put on her jogging clothes. She glanced curiously around at him. He sat leaning forward over the wheel, peering out. The car's headlights were like pencil flashlights penetrating the darkness.

"Would you mind too terribly much telling me where we're going?" Joanne asked.

Bryant kept his narrowed eyes staring intently forward. "You'll see," came his cryptic reply.

Well, there was no use both of them worrying and straining to see. Joanne forced herself to relax. She leaned her head back and closed her eyes, soon drifting off into sleep. She had no idea how much time had passed before Bryant shook her arm, waking her.

"Wake up, Joanne, we're here."

"And where is here?"

Bryant grinned. His broad, lightly freckled face was only inches away from hers as he leaned across to throw open her door. "Climb out and you'll see."

Joanne did as instructed. Her foot hit a curb and she climbed onto a walk. Straining to see, she could make out what appeared to be a railing. She caught a strong saltwater smell of the sea. She heard ocean breakers, and the eerie sound of foghorns ahead or below or both. Suddenly she knew where she was: on the pedestrian walk of the Golden Gate Bridge. She swung around and peered at Bryant in the car.

"I'll meet you on the other side," Bryant yelled, motioning forward, then he pulled the car door closed. Shocked, she watched as the red taillights of his car moved off and were quickly gobbled up in the fog.

She stood a moment too stunned to move. How dared he do this to her? Feeling suddenly cold, she wrapped her arms around herself. Then she thrust her chin up in defiance. All right, she could see what he had in mind: a test to see how well she could handle herself under stress. Joanne began gingerly walking forward. Well, she would show him. She would not become frightened or confused, but would walk or jog unseeingly through this thick haze until she had crossed the bridge and was picked up by him on the other side. The distance, just over four thousand feet, was no challenge at all, if it hadn't been for the blinding, enveloping fog.

After she'd walked a dozen feet, Joanne broke into a jog. The rhythmic movement gave her increased confidence, and she was soon running along quite easily, her lips set in grim determination. As she moved she was aware of the railing to her right and tried to run parallel to it without running into it. She could hear the frequent lonely wail of foghorns. Occasionally the headlights of a car came bursting briefly into view, then it would move on past and be quickly swallowed up again. She doubted if any driver could see her.

Less than a mile to run. She began to feel warm and happy. One more test to prove her fitness to climb Dhaulagiri, the mountain of storms. Snow swirls at high altitudes could cut off vision even more effectively than a heavy fog. Any climber who became disoriented or frightened was a life-threatening liability. She'd show Bryant how little he need fear this would happen to her.

As she ran it seemed to Joanne that the fog

got even thicker, if that was possible. She tested by putting a hand up before her face and found that she could not see it. Her hand all but brushed her nose before she could distinguish it. It was like running blindfolded. When she was about halfway across, in her own estimation, she hit a sudden clearing, but twenty feet farther the fog closed in again.

As she passed the second tower, the haze began to thin a bit. More and more cars were driving by, the noise of their engines eerily muted. Joanne reached the end of the bridge and ran into a bulk standing squarely in her path, a form she hadn't seen. Her pulse jumped excitedly as she instantly recognized the voice.

"Good enough," Bryant said. "Come along, my car's right here." He led her to it and helped her in.

As he drove forward through ever lighter fog, Bryant asked whether she'd like him to look for an open café where they could have some coffee.

"Thank you, no," Joanne answered in a friendly but formal voice. "I'd rather head back, if you don't mind."

He glanced around with a shrug. "Whatever you say." He turned around and headed back toward the Golden Gate, which would take them home.

To Joanne's profound shock, he drew the car over and stopped just before they reached the bridge. Leaning past her, he threw open her door. "All right, out you go. I'll meet you on the other side."

"But—"

"No buts. Unless you're afraid, of course."

"Go to blazes!" Joanne jumped out of the car.

She had run only a few hundred feet when she suddenly slowed, a tentative smile tugging at her lips. Her heart began racing excitedly as the smile broadened into a grin. Without further thought she swung around and began jogging back along the walk she had just traversed. She'd show Bryant who was afraid!

After she left the bridge behind, she followed the bay into the charming little town of Sausalito. There she hired a cab to take her back across the bridge and home.

Arriving at work at eight-thirty that morning, she stopped to talk to Ellie, the receptionist.

"Ellie, I'm expecting a call this morning from a man by the name of James Bryant. If he phones, here's what I want you to do. Tell him you think—and stress that word, please—you *think* I've come in and you'll ring my office. But then don't ring it. After a minute or so, go back on the line and explain that I must be out of my office at the moment. No matter how many times he phones, please do this each time. Do you mind?"

"Gotcha, Miss Patton," Ellie said with a grin. Joanne laughed, thanked the young woman and went striding happily down the hall.

Her apartment phone had rung insistently three different times before she'd left for work. She had let it ring on and on without answering. Let Mr. James A. Bryant sweat it out for a change!

At eleven that morning Joanne buzzed the switchboard and asked Ellie whether or not Bryant had phoned. Ellie laughed. "Eight times so far. Each time he sounds a little bit angrier."

"Or a bit more frightened?" Joanne suggested, laughing. "Well, thanks, Ellie. Keep up the good work."

At 11:20 A.M. the door to her office was thrown open and a whirlwind came hurtling through. Bryant's broad face, pale and strained, was set in rigid lines. At the sight of her, fury charged his eyes.

"Where have you been all morning, dammit? Why didn't you answer your phone? Have you the least idea what you've put me through?"

He stood in front of her desk, glaring across at her, his nostrils flaring in rage. Joanne leaned back in her chair, innocently returning his gaze. She tried to keep a smile from her mouth, but in the end it broke free. She started to laugh. A flush swept up Bryant's face. A moment later, to her relief, he grinned. He joined in her laughter. The next moment, his laughter died away as he came striding around the desk, taking her completely by surprise. Grabbing onto her arms, he pulled her to her feet, then drew her close, pressing his warm mouth down on hers.

Joanne's laughter was silenced abruptly. Held tightly against Bryant, she was aware only of her body melting into his. As his soft lips pressed hers with their silken caress, a hot shiver raced through her, and she trembled with anticipation. Then just as suddenly he drew away. Joanne felt an almost irresistible urge to fling herself forward against him again, but she held herself stiffly back. Bryant ended the kiss and stood gazing furiously down at her.

"All right, this time I had it coming, so we're even. But don't you dare ever do that to me again."

He leaned down, kissed her a second time—so quickly, so lightly—then dropped hold of her arms, rounded the desk and was gone.

A WEEK LATER Joanne received an unexpected call.

"Hello, Joanne. How are you? This is Jim Bryant."

Joanne tried not to notice the way her heart began to race or the sudden dry feeling in her mouth. "Well, Mr. Bryant, hello. I didn't expect to hear from you again this soon."

After their most recent encounter, when he'd unexpectedly grabbed her and kissed her before storming out of her office, she had heard from him only once, indirectly. Two mornings later, he'd phoned when she was out and left the message that he was returning home to Seattle and would contact her sometime after the year-end holidays to give her specific dates about the Himalayan expedition. Now here he was calling in mid-December, before not after the holidays.

Bryant laughed. "I know. I didn't expect to call this soon again, but things have been going so well I find I have a few days free. How have you been?"

Joanne's heart was no longer racing wildly; it had settled down to a quick hard beat, but she still felt tense. The day would probably never come, she supposed, that she would hear this man's voice without a reflexive tensing. No, that was nonsense, she scolded herself. Once the Himalayan climb was over, everything would change. It was simply that at the moment Bryant held the reins of power; he could help or hinder her in the pursuit of her most cherished dream. That was the one and only reason he had such an unsettling effect on her.

"Oh, I've been fine, thank you. And you?" Joanne was pleased at the firm cool ring to her voice. No one listening would have had the least suspicion she was in any way perturbed.

"I've been fine, too. Terribly busy, of course, but as I said, things are falling into shape, and I find I'll have a few days off over the holidays. Can you fly to Seattle a day or two after Christmas so we can have a go at climbing Glacier Peak?"

"What?" Joanne had been listening intently, yet she had the feeling that her ears must have

blanked out. She couldn't believe what she'd heard.

Bryant laughed again, as though with deep enjoyment at her momentary confusion. As his brief burst of laughter died away, he spoke with great precision, as though to a child. "I asked, Joanne, if you could possibly get away for a few days between Christmas and New Year's and fly to Seattle so that you and I could have a go at climbing Glacier Peak."

Joanne's face burned with anger at Bryant's patronizing tone, at the fact he'd been able to throw her off balance as thoroughly as he had. She fought to keep her voice stripped of both embarrassment and rage. "Just the two of us, you mean? Or will other climbers from the team be joining us?"

He sighed, a deep rich sigh full of complacent amusement. "Just the two of us, I meant. It hadn't occurred to me to ask anyone else, and even if it had I would have rejected any such notion. So can you make it, Joanne? I really feel it's quite essential that you do."

You devil, Joanne thought in fury. Naturally he wouldn't suggest this kind of nonsense to any of the other climbers, all of whom were men. It was just his way of testing her further, punishing her; his way of throwing into her face the insulting insistence that she *needed* testing. Still, on those two prior occasions when she'd humored him it had worked out rather well. Especially on the second occasion. Remembering the way he'd come storming anxiously into her office in an uproar, Joanne felt a slight smile curl her lips. Putting her anger to the side, she answered as pleasantly as possible. "Well, in all truth, Mr. Bryant—"

"Call me Jim, if you like."

Joanne allowed herself a cool little laugh. "Well, if you'd prefer—"

His words were suddenly clipped as he cut in again. "No matter. Whichever. But I'd appreciate a straight answer one way or another. Can you make it?"

Joanne felt a renewed burning anger speed up the back of her neck. How this man infuriated her! "Unfortunately I can't give you an answer," she responded quickly, bitingly, "until I've had a chance to check it out. Give me your number and I'll phone you back."

"Never mind. I'll call you back. How soon will you know?"

"By early afternoon. I'll check with Ted Myers as soon as he gets in."

"Fine. I'll call you back." And with that, Bryant hung up.

Joanne slammed her own phone down. She sat for a moment pressing her hands against her desk, then jumped up to walk off some of her rage. She strode to her office window and stared unseeingly down at the parking lot, just as Bryant had stood there one afternoon staring down. The memory of their most recent encounter moved in slowly to calm her down. That morning she'd had the whip hand and would again. Her lips curled into a slight satisfied smile. She didn't have to check with Ted Myers or with anyone else about taking the time off. Coghill and Myers traditionally closed down between Christmas and New Year's, and Ted had already verified that they'd be closed again this year. The official memo would circulate any day.

But Bryant didn't know that. Surely there was no way he could know. So when he phoned back in the afternoon, she'd tell him regretfully that she was sorry, but the office was so busy there was no way she could get away. *My apologies, Mr. Bryant, but there it is. Find yourself someone else to torment.*

Joanne felt keyed up the rest of the morning, anticipating Bryant's return call. She'd been so obliging on his earlier test runs, giving in to his whims without argument, that he'd apparently misinterpreted and assumed that she was a spineless patsy who'd put up with any and all kinds of nonsense. Well, when he phoned back today he'd learn better. No matter how he insisted, badgered, verbally browbeat her, she'd remain coolly in control. *Sorry, Mr. Bryant, I just can't make it.* That should put a permanent crimp in his patronizing attitude toward her. Joanne relished the thought.

Ordinarily she took a late lunch, sometimes not leaving her office until one-thirty or two, but not today. She left a little after twelve and returned before one, not wanting to miss Bryant's call. She had barely gotten seated on her return when the phone rang. Her pulse instantly racing, she swooped it up—to find herself confused by the sound of Scottie's voice.

"Oh—Scottie. Hi. I thought it was someone else."

"Sorry. If you're expecting an important call, I won't hold you. I just called to say I'm going to be down in your area and wondered if you could possibly meet me for lunch."

"I'm sorry, my schedule was such that I went out early today and I just got back. Sorry."

"No problem. I'll see you tonight. I love you, Joanne. Bye."

Joanne somewhat reluctantly replaced the receiver, feeling a soft wave of nostalgia.

When the phone rang again a few minutes later, she had herself under much better control. Again it wasn't Bryant. She was deluged with calls all afternoon, but not a single one came from Seattle, from the man who had said he would call. As five-thirty came and went, Joanne rose rather tiredly and gathered her things. She felt more depressed than angry, though she didn't quite understand why. She should have been pleased that the man didn't call.

She was headed out the door when her phone rang again. This surprised her as Ellie, who operated the switchboard, always left right on the dot of five-thirty, and her phone didn't have a direct line in or out. Obviously someone had been out in the reception area to put the call through. Certain it would be a business call that she'd really rather miss, Joanne hesitated and almost left without answering. Then with a sigh she walked dutifully back to pick the receiver up.

"Hello. Joanne Patton here."

"Hi." It was Bryant's voice. "I'm relieved to have reached you. I tried half a dozen times, but there was some kind of problem on the lines. Can you get the time off?"

As though that was the only consideration, Joanne thought in immediate anger. She had half a mind to change her story, to admit she would be off work those days, but then add coldly that that didn't mean she would join him in Washington State or anywhere else. She had her own plans, thank you, and they did not include climbing Glacier Peak with him. In her angry indecision, she bit at her lip for a moment without answering.

"I asked if you could get the time off." Bryant's voice was openly impatient.

"No, sorry, I couldn't," Joanne snapped, deciding again on the lie she'd planned earlier.

"Sorry to hear that." He didn't sound particularly sorry. "Would it help any, do you think, if I were to call your boss, whom I met that day, to intercede for you?"

"Don't you dare!"

"All right, no problem. Have a nice holiday, and I'll talk to you again after the first of the year." He hung up.

Joanne stared at the dead receiver, feeling hot all over and angry. Just like that—no problem, goodbye. Oh, how that man infuriated her!

Joanne went out to dinner with Scottie that night, then to a movie. After she returned home and went to bed, she found she couldn't sleep. Her mind insisted on reviewing time after time every word that had been exchanged that day between Bryant and herself. Had she made a mistake in turning down his invitation? He had seemed to accept her refusal so placidly, which wasn't like him. Did he have some card up his sleeve, some scheme to rid himself of her? He had vowed that he would, that he would wring her out and cast her off. Would he be able to make good on his threat? Joanne tried frantically to shut off her mind and settle down for sleep, but sleep wouldn't come.

Two days later, on Friday, when a man stepped unexpectedly into her office, Joanne was so engrossed with the brief she was studying that it took her a moment or two to glance up. She had assumed that the man was Ted, though the step hadn't sounded like him. If not Ted, then it must be Leroy, the thin short retired man who was the office messenger, or possibly some client who, looking for Ted's office, had taken a wrong turn. Joanne hastily scanned an additional line or two of the brief, then glanced up, ready to don a friendly courteous smile. The incipient smile froze on her lips, and she felt instantly tense when she saw James Bryant looming over her.

"Oh, my God." She rose instinctively to her feet, motioning him in.

Bryant's face looked paler than she'd remembered, and he wasn't smiling. He greeted her with a slight inclination of his head. "Good morning, Joanne. You're looking well."

"You, too." *What a lie,* she thought. Bryant looked more anxious than she'd ever seen him. Her heart sank as she wondered if his expression in any way reflected the purpose of his visit. Joanne's hand trembled slightly as she motioned toward one of the chairs in front of her desk. "Have a seat, if you like."

"Thank you." As Bryant seated himself, Joanne sank down on her own chair. Her eyes sought his. He looked so subdued, so quiet, and her uneasiness grew.

"Well, this is—needless to say this is a tremendous surprise." Joanne's lips parted in an attempted smile.

Bryant's eyes met hers, but he did not return the smile. She had never seen him before when he wasn't all smiles: broad friendly ones or tight hard ones. She gazed across in growing panic. How had he managed to dump her so soon, for surely that was what his visit, his unsmiling visage meant.

He held a sheet of pink paper, the type of paper that office memos were printed on. He rose momentarily and handed the paper across the desk to her. Before Joanne could focus her eyes to read the words, Bryant spoke.

"I happened to stop by the bulletin board just past the reception area, and I saw that posted, so I borrowed it. It seems that the offices here are going to close down over the holiday, after all."

Joanne stared down at the memo for a moment—already knowing what it said, then her eyes rose to meet his. "Yes, so it seems."

"So you will be free for a few days after Christmas after all?"

"Well, I—I had already made other plans." That wasn't precisely true! She and Scottie were driving down to San Carlos to spend Christmas Day with her mother, but apart from that she had planned to rest, catch up on her reading, give her apartment a thorough cleaning—plans, yes, but not very pressing ones.

"Plans that you can't change, you mean?" Bryant still spoke in that odd quiet voice.

Joanne felt a warm flush rising to her face as she searched frantically for a suitable reply. "Well, I—I suppose I could change them, if it came to that."

"I suggest that it should come to that." Bryant drew out a pamphlet from his coat pocket and handed it to her. "Glance at this, will you? It's a picture of Glacier Peak and a map of the area. Have you ever climbed in Washington State?"

Joanne's eyes were infuriatingly misty. She blinked nervously, lifting her gaze to Bryant's somber pale-looking face. "Well, I've climbed

Mount Rainier. The first time when I was twelve. It was just a few months prior to my father's Himalayan climb, and he took my brother and me there as sort of a training ground for the big one. Only, even though I did wonderfully well on Rainier, my father still wouldn't let me go on the Himalayan climb.''

Bryant's narrow, dark green eyes stayed steadily fixed on her as she said this. When she had finished, his soft lips curved in a very slight smile. "So naturally you've hungered to climb in the Himalayas ever since."

"Of course," Joanne replied cautiously.

"That's the only time you've climbed Rainier?" he asked. "That time when you were twelve?"

"No, one other time, when I was fourteen."

"And Glacier Peak?"

Joanne felt as though she had sunk into deep cold water. The cold water was slowing her reactions, her ability both to think and talk. Frowning, she said, "No, I don't think so. I'm sure that I never did."

"And any other peaks in the Northern Cascades?"

"No. I guess Washington State was just too close to home. Whenever my father had time off, he always wanted to head toward far-off places, I guess figuring that when he got old he could tackle the mountains closer to home." Joanne sighed. "But before he got old enough, he became ill and died."

A momentary silence followed, then Bryant rose to his feet, his face still looking pale and somber. Joanne rose too.

"Mount Rainier is often used as a training ground for those headed toward the Himalayas, as your father used it, but since you've already climbed there twice, I'd rather we tackle Glacier Peak. I think you'll enjoy it. I know I will. Won't you please change your mind and agree to go? That's why I came here today, you know—to try to convince you."

Joanne hesitated only momentarily before saying, "All right, yes. If you like."

Bryant stepped forward, extending his hand. His face glowed with a warmth now that spilled over Joanne like an uninvited caress. In surprise she rose, slipped her hand into his and shook on the agreement. Suddenly Bryant looked the picture of radiant health.

"Thank you, Joanne. I'll do my best to see you never regret it. I'll be in touch." He gave her hand a hard warm squeeze, then turned and walked from the room.

Joanne stared after him, stunned. She dropped into her seat, then a moment later jumped up nervously and wandered over to her office window. What had she done? She hadn't had the least intention of consenting to climb with him over Christmas. Had he come striding in ready to steamroller over her she would have been able to handle him, would have stuck by her decision and told him to go jump. But this was a new side of him he had presented her with and the technique had worked. She'd been completely unnerved.

Joanne stared blindly down at the parking lot, nervously biting her lip. A minute later she saw a tall broad-shouldered figure come striding out from the building: James Anthony Bryant, her adversary, her nemesis. Staring down at him, Joanne unconsciously straightened her shoulders and took a deep resolute breath. Bryant was one up on her now, but she'd see that that state of affairs didn't last. Obviously he was a subtle and tricky fighter, more so than she'd given him credit for. But just because she'd agreed to go on the holiday climb with him didn't mean he had come out on top. She felt reasonably sure she'd enjoy the climb; she always loved climbing, but before the trip was over she'd find some way to even the score.

CHAPTER FOUR

BRYANT MET HER AT THE AIRPORT when she flew into Seattle on the morning of December 26. Again his manner was quiet and subdued—no big smile of welcome even as he shook her hand in greeting. It was as though he wanted to show her that for him this was all business, no pleasure. *Good enough,* Joanne thought, climbing into his dark blue Mercedes. For her it was all business, too.

From the moment she'd agreed to come on this climb—was tricked into it, she amended—she had determined to gear herself up for it, to fly up here to meet Bryant feeling rested and confident. Unfortunately all of her well-laid plans had been for naught. Though she'd cut down on all social activities, had seen Scottie only one night a week and had retired early each evening, she'd rarely gotten a good night's sleep. Had she added up all the hours she'd lain awake in bed, feeling frightened and anxious, then becoming furiously angry at herself for feeling that way, they would have far outnumbered the hours she'd managed to fight her way into fitful sleep. *What in the world is the matter with me,* she asked herself repeatedly at two or three in the morning, but no answers came. Then she'd resolve to call the whole thing off. If she was going to suffer anxiety attacks before the climb, what would she be like when they were halfway up the mountain. *Just forget the whole thing, you're not going anyway,* she'd tell herself, hoping this would do the trick, but it never worked. In the morning, reaching her office at work, she'd stand with her hand on the phone, debating whether to phone Bryant to cancel the climb. On three occasions she lifted the receiver and dialed information to get his number in Seattle, but on each occasion she changed her mind and didn't go through with it. *He won't believe my excuses,* she thought, her knees going weak. *He'll think that for some reason I'm chickening out. Which is exactly what you would be doing,* a part of her mind mocked.

So she hadn't called it off. Instead she'd gone doggedly ahead trying to rest up, to regain her confidence, to look forward to the climb with eagerness and excitement. Glacier Peak. Even the name was enchanting. On the Friday evening after Bryant's unexpected visit to her office, she'd dropped by the Alpine Club to pick up what information she could on the mountain. It turned out that an acquaintance of hers had been in Washington State the previous fall and had maps and information on all the larger peaks in the Northern Cascades. He'd magnanimously offered to mail to her everything he had.

The following Tuesday, true to his word, a large envelope was delivered to her at the office, and out of it tumbled maps, photos and printed material.

Her heart had raced with excitement as she began eagerly searching for a picture of Glacier Peak. Finding one, she sank down on her chair and stared at it while her heart thudded. When she could finally tear her eyes away, she studied a map of the peak attached to the back of the photo and hurriedly read the information given. Glacier Peak was 10,436 feet high, the fourth highest mountain in Washington State. It was located in the Glacier Peak Wilderness area northeast of Seattle and could be climbed in two days from the end of the road along White Chuck River; the route was by way of Kennedy Hot Springs, Sitkum Creek and Sitkum Glacier.

After reading this, Joanne let the material fall out of her hands and sat staring unseeingly across the desk top to the chair in which Bryant had sat during his brief visit with her the previous week. *A two-day climb. Glacier Peak could be climbed in two days.* That meant they would be spending a night together camped on the slopes. She and James Bryant.

Thinking this, Joanne shivered. She remembered the morning that Bryant, furious at her for frightening him, had come storming into her office, and had unexpectedly strode around her desk, pulled her up and kissed her—not once, but twice. And the outrageous way her body had responded, aching for more, betraying her. *And now she would be spending a night alone with him camped on the slopes of Glacier Peak.*

Oh, for heaven's sake, so what, Joanne snapped angrily at herself. In a fury, she rose and hastily picked up all the material her friend had sent her and stuffed it back inside the large manila envelope. Few of the higher peaks could be scaled in one day. She had rarely gone on a climb and not spent at least one night camping out. Yes, but that had been with her father or brother, a voice inside her reminded her. These fears were ridiculous Joanne thought impatiently. Besides, climbing Glacier Peak with Bryant would give her a chance to prove she was as good a climber as he was, maybe better.

Unfortunately her doubts were not effectively silenced. As she climbed into bed each night, Joanne would find herself remembering the one thing on earth she most wanted to forget: Bryant's kiss. As she relaxed and began drifting off into sleep, she'd suddenly feel his hands, so incredibly strong, pulling her close, then she'd feel his soft lips pressing down on hers—and would snap wide awake again in a cold sweat to find herself faced with hours of sleeplessness.

But even if he did kiss her again, she reasoned irritably with herself, and she would make absolutely sure he didn't, she wouldn't react the same way again. He had caught her off guard. That was all.

On the nights that her insomnia was the

worst, she'd give up about two in the morning, sit up, snap on the light and begin poring over the material on Glacier Peak. Never before had she taken the time to study a mountain she was planning to climb. Her father had always taken care of everything. But this time she'd be prepared. After thoroughly digesting all the information she had, she returned to the Alpine Club to search for additional material. Soon she knew every possible approach to the area, every possible route up the mountain. Glacier Peak, like Mount Rainier, Mount St. Helens and the other mountains in Washington State, was a volcano, so Joanne read everything she could about volcanic peaks. She'd never been so informed, so intellectually prepared. If Bryant thought he was going to trick her or in some way show her up, *she'd show him*!

The day of their departure arrived, and Joanne found herself riding smoothly along in the passenger side of Bryant's Mercedes, her bags stowed safely in the trunk. Surreptitiously she studied the man beside her. Seated behind the wheel, his large hands casually gripping it, Bryant looked slightly less physically intimidating than he did when standing. Gazing steadily at him, Joanne noticed the pale freckles sprinkled across his cheekbones, and for no particular reason the sight made her feel happier. Tom Sawyer...Huckleberry Finn...Jim Bryant. At the unlikely comparison Joanne felt like laughing. Her accumulated fatigue seemed to dissolve away and she was freshly energized.

Regardless of how she'd made it onto the team, she was now a climber on Bryant's scheduled Himalayan expedition. Once the trip got under way they'd be spending the better part of four months together. It was time she put to rest her silly fears and learned to like and accept him.

"Joanne, are you hungry?" Bryant asked, turning to look at her.

His gaze hit her with a jolt. When he faced her fully, it was harder to notice the light sprinkling of freckles, which made it harder to think of him as in any way a boy. All she felt, instantly, instinctively, was the tremendous inner power of the man, which stemmed, she knew, not solely from his physical strength.

"Joanne," Bryant repeated, "I asked you if you're hungry." There was an edge to Bryant's voice as his eyes swung back to the road.

"Sorry. Yes, I am."

He nodded. In the morning light the reddish tint of his dark brown hair was more noticeable than usual. "Fine. There's a restaurant a few doors down from my business offices. I'll drop you off there, stop by the office long enough to tie up a few things, then I'll pick you up. We'll go by my home to pick up my camper and head for the mountain. We'll camp near the base tonight, then hit the slopes early tomorrow morning. If all goes well, you'll be back home in San

Francisco in ample time to usher in the New Year."

"Fine."

No more was said.

Bryant was obviously not indulging in any idle chitchat. Joanne turned her gaze from him and sat staring absently out the car window. His businesslike manner suited her to perfection. Now that she was here, she felt confident that her irrational anxieties had died away. She'd get a sound night's sleep and be fit and energetic for the climb in the morning.

At the restaurant she ordered and consumed a delicious breakfast—grapefruit wedges, a mushroom omelet, toast and coffee—which left her with an even greater sense of well-being. By the time she'd finished, Bryant had not yet appeared, so she left the restaurant and walked briskly down the sidewalk, having informed the cashier that she'd gone to the Bryant Company offices. As she rode the elevator up to the sixth floor, Joanne smiled to herself, remembering the earlier time she'd been here. She sighed. No wonder Bryant was acting cool and formal with her. He must still resent the fact that she'd forced him to bend. She was quite certain he disliked her, yet that didn't mean they couldn't work well together on their climb. Besides, she wasn't sure she liked him much, either.

She arrived at Bryant's outer office and gave her name to his secretary, a stylishly sleek, middle-aged woman. Joanne wondered if she had been the one who had eliminated both her applications. The woman waved her to a seat, then went in to speak to her boss. She returned shortly to say that Mr. Bryant sent his apologies, but he'd been unexpectedly held up and wouldn't be able to get away for a few minutes yet.

It was almost half an hour before he came striding out, scowling. He nodded to Joanne, spoke briefly to his secretary, then waved for Joanne to join him when he was ready to leave. As she walked over to him, he put his hand to her back, not in friendliness or affection but impatiently, as though to prod her into greater speed.

"Sorry I'm late. Damn, we'll be getting a later start than I wanted to." His hand stayed against her back, pushing her along.

Joanne found the pressure of his hand intensely irritating. *She* wasn't the one who had held them up! She walked along as rapidly as possible, trying to pull away from his touch, but the faster she walked, the faster Bryant walked, keeping his hand against her. Finally, feeling outraged, she stopped walking and swung around to face him.

"Would you kindly stop pushing me that way?" Her voice was icy.

Bryant's dark green eyes caught hers. "Sorry." As he dropped his hand a slight smile tugged at his lips. Joanne immediately dropped her own gaze and started briskly forward again, fighting down a sudden trembling. She was furious with herself for allowing this man to affect her in such a way.

Neither spoke again until they were rolling smoothly forward once again in his Mercedes. "My home is about a forty-minute drive. We'll exchange this car for the camper, which I've already loaded, then off we'll go."

His words seemed to envelop Joanne in a caress, and she tensed. "Fine." She turned to gaze out the window, ending the brief exchange. They were both silent until they reached Bryant's home.

His house was lovely, somewhat rustic on the outside and rather reminiscent, Joanne thought, of a weathered Swiss chalet. It was a half mile off the road in a luxurious forest setting. Bryant led her inside. To the left off the entrance hall was a long low-ceilinged room with a huge fireplace and tall windows that embraced the picturesque outdoors. Joanne couldn't hold back an exclamation of how attractive yet comfortable everything looked.

Bryant grinned. He stood a few feet from her, looking impossibly bright and warm, vibrating with life. "With no credit to me. I bought the place from my older sister. She married when I was thirteen, and she and her husband used to invite me here for weekends and over vacations. I fell in love with the house and the setting—the woods, a stream that runs out back, everything—so when Carol and her husband tired of it, I talked her into selling it to me. Everything is pretty much the way she left it; I haven't changed anything. But I'm glad you like it.''

"Love it,'' Joanne murmured, surveying the room appreciatively.

In the kitchen, which was modeled in the same rustic style as the living room, Bryant made coffee and fixed himself a sandwich. He offered Joanne one, but she shook her head in refusal, murmuring that she was still full from the huge breakfast she'd had.

At last they were on their way again. After finishing his sandwich, Bryant had brought out some fruit and cheese, and Joanne had partaken of both. Now she felt quite drowsy. Bryant drove without speaking, his eyes steadily on the road, and Joanne leaned her head back and dozed off.

When she woke it was fairly late in the afternoon. She straightened up, yawning, and glanced around at Bryant. She thought about asking him what time it was, where they were, how much farther they had to go to reach the campground, then decided against it. He seemed rather a forbidding figure at that moment. A few miles farther along she noticed a sign that indicated they were traveling on State Highway 542.

She frowned. *542?* She had studied the various ways to reach Glacier Peak Wilderness and that route rang no bell. "How far away are we?'' she asked, turning to Bryant.

"From the campground? It's a couple of hours' drive yet. We ought to arrive just after dark. Did I mention there's been a change in plan and we're not headed for Glacier Peak after all?"

"*What?*"

Bryant's expression was sober and reflected his annoyance. "You heard me, I'm sure. I changed my mind about Glacier Peak and decided that we'd climb another mountain instead."

Joanne was furious. "You switched mountains on me—without even telling me?" She glared at him, sure that he'd done this deliberately, hoping to throw her off balance.

"Yes. I switched mountains," Bryant admitted. "The more I thought about it, the less point there seemed in our bothering with Glacier Peak. Glacier's too easy a climb. Also it would take us two days, and I thought you might prefer not to camp out overnight."

"So—where *are* we going?" Joanne demanded, speaking between clenched teeth.

Bryant's eyes challenged hers. "Mount Baker. It's a climb we can make in one day. Also it has a glacier system second only to Mount Rainier's—thirty-one square miles of ice. The route up is through Coleman Glacier, which is heavily crevassed. It ought to give us a good workout."

Joanne stared out the car window and did not speak again.

Darkness fell. By this time they were traveling on a narrow mountain road. Joanne began to feel cold and pulled on the jacket she had earlier tossed onto the back of the seat. Gazing out, she could see little. At home she had spent hours gazing at photographs of the North Cascades. Although they were not the highest mountains in the world, they looked wonderfully imposing; craggy walls of granite rising nearly vertical mile after mile. As chilled as she felt outside, inside she began to feel warm and happy. She loved mountains, the look, feel and smell of them. She loved to be near them, driving through them, most of all climbing them. All of her earlier anger at Bryant died away. Maybe he hadn't switched destinations as a mean trick; maybe he really *had* thought she'd prefer a one-day climb. She glanced across at him.

"I love the clean mountain smell. As far as I'm concerned, there's nothing in the world that compares with it."

Although Bryant didn't answer in words, he glanced around to respond with a friendly affirming smile.

Before too long he drew off the road into a fairly large clearing. Two vehicles were already parked there. Joanne climbed out, stretching, and breathed in deeply. The snow underfoot was soft and slushy. A male voice called out a greeting. She turned and waved. It was comforting to know that others were nearby. She wasn't entirely alone with Bryant.

They joined the other campers around a low camp fire. There were five men in all, counting Bryant; Joanne was the only woman. None of the others planned an assault on Mount Baker. After a delicious meal of franks, beans, French bread and coffee, Bryant suggested that they should turn in early as they had a strenuous day ahead of them.

Bryant's camper was a large and comfortable one. There was one bed up front and another pull-down one along one side. "If you'd feel more comfortable, I'll sleep outside," Bryant offered, but Joanne, her pulse racing, responded casually that that wasn't necessary, she trusted him. She crawled into the bed at the front and settled down for a sound night's sleep.

"Good night," Bryant said softly to her and doused the light. She could hear him climb into the other bed.

"Good night."

She felt wonderfully relaxed and irrationally happy, and almost at once fell asleep.

WHEN BRYANT SHOOK HER AWAKE, Joanne was convinced that she couldn't possibly have slept more than three or four hours.

"Wake up, Joanne. Time to get cracking. We've got a very long day ahead of us."

"Right. Okay." Joanne struggled up, doing her best to shrug off sleep and be instantly awake and alert.

She took a quick shower and pulled on her

clothes: a down-insulated suit, three pairs of wool socks and high boots. She strapped her sun goggles on, adjusted the fit, then pulled them down to dangle around her neck. She slipped on her headlamp and pushed her fine black hair under a wool cap. Bryant offered her a cup of hot coffee, which she gratefully accepted.

A few minutes later, their coffee cups emptied, she and Bryant gathered their equipment, strapped on their backpacks, climbed down from the camper and were on their way, hiking along a pitch-dark mountain road.

Joanne walked a few paces behind, breathing deeply, trying to shake off a slight buzz in her head. She'd fallen into a deep sleep very quickly, and it seemed impossible that many hours had passed.

"What time is it, anyway?" she called out. To her chagrin, she had forgotten to bring her watch.

Bryant tossed the answer over his shoulder, not slackening his pace. "It was eleven when I woke you and it's about twenty after now."

In shock Joanne stopped walking. *Eleven o'clock!* She was used to getting up by three, or even two o'clock, when climbing with her father, but this was crazy. As Bryant pulled ahead of her, she broke into a brief run to catch up. "Why so early? Surely we don't want to attempt too much before daybreak."

Bryant glanced around, and the gleam of Joanne's headlamp lit his face. His expression was hard and determined. "Of course not. But we're still several miles from our destination. We ought to reach the base of Mount Baker about three in the morning, which is just about right."

"I see!" Seething with anger, Joanne dropped the beam of her light. More testing! Obviously they could have driven miles closer to the mountain, but Bryant, without consulting her, had chosen not to. Arrogant devil! Dom had been right: she should never have put herself in this position, under James Bryant's leadership.

She allowed herself to fall behind. Her breathing was hard and quick, but after a few minutes she warned herself that if she kept that up, she'd tire far too easily. Hiking and climbing on a few hours' sleep would take all the energy she had; she mustn't waste it waging a futile mental war against Bryant. She forced herself to breathe more deeply, to calm down. So Bryant wasn't satisfied merely to climb with her; he had set it up so they would take a four-hour hike beforehand. Well, that was fine with her. She'd prove she was up to it, that she had energy reserves enough to make it through a long strenuous day—a day that might prove to be almost twenty hours long before they were through—on a few hours' sleep. If Bryant could do it, then so could she!

Time passed in fits and starts for Joanne. Occasionally she drifted into a half sleep, one leg automatically striding after the other while her mind was in a dreamlike state. At other moments she was wide awake, excitedly aware of the thin, exhilarating, high mountain air, intently aware of the sound of Bryant's steps and her own. A couple of hours after they'd gotten under way, Bryant, without breaking his stride, uncapped his thermos and poured them each a cup of steaming liquid. With her first sip, Joanne was surprised to find it wasn't coffee but hot chocolate. How delicious it tasted! For more than an hour she hiked along at Bryant's side. He glanced around at her a few times but neither of them spoke. There was still no hint of the approach of dawn as they reached an open parking area, where Bryant touched her arm and drew her to a stop. He pointed toward a trail ahead.

"Two miles up is a cabin, available for the use of climbers. We can stop there, freshen up, and have breakfast."

"Great. What time is it?"

Bryant flashed his light onto his wrist. "A few minutes of two. We've made good time."

"Great," Joanne murmured again, fighting to push away awareness of all bodily fatigue.

Bryant did not once hesitate on the two-mile ascent to the cabin and Joanne forced herself not to falter, either. At last she took a final upward step into a cleared area where she could stop and rest. She glanced around, feeling excited and pleased.

Bryant stood before a small cabin. He motioned her forward, smiling. She caught one quick glimpse of his handsome, freckled face before he turned and entered the cabin. When he smiled it was impossible to dislike the man. All her defenses dissolved as she felt again the familiar quickening of her pulse.

There were no cooking facilities in the cabin, but Bryant pulled a small one-burner kerosene stove out of his backpack and filled it with the flammable liquid. As he moved about, preparing them a light breakfast, Joanne noticed how powerfully yet gracefully he moved. Watching him, she began to feel stifled and claustrophobic, so she walked outside to calm herself. She stood before the cabin, staring out into the dark, lost in thought, until she heard Bryant's voice call her name and she went back inside.

They ate sitting on upturned wooden crates and placed their headlamps on a nearby carton to provide light. As Joanne sipped her after-breakfast coffee, Bryant's dark eyes caught hers and he smiled. He reached across the small space between them, his large hand clasping her shoulder. "So how you doing, friend?" There was a hint of mocking laughter in his voice.

Joanne was annoyed by her reaction to his touch. Why did she always tremble when he touched her? Surely she wasn't afraid of him. She moved away to break his hold. "Oh, I'm fine, thank you. And you?"

Bryant grinned even more broadly, his eyes

sparkling. "Fine, too, thank you." He rose and began clearing their plates away.

By twenty to three they were ready to leave the cabin. "We've got a fairly steep and strenuous climb ahead of us," Bryant warned her.

"How many hours?" Joanne asked.

"If all goes well, seven to eight, then one-third to one-half of that to come back down. Ready?"

"Ready," Joanne agreed.

Bryant again led the way.

The day passed easily enough for Joanne. It had been more than two years since she'd been on a strenuous climb, and she'd almost forgotten how much she delighted in that challenge. As she began to distinguish the outline of the mountain in the predawn glow, she felt an old familiar thrill. Her father had once told her that mountains have gender, just as people do. Some were stern old men, rising straight and austere. Others were flirtatious young maidens, spreading their skirts in a friendly bow. Mount Baker was—to Joanne's enchanted eyes—a dignified broad-bosomed matron, far too proud to bow to anyone, yet with nothing the least forbidding about her. She was a large mountain, with many glaciers and snowfields rising to a flattened dome. She was dressed all in white, a very bright and gleaming white, except for a decorative ridge of dark rock here and there and a few sprigs of green forest very low along her full skirt. A lovely lovable matron.

As dawn broke, Joanne feasted her eyes with even greater pleasure. She reveled in the exhilarating tang of the air, breathing it deeply into her lungs. The cabin in which they had eaten was so close to the timberline that they'd begun their climb in an alpine region of moss, heather and lichen and had hiked through clumps of dwarfed and flattened mountain hemlocks and alpine firs. As the stars twinkled one last time, then faded away, they arrived at the edge of the glacier for the start of the day's real climb.

They took a few minutes to rest and prepare: drinking water from the canteens they carried, munching chocolate bars, smearing sun cream generously on their faces and all other exposed skin, strapping crampons—steel frameworks with spikes attached—onto their boots, roping up, fitting their sun goggles into place. Without goggles they ran the danger of becoming snow-blind, a painful and dangerous condition. They drank water freely, for dehydration posed an ever-present danger to those climbing in high altitudes. During the climb they would lose a lot of liquid through perspiration. Climbing was a strenuous activity and the decreased air pressure of the heights caused perspiration to evaporate more quickly, so that the body had to perspire even more profusely to maintain a sufficient cooling effect. In addition, the cold, thin, high mountain air was very dry. With each breath a climber took he was drawing in very dry air, following which he exhaled the warm moist air naturally present in his lungs. This meant that with every breath a climber took he was drying himself out a little more.

Melting snow to obtain the needed water was time-consuming and a lot of work, so for a one- or two-day climb, carrying a canteen made far better sense. Both Bryant and Joanne had brought along plastic bottles filled to the brim, which they carried in outside pouches of their backpacks for easy access.

They also carried nuts, chocolate bars and other candy for snacking during brief rest periods. The sun cream they smeared on was another essential. Even on hazy or cloudy days the sun burned fiercely at high mountain altitudes. The thin air above the snow line didn't filter out ultraviolet rays. The snow reflected these rays and gave climbers a double dose, which could cause painful burning. Joanne made sure that every inch of exposed skin was protected by a thick sun cream.

The ropes were another safety precaution. To climb on a glacier alone without being roped to one's companion was to invite disaster. The purpose of roping up was not to pull one another up or down a mountainside but to limit and control a possible fall. Before a fall could be safely stopped, it had to be slowed. An abrupt jerk on the rope to stop a falling climber could cause more injury than the fall itself; in fact, a too-powerful yank to stop a fall could kill a man. Joanne had been well schooled by her father in the proper techniques of rope use and knew she could handle the situation well if Bryant should fall.

Ordinarily, just as it was considered risky for one person to swim alone, it was considered unsafe for fewer than three people to climb at high altitudes alone, especially in winter. Joanne knew of this safety "rule" and knew that she and Bryant were breaking it. However, if they weren't experienced enough to make the climb safely with just the two of them, then they certainly did not belong on the treacherous slopes of Dhaulagiri. On the Himalayan climb there were certain to be numerous two-person teams ascending together, scouting for camping sites or carrying supplies from a lower camp to a higher one. One of the things Bryant was testing now, Joanne felt sure, was how well she could handle herself with only one climbing partner.

"All set?" he asked, after the rope was securely in place around their waists.

"All set," Joanne agreed.

Bryant waved for her to precede him, to act as lead. This momentarily surprised her, but on further thought it seemed sensible. Bryant didn't doubt his own expertise; they were there to test *hers*. And before the climb was over she would prove herself once and for all!

Joanne began moving slowly up the glacier. It was covered with frozen snow, and she kick stepped her way up, ice ax firmly in hand. First she would lift her foot a small distance and kick with her boot gently against the snow until she had secured a step. Next she would place her boot on the step, test it, then slowly put her weight on it. Lifting her other boot, she would repeat the process. It was a slow but safe procedure and not overly strenuous. If Bryant was as experienced a mountaineer as she supposed him to be, he would soon realize that she too knew what she was doing. Slow, steady, tortoiselike progress up a mountainside was always more profitable than harelike bursts of speed that couldn't be sustained.

An open crevasse, a crack in the glacier, briefly slowed their ascent, but soon they were crossing a beautiful snow bridge. As they climbed, Joanne carefully crisscrossed the glacier, the safest procedure. While some crevasses were visible, many others were not. To minimize the danger of Bryant and herself both falling into one, they climbed in a zigzag pattern with the full fifty feet of rope stretched out between them. If one of them fell in, he or she could use spring-loaded handles to climb out again while the other anchored the rope. If both fell in, there'd be no anchored rope to use in climbing out.

The day was bright and clear, with an early-morning breeze that kept them pleasantly cool. Then the breeze died away, and the sun became an oppressive weight, pressing down on them from a cloudless blue sky. Joanne stopped long

enough to drink water slowly from her canteen
and eat another chocolate bar. Bryant stopped
when she did. Fifty feet away from her he also
ate and drank. Within a minute or two they
were on their way again.

They reached the ice wall they had been
heading toward, and Bryant climbed up to consult with Joanne. With a minimum of words
they agreed to climb along the left edge, a ridge
rising at an angle varying between fifty and sixty
degrees. They would belay each other up the
wall.

Again Joanne went first, while Bryant, in an
anchored position, slowly played out rope to
her. If she were to fall, he would immediately
limit and control her fall by means of the rope.
In time she stopped, anchored herself and be-
layed Bryant up to her. While climbing, Joanne
used the rhythmic rest step her father had taught
her. She raised one foot, then placed it against
the wall, knee bent, while the weight of her body
remained on the downhill foot. Two deep
breaths. Then she lifted the lower leg, up past
the higher one, bent it, placed it against the wall
and took two deep breaths while this leg rested.
Repeat...repeat...repeat. Bryant was using
the same step in almost precisely the same
rhythm. *We climb well together,* Joanne
thought, and she was filled with an odd pleasure. *Did Bryant realize this, too?*

They reached the top of the ice wall. A few
hundred feet above, the summit was visible. A

giant *bergschrund*—a large crevasse—blocked their direct path to the peak, so they veered to the left between other crevasses. At last, in a little less than eight hours after they'd left the cabin, they stood on the summit, breathing deeply as they gazed admiringly at the panorama below them: islands to the west, forests all around, glittering mountain peaks to the east.

Mount Baker had an elevation of 10,778 feet, which meant they were now standing over two miles above sea level. It was so clear that to the west they could see the Pacific Ocean rolling in. Watching, Joanne smiled to herself, feeling wonderfully happy. There was nothing in the world like being on top of a mountain, on top of the world!

They lingered on the summit for close to an hour, then started down. Bryant said he would lead the way, and to Joanne's surprise he did not take them down the same route they'd used coming up. To her chagrin, after the first hour or two she lost all sense of direction as well as time. An eight-hour ascent should have meant no more than a three-hour descent, but her mind and her aching body insisted that it was taking far longer than it should. She began to feel angry. Bryant was playing games again, taking them on a roundabout route, doing his best to exhaust her. Or was her mind playing tricks on her? She began to feel light-headed and unsure. By now her body was so numb with fatigue it was hard to force it to obey her commands. Or

was it her mind that was slipping away, toward
escape into sleep? If only she could catch a second wind! She was getting so tired.

At last they had left the icy slopes and hard
snow behind and once more were hiking across
a field of moss, lichen and heather. There were
hemlocks and fir trees. Bryant motioned toward
a structure Joanne could just make out in the
distance. Her heart leaped up. A mountain
lodge! So that's why Bryant had brought them
this way—a hot bath and a soft bed to rest on!

The sky was darkening with heavy clouds
when they at last reached the building. Few sights
had ever been as welcome to Joanne. As they
stepped up onto the porch of the lodge, Bryant
threw his arm across her back and grinned at her.
Joanne grinned back. Her legs, coming back to
life again, felt wobbly and weak. For the better
part of eighteen hours Bryant had kept her hiking
and climbing, but she'd made it! Exhausted she
might be, but so was he. It showed in his eyes, in
the lines of his sunburned face. They walked into
the lodge on their weary aching limbs, moving
slowly in their stiff heavy clothing.

A warm bath, clean clothes and a delicious
dinner in the small dining room did wonders to
revive Joanne. Bryant appeared equally re-
stored. His face glowed as he smiled across at
her, his light sprinkling of freckles dancing
across his cheeks as he laughed. Joanne felt the
same deep sense of satisfaction she always did
after a long and strenuous climb. No feeling on

earth matched it, as far as she was concerned. Though she and Bryant talked very little over dinner, they kept smiling and laughing for no particular reason except sheer fatigue. They had shared a long day, a day that had begun in the middle of a long cold night. Bryant didn't tell her in so many words that she had climbed exceptionally well, but he didn't have to. A new warmth in his smile said it, a look of admiration in his dark green eyes. After a long leisurely dinner, they walked outside to stroll a few minutes before heading to bed.

By this time Joanne's sore legs were stiffening a bit, but so were Bryant's. They walked very slowly, just a few feet from the porch of the lodge, and then stood contentedly gazing around. The world was fast losing the slight afterglow of the setting sun.

Motioning toward the outline of a soaring peak to their left, Joanne murmured that it appeared an entirely different mountain from this viewpoint. It did not look at all like the broad bosomed matron they had set out that morning to climb.

Bryant laughed. He slipped an arm around Joanne's waist, which caused her instantly to tense. "Because that *is* a different mountain," Bryant informed her. "That's Mount Shuksan, not Baker. The two peaks are almost exactly ten miles apart." He motioned toward the right. "That level summit over there hides Mount Baker from our view here. We skirted it to get here, which is why the descent took us rather long. But I felt it was worth it.''

"Yes," Joanne agreed. At the same time she felt a cold wave of anger. She had spent so many hours studying maps and photos of Glacier Peak, the mountain Bryant had told her they were going to climb, that she would have known exactly where she was at all times. Bryant had cheated her out of this by his last-minute switch, which is probably exactly why he'd pulled it. It was fine for him to be warm and friendly now, but he had played a mean trick on her.

As though sensing her anger, Bryant dropped his arm from around her waist. He stepped past her and stood staring out at the darkening scenes before them. After a minute, forcing her anger away, Joanne moved up to join him.

"Where we are now is just about as far north as we can go in the United States except for Alaska," Bryant told her. "The road that leads up here to the lodge runs parallel to the Canadian border about five miles from it. Mount Shuksan is about twelve miles from the border, and the view to the north from its peak is of Canada, including the city of Vancouver and the peak of Mount Garibaldi, which can be seen on a clear day though it's a hundred miles away.''

"You've climbed through here before then?" Joanne asked.

"Years ago, when I was a kid.''

A moment later Bryant took her arm and suggested they go back inside. "A good night's sleep is what we both need right now."

To Joanne's surprise, just before they reached the lodge steps, Bryant pulled her over to one side. The next thing she knew his arms were around her. He lowered his head, and his full soft lips came pressing down on hers.

Joanne felt a surge of fury. Her heart raced. Why was it that his lips felt so soft, yet hot and demanding at the same time? Joanne was aware of her knees weakening, and she feared she might fall. She tried to back away and pull free, but Bryant's hold tightened. She managed to swing her head around.

"Stop it! Right now!" she hissed, her head ringing with odd jangly noises. Her blood pounded through her in fury and fright. "Bryant, let go!" She jerked even harder against his hold, and his arms fell away. He stood gazing mockingly down at her, his green eyes glittering, then he lifted one hand to push up a stray strand of her silky black hair, the touch oddly gentle, belying the coolness of his eyes.

"Don't you ever—ever—do that again!" Joanne could feel a mist of tears move into her eyes as she glared at him, which only upset her more. "I'm here at your invitation, at your insistence, but solely as a climber, a member of your team—nothing more! And I will not be treated this way, do you understand?" She whirled around, stepping blindly toward the stairs. Her progress was halted by Bryant, who grabbed her arm.

"Hold it a minute, Joanne, please." His voice was gentle, his eyes no longer dancing with glittering amusement. He pulled her back toward him. When she came to a stop before him, he held her by both arms and stood gazing steadily down into her eyes. After a minute he added, in an even softer voice, "As you obviously feel insulted, I apologize. I'll try to keep from upsetting you in like fashion in future." A smile broke across his full lips as he dropped hold of her arms and extended his hand. "Friends again?"

"Well—"

"My word on what I said. No more upsetting you like that."

"Well—" As her eyes flicked up to meet his, Joanne felt a rather embarrassed smile part her lips. Her cheeks had flushed. She'd made rather an idiot of herself, she supposed, but at the same time she'd meant every word. Bryant could play all the games he liked with her when it came to the expedition and she had little choice but to put up with them. That didn't mean she had to allow *this* kind of meaningless game, putting up with kisses and embraces she had not invited and did not want.

After the briefest of hesitations, she slipped her hand into his. "All right. I accept your apology and will take you at your word. Friends again."

"Good." Bryant smiled warmly at her, then leaned down to press a friendly kiss on her cheek. The next moment he wound her hand over his arm and led her into the lodge.

CHAPTER FIVE

"JOANNE, WAKE UP!"

Joanne woke abruptly to find herself staring up into Bryant's face. "What are you doing in here?" she hissed, her pulse pounding. The lodge was full of skiers, and she hadn't gotten a room of her own but was sleeping in a dormitory with numerous other women. What did Bryant think he was doing barging in here in the middle of the night?

"Obviously I'm waking you. Now get up." With that, he turned and walked quietly out.

Joanne hesitated only momentarily, then slowly moved her aching body out of bed. She dressed quickly, making as little noise as possible, and left the room. She found Bryant waiting for her downstairs. The lodge clock read a quarter to three. He handed her a cup of hot coffee.

"Couldn't this have waited until dawn?" Joanne asked sarcastically, before cautiously sipping from the cup.

Bryant's lips curled into a tight smile. "I always like to get an early start."

"On what?"

"We're climbing Shuksan today."

Stunned, Joanne lowered the cup with a sudden jerk and coffee splashed over the brim. "We're what? You're crazy!"

Bryant's dark green eyes cut into her. "No, Miss Patton," he said icily, "you're the one who is crazy. Do you think climbing Dhaulagiri will be a picnic, one long day of exertion, then weeks of rest? Go back up to get your pack, and I'll meet you out on the porch in five minutes."

As they started off, Joanne alternated between feeling furious at Bryant and feeling upset with herself that she'd shown resistance to his plan. It wasn't back-to-back days of climbing that upset her, she insisted to herself, it was Bryant's sneaky way of never keeping her informed. This was his way, she was sure, of throwing her off balance, of trying to force her to break. He'd done everything possible to make their climb yesterday as arduous as possible: starting them from miles down the road, then lengthening their descent by taking them around to the lodge. Joanne sighed. Well, this was as good a way as any, she supposed, of testing her endurance, of finding out how much she could take. The only sensible thing to do was swallow her resentment, gather her strength and make it through another day of climbing with him.

From the twilight look she'd had of Mount Shuksan the previous evening, she knew that while it wasn't quite as high as Mount Baker, it was a more spectacular mountain and would be more difficult to climb. Where Mount Baker was white, rounded and beautiful, Mount Shuksan had looked dark, jagged and forbidding. Or maybe it was only because she'd been very tired that it had seemed so threatening. Of all the mountains she'd ever seen close up, it was the first that she'd felt no impulse to climb. But, Joanne assured herself determinedly, climb it she would. If that's what Bryant wanted, that's what he'd get. She could handle a difficult, hard-edged "masculine" mountain quite as well as he could, and before the day was out she'd prove it.

With the dawn, Joanne got a clearer look at the mountain they were challenging. It had several high, hanging glaciers, its craggy summit rising steeply above them. It would be a slow tricky climb. Bryant had mentioned as they were leaving the lodge that Mount Shuksan was one of the great tourist attractions of the state of Washington. Although less than ten thousand feet high, it was starkly impressive and looked exactly the way people imagined a mountain should look. Some mountaineers found it too jagged and threatening and for this reason steered clear of it, while others found it just frightening enough to be irresistibly attractive. Joanne could tell from the sound of Bryant's voice as he told her this that he belonged to the latter group: the more dangerous the climb, the more appealing.

As daylight overtook them, the weather became a repeat of the day before: bright and clear with a refreshing early-morning breeze. After a few delightful hours, though, the breeze deserted them and the sun became oppressive. Part of the time Bryant led the way, other times Joanne did. In most respects the climb was a repeat of the previous day, except more difficult. By late morning the sky had become almost completely overcast, and the grayness was chilly and depressing. Joanne's limbs ached. As frequently as she drank from her canteen, she felt increasingly dried out. Hour after hour she and Bryant climbed, fifty feet apart.

At one point Bryant slipped into a crevasse, but the crack was sufficiently narrow that he could use his crampons against one wall and chimney himself back up. When they finally reached the summit, Joanne felt a tremendous sense of relief but little triumph. The sky was so cloudy that visibility was poor. Bryant, climbing behind her, looked as grim faced and tired as she felt.

The way down was slow and torturous. By the time they reached the lodge, Joanne felt too exhausted to talk. She parted from Bryant and went upstairs to soak in a hot tub. Dinner was quiet and for the most part silent. When Bryant suggested a short stroll outside after dinner, Joanne, remembering what had happened the evening before, coolly declined. She relaxed in the entry room of the lodge, reading the morning paper. Bryant sat in the chair next to her. When she caught herself nodding off, she said her good-nights and went upstairs.

"See you in the morning," Bryant called after her.

"Right," Joanne called back. She was pleased with her day's performance and felt completely exhausted and ready for sleep.

She woke just before dawn the following morning and after lying in bed for a few minutes rose and dressed. When she went downstairs, she was delighted not to see Bryant anywhere around. He must be sleeping in later than she. She went outside and stood gazing happily at the mountainous country surrounding her: the rugged jagged Mount Shuksan, on whose peak she had stood just yesterday, and the level summit of Table Mountain, behind which Mount Baker was hidden. She rose on tiptoe, exuberantly inhaling the marvelous mountain air. Bryant had put her to the test and she'd passed, no problem. Smiling to herself, she turned and went back inside.

Bryant appeared about half an hour later. After a leisurely breakfast, they started down the road. "It'll be quite a walk back to where we parked the camper," he remarked. "Are you sure you can make it?"

"Do I have any choice?"

Bryant laughed. The sound was warm and enveloping. "A beautiful young woman always has choices. Wait here, if you like, and I'll drive back for you.''

Joanne's response was immediate. "Thank you, but no thanks. I'm quite able to make it. In fact, give me the camper keys and I'll hike down and return for you."

At that, Bryant laughed even harder. Momentarily he put his arm around Joanne's shoulder and pulled her to him, but before she could protest the embrace he released her again.

They walked at a friendly leisurely pace. Not far below the lodge, they passed a small lake, on the surface of which the starkly beautiful Mount Shuksan was reflected. Joanne felt hushed by the imposing image. She stopped walking to let its grandeur sink in. Bryant stood silently beside her, then after a moment he moved behind her. He advanced slowly, slipped his arms around her and pulled her back to rest against him. Joanne was momentarily startled, then felt an irresistible impulse to relax and allow him to hold her. It felt so comfortable, his arms around her, her body pulled back to where she felt the gentle presence of his.

Just before she stirred at last to pull free, Bryant pressed a kiss on her cheek, then whispered into her ear, the warmth of his lips tickling her, "I'm proud of you, Joanne. Your father was right: you're one hell of a good climber."

Exhilarated by these words, Joanne spun around and faced him, her eyes sparkling with the thought: *I told you so!* Bryant's lips moved apart in an answering grin. Joanne's pulse raced. Suddenly his smile died away and he pulled her close, his hands no longer holding her gently but clasping her harshly, insistently. He drew her against him and his lips lowered demandingly on hers.

In shock she tried to break his hold. Just two nights ago he had promised, had given his word.... After a momentary struggle Joanne felt the familiar weakening in her knees. Her skin flushed hot and cold, and her heart pounded. She wanted to pull free, shout at him, curse him. She wanted to let go, melt against him, become one with him. Tears stung her eyes. With a will of their own her arms slipped around his shoulders, and she began kissing him back.

At last Bryant released her. As he drew away he caught her hands and held them tightly. His dark green eyes gazed into hers, and his broad handsome face held a sad troubled expression that made Joanne's heart race even faster.

"What's the matter?" she whispered, her voice hoarse.

At first he didn't answer, then he shook his head slowly and, turning aside, muttered, "My apologies. Come on, let's be on our way."

Joanne felt severely shaken as they continued their downhill walk. Tension gripped her. She did not like James Bryant. She objected strongly to his tyrannical manner and the way he ordered her around. Maybe she should admit she'd made a mistake and back out, turn to Bryant right this minute and say, *Look, I now realize that this has all been a big mistake. I don't want to join your expedition after all.*

As she thought this, Joanne's eyes wandered across to the tall, powerfully built man striding along at her side, and a shiver ran through her. What was the matter with her? Their two days of climbing together had gone extremely well. Hadn't Bryant admitted as much, telling her she was "one hell of a good climber"? What was it that was really worrying her, frightening her to the point where she wanted to run? Her eyes stayed fixed on Bryant's face.

He glanced around and caught her staring at him. A slight smile tugged at his lips. He moved a bit closer to her and asked in a very soft voice, "Joanne, I'll ask you what you asked me a minute ago: what's the matter? Can you tell me what's troubling you?"

Joanne stared into his broad sunburned face for a moment, then suddenly shook her head hard. A light shudder ran through her. No, she couldn't tell *him*, but she realized now what was bothering her. It was this silly schoolgirl reaction to Bryant: she had not yet learned how to control her physical reactions to this man. When he touched her, it caused wild uninvited sensations. Her body took over and reacted in a way completely at variance with her thoughts. This had been true from their very first meeting;

the slightest touch of his hand sent weird chills through her.

Joanne smiled, still looking straight across into Bryant's eyes. Now that she knew what the problem was, now that she had identified it, she knew it would be a problem no more. For some unfathomable reason, she found the physical attraction between this overbearing man and herself uncomfortably strong, but now that she had faced it, she knew she could handle it. She wouldn't allow it to throw her again. He was not the type of man she'd ever seriously love, though she did find him physically attractive. But she *did* want to join his team and climb in the Himalayas with him, and with that goal in mind she would certainly learn to control these overpowering sensations.

"Nothing's the matter," Joanne replied coolly. "Everything's fine."

Bryant smiled at her. "Good."

Before noon they reached the parking area where Bryant had left the camper. With a sigh of reluctance, Joanne climbed in for the return to Seattle.

Instead of going into the city, Bryant drove them to his home. Joanne tensed when she saw where he'd taken her, but she told herself that was silly.

"We can rest and relax this afternoon. I'll fix us dinner here tonight, then in the morning I'll drive you into the city if you have to catch a flight back."

Joanne smiled. "Not *have* to," she mocked lightly. "*Want* to."

Bryant looked momentarily startled, then he grinned. His green eyes sparkled animatedly and his thick reddish brown hair tumbled about his head. Joanne felt her breath catch, he looked so attractive.

"My error," Bryant said, laughter bubbling in his voice. "*Want* to, not *have* to. I'll remember that."

They climbed into the camper and retrieved their packs, then Bryant led her into the house, remarking that he'd unload the rest of their equipment after he'd gotten her comfortably settled in.

He led her into the guest bedroom, a lovely, large blue-and-white room with an adjoining bathroom.

Joanne took a long leisurely bath, then slipped on a soft black turtleneck sweater and black slacks. She carefully brushed her fine black, freshly washed hair until it gleamed. Pulling it tightly back from her face, she pinned it into a knot at the back of her head. Glancing at herself, she frowned and decided that she really did not feel in such a severe mood. She unpinned it, allowing it to fall freely down to her shoulders. After a moment she decided she didn't like that either. She walked over to the bed, picked up her purse and pulled out a black grosgrain ribbon. Ordinarily she never appeared in public with her hair tied back with a ribbon.

She felt it made her look too girlish. But at home, doing housework, that was the way she customarily wore it. Seating herself at the vanity mirror, she tied her hair back and immediately decided that for the moment this suited her fine.

She found Bryant in the kitchen. He was sliding a roasting pan into the oven as she walked in. "You didn't know I was the best cook in these parts, did you?" he greeted her.

"Are there no limits to the man's talents!" Joanne declaimed, waving her arms for dramatic emphasis.

As Bryant burst forth with his full rich laughter, Joanne broke down and joined him. It was one of the warmest moments they'd ever shared. As their laughter died away, there followed a slightly constrained silence in which Joanne experienced both embarrassment and an indefinable loneliness. She kept her eyes away from Bryant, afraid to look at him.

He offered her a drink then led the way out of the kitchen, remarking that the bar was in the den.

Every room in the house struck Joanne as so attractive, so charming, she felt she was repeating Bryant's experience: she was falling in love with someone else's home. "I really love your place," Joanne remarked lightly. "I don't suppose you've ever thought of selling it?"

Bryant was pouring their drinks. He glanced around with a surprised, pleased look. "I'm afraid not. I could never understand how my sister could bear to give it up.''

As Bryant handed her the Scotch highball she'd asked for, Joanne said, ''Well, if you ever do decide to sell—''

''Which I never will, believe me.''

''But if you should—''

''It won't happen.''

''Well, keep me in mind, anyway. Promise you'll give me first chance.''

Bryant laughed. He picked up his own drink and motioned for her to follow him.

He led the way outside, and they settled down into comfortable patio chairs, facing the woods. ''Listen carefully, and you can hear the scurrying of the squirrels,'' Bryant remarked softly. ''Watch, and you can see them dash from one tree to another. Often, on a Sunday afternoon, I'll sit out here for hours, no matter how much work I've brought home, no matter what problems are waiting inside. Within a few minutes I'm totally relaxed. The world fades away and I haven't a care. You don't imagine I'd ever willingly part with that?''

Joanne smiled. ''No, I don't imagine you would.''

They sipped their drinks companionably, gazing out on the woods, and Joanne felt the same peace fill her that Bryant had spoken of. The world before them was darkening into evening when Bryant casually asked her what was waiting for her back in San Francisco that made her want to return before she had to.

"Oh—lots of things," Joanne murmured, a slight frown drifting over her face. "For one thing, I want to drive down to see my mother before the holiday ends. Apart from that, I'd like the chance to rest and relax a day or two before I have to return to work."

"You don't think you could relax here?" he asked in a quiet voice.

Joanne glanced around at him and grinned. Of course she could relax there, she thought, as long as Bryant wasn't around. He had fixed her a second drink, and she could feel the tensions of the past couple of days begin to fade. At the same time deep within her stirred waves of excitement. She'd successfully passed another of Bryant's tests and could hardly believe she would soon be leaving to spend four months climbing in the Himalayas!

Bryant's voice interrupted her thoughts. "I'd wager you've got a big New Year's date to get ready for. Am I right?"

Joanne felt a slight stir of discomfort. She hadn't given a thought to Scottie lately. "Well, I do have a date, but whether it's a big one—" Her voice died away as she frowned. Had she ever, even once, had what she'd thought of as a big date with Scottie?

"What are your plans for New Year's Eve," Bryant inquired, "if I may be so bold as to ask?"

"Well, they're pretty much the usual."

Joanne's frown deepened. "We have dinner reservations, then later we'll drop by the home of some friends. Nothing spectacular."

"We?" Bryant echoed. "You and a friend?"

"Yes."

"The same friend who was with you at Penny's the night we met?"

"Yes. That's the one."

"He's a close friend?"

Joanne circled her eyes around to meet his. "Yes, a very close one." *But not a man I'm in love with, not my lover!*

Bryant grinned.

"And you?" Joanne asked, her pulse picking up. "What are your plans?"

Bryant shrugged. "Pretty much the same. Dinner first, then a party. Just as you said, nothing spectacular."

With a friend, of course, Joanne thought. *And is it some woman you're in love with,* she wondered. Her face warmed as she lowered her gaze. Naturally she did not ask.

Silence fell as the world darkened before them.

They ate dinner by candlelight at the dining-room table. Bryant sat at the head, placing Joanne to his right. He had fixed a zucchini dish, baked with tomatoes and nuts and smothered with melted cheese. They sipped wine with their meal, and for dessert Bryant carried in a plate of fruit, nuts and cheese.

In the flickering light from the candles,

Bryant's face glowed as he talked quietly with her. He seemed so different here in his home, so friendly, charming and attentive. She could scarcely believe it was the man she'd known up to now. *This must be the real Jim Bryant*, she thought in surprise. *If she hadn't had to force herself into his life this was the man she would have gotten to know.* Except, if it hadn't been for the expedition she probably wouldn't have gotten to know him at all. And she found this Jim Bryant, the man who sat at the candlelit table talking and laughing quietly with her, all but completely irresistible.

As they rose at last, Bryant suggested that she go into the living room to relax while he cleared the table.

"Oh, no, I'll help, of course," she protested, and picking up her plate, silverware and wineglass she followed him into the kitchen.

After he'd rinsed the dishes off and placed them by the sink, Bryant turned to face Joanne, his dark eyes gazing steadily, almost somberly into hers.

"You've proved you're not only a beautiful young woman, you're also a fearless adventurous one," he said softly. "Being the good sport that you are, how'd you like to go on one more climb?"

Joanne's face registered her shock. "What! When?"

"Tonight."

"You're kidding!"

Bryant laughed. The laugh was deep yet soft, sending velvety shivers through Joanne. His large strong hand touched her arm. "No. Please, go grab a jacket and gloves and we'll go."

Joanne did as requested, though she couldn't imagine what he had in mind. When she rejoined him, instead of leading her out to the garage where the camper was parked, he walked out onto the patio. Using a large flashlight, he led her across the back lawn, the damp grass squishing under their feet. They entered the woods, Bryant flashing his light on the tree trunks they walked by. He stopped before one tree and stood grinning down at her.

"Here we are. An easy climb, as you'll see, with short steps all the way."

In surprise Joanne looked more closely at the huge trunk and saw that there were strips of wood nailed in, one above the other, to form a ladder.

"Up you go," Bryant said. He put his hands to her waist and gave her an initial boost up the steps.

The climb was every bit as easy as Bryant had said it would be. He was a few steps behind and kept the light flashing up the trunk so she could see her way. Within minutes she reached a platform high up in the tree branches. After climbing onto it she looked up and felt her heart swell at the clear bright sky overhead. A million stars sparkled down on them. Bryant followed her onto the platform and sat down cross-legged across from her.

"It's delightful," Joanne said. "You built it, of course."

"With more than a little help from Peter, my sister's husband," Bryant told her. "We built it the first summer they owned the house, the summer I was thirteen, and it was my favorite spot from then on. I'd bring my books up here, my transistor radio, anything and everything. In fact, I always wanted to sleep up here, but my sister was frightened and wouldn't let me. She was afraid I'd roll off."

"A good thing one of you had some sense," Joanne said, laughing softly.

Bryant laughed too. "Right you are. The first summer I didn't have steps. When Peter suggested them I thought that was far too sissy. I just shinned up the trunk, like Tarzan. But then—then I got to know this girl—" Bryant's eyes circled up to the sky as his voice cut off. Suddenly he seemed far away, lost in his adolescence, yet at the same time he'd never seemed so close, as though his words, wrapped in nostalgia, had successfully drawn Joanne into that other world in which he'd once lived.

Bryant remained silent for a moment, still staring at the stars. Then slowly he lowered his eyes and smiled. "Her name was Sara, and her family had a summer home up the road. She was a few months older than I, and the most beautiful girl in the world, I thought then, with the deepest gray eyes. Hour after hour I sat up here, thinking about her, mooning the summer away. I may have dragged up my books and radio, but I'm not sure I read one page or heard one song. All I did was dream the hours away, hungering for Sara.''

Bryant fell silent again, a faraway look in his eyes. ''So?'' Joanne prodded softly after several moments.

''So?'' Bryant grinned. ''So the following summer, when I was fourteen, I told Pete I did want steps up to my treehouse after all, so he got me the wood. I carefully measured and cut the steps, nailed them on and then the big day— I actually talked Sara into climbing up the steps.''

''Good for you,'' Joanne murmured, a tumultuous mix of emotions from sympathy to envy filling her. ''So what happened?''

''What happened?'' Bryant burst out laughing. His eyes sparkled, brighter than the innumerable stars above them. ''What a day that was! A Sunday, and Sara's family was here visiting. It was almost the end of summer, and I'd been begging her for weeks, for months, to climb up here. If only she would, she'd love it, I swore. She was about to leave for the city just as I was—this was my final chance. At last, late in the afternoon, she agreed. My heart almost burst. I led her out here, kept assuring her she'd find it easy to climb up here, no problem. She stood at the base of the trunk for what seemed like hours, then finally grabbed hold of one of the steps and started up. Up she went, with me right behind her, my heart almost bursting. She got up to where her eyes were on a level with the platform, took one look across it, murmured, 'Yes, Jim, it's very nice,' then started down again, irritably telling me to please hurry up or else get out of her way. That's what happened.''

"Poor Jim,'' Joanne teased. "Maybe she was afraid of heights.''

"It's far more likely that she was afraid of me and rightfully so. Once I got her up here, my plan was to throw myself on her, plead my love and steal a few kisses, or anything else I could get away with. That's all I'd thought about all summer, and I came so close! Or thought I did.''

"Poor Jim,'' Joanne murmured again, smiling.

Bryant grinned. He leaned across the short distance between them and lightly kissed her cheek. Then he put one hand to the back of her head, his fingers tangling in her hair, and drew her slightly toward him as his lips sought and found hers. Joanne's heart all but stopped. Bryant's lips were so soft; she could feel their softness all through her. He moved closer, put his arms around her and the kiss became more intense, his mouth pressing hungrily against hers. When he drew away at last, the look in his eyes set her senses afire.

"A dream come true,'' he said softly, "all the

better for the delay." Again he put his arms around her and kissed her.

They stayed up on the tree platform for close to an hour. For most of that time Bryant sat behind Joanne, his strong arms around her. She gave up trying to interpret the conflicting emotions she felt toward him and was content to luxuriate in the feeling of warmth and security that leaning against him gave her. A three-quarter moon rose high enough to flood their perch with silvery light.

"I ordered a full moon," Bryant whispered into her ear, "but apparently there's been a mix-up. Sorry."

Releasing his embrace, he turned her around and kissed her, his hands holding her arms. In the magical light, Joanne found herself staring into his shadowy face, transfixed by how handsome it was. Suddenly she shivered.

Surprise darkened Bryant's eyes. "You're cold. We'd better climb down and go back inside."

"Oh, not quite yet, please. It's so very beautiful here."

He cradled her in his arms, smiling down at her. Joanne felt so warm and happy inside she couldn't believe it when she suddenly began to shiver uncontrollably.

"That does it. Down we go," Bryant announced. "I'll lead the way to give you light."

The climb down, with Bryant's flashlight outlining each step for her, was every bit as easy as the climb up. Within minutes they were crossing the back lawn. Bryant's arm was draped around her, but still Joanne kept shivering, even after they'd stepped back inside the warm living room.

"It didn't seem that cold to me," Bryant said. "I hope you haven't caught a chill."

It hadn't been that cold. As Bryant stood gazing down at her with concern, Joanne made an even stronger effort to gain control and stop trembling, but it didn't help. Dismay filled her. She'd gone through two days of strenuous climbing in the ice and snow without even a moment's chill, and now to have this happen— what a fool she was making of herself!

Suddenly Bryant swooped her up in his arms. He carried her into the guest bedroom, where she'd left her things, and placed her gently on the bed, then sat beside her. He unzipped her jacket, pulled it off and began tenderly chafing her arms with his large strong hands.

"This should help. We'll have you over it in a jiffy," he said, smiling.

Joanne blinked against the stinging mist in her eyes. Her shivering was dying down. It seemed to her as if she'd had to shiver and shake to cast off the hardness she'd been forced to encase herself in to make it onto Bryant's team. As Bryant tenderly rubbed her arms, she felt all her anger and resentment toward him flow out, leaving her feeling refreshed and newborn.

"There," Bryant said, smiling down at her as

the last of her trembling died away. His dark gleaming eyes said that he understood. He leaned down and pressed his mouth against hers.

This kiss was the softest, sweetest one yet. Joanne felt joy wash over her. She put her arms around Bryant and pulled him down closer. His lips left her mouth and he pressed his cheek to hers.

"You're a beautiful young woman, Joanne," he whispered softly, "and every bit as strong as you are beautiful."

With his tongue he traced along the delicate edge of her neck, and this time the shiver Joanne felt was one of pure delight. Instinctively her arms around him tightened.

"And you're wonderfully attractive," she murmured.

Bryant drew back and gazed at her, his dark eyes gleaming. His large hands slid down over the curves of her breast to her waist. With excruciating slowness he eased his fingers up beneath the woolen fabric of her sweater and deftly slipped it over her head. Leaning down, he pressed kisses along her bare shoulders and arms, and Joanne felt a hot rush of desire surge through her. Pulling her into his arms, he held her tightly a moment, his breath coming hard and fast. Then his fingers found the clasp of her bra, and the silky garment fell free.

"Beautiful," he murmured, his voice husky with desire. As he pressed his face down against her rounded breasts a wild pleasure filled Joanne. His lips caressed her nipples into hardened peaks while his hands cupped the soft creamy fullness. At his touch she bit back a moan.

Her hands trembling, Joanne reached up and began to undo the buttons of Bryant's shirt. With gentle kisses and caresses they swiftly undressed each other, then Bryant slid from the bed. Crossing the room, he switched off the light, then walked over to the window and pulled back the draperies. Moonlight flooded the room, falling over Joanne where she lay on the bed, fully naked. With a gasp of delight she sat up and stared out at the moon, incredibly bright in the night sky.

Bryant moved onto the bed beside her. Again he held her as he had on the platform, sitting behind her, his arms around her. But now his hands cupped her uncovered breasts, and she rested against his bare chest. His fingers tenderly teased her nipples until they rose with an aching stiffness. With a cry Joanne swung her head around.

"Oh, Jim," she moaned.

He drew away then and, pushed her gently down onto the bed. Leaning down he buried his face against the soft curve of her hips. With one hand he began tracing small circles along her inner thigh until Joanne felt her blood had turned to liquid fire.

Raising himself up, he found her lips once

more. "Oh, Joanne, you're so very beautiful," he whispered, then his mouth passionately captured hers as his hand pressed against her yearning softness.

Joanne's head whirled, and she was lost in sensations so exquisite she could not begin to sort them out. She lifted herself to meet him and let out a cry of delight as Bryant thrust within, drawn by the aching power of his need.

"You're so lovely," he said hoarsely, then his mouth hungrily captured hers again.

Their passion crested as they reached their peak. Cascading down, they lay quietly in each other's arms, their glistening skin lit by the silvery moonlight streaming in.

CHAPTER SIX

WHEN JOANNE WOKE in the morning she was alone.

She pulled over the spare pillow and, propping her head up, lay in bed staring out the window. Bryant's image seemed to hover in the clear morning air, so close she felt she could reach out and embrace him. Why wasn't he still here so she *could* embrace him? She'd wakened once during the night and Bryant had still been beside her, but sometime after that he had obviously slipped away, without disturbing her.

Joanne sighed, feeling warm and contented, then slowly, though she fought against it, a cold apprehension spread within her. Bryant had seemed so different the night before, so charming and friendly, attentive and appreciative of her, but could that simply have been one more way of testing her?

Bryant had never taken any pains to hide the fact that he felt physically attracted to her—and had from their very first meeting. During two days of climbing they had developed a strong underlying sense of companionship and mutual trust. They could not have made it through their climbs if this had not been so. And what had happened the previous night had seemed so natural, so right—an extension of the intimacy they had shared on the mountainside. But if it *was* a test.... Frowning, Joanne tossed the covers back and climbed out of bed.

As she showered and dressed she tried to dismiss all worry. Last night had been so lovely, and the man she had been with on the platform high in the tree, the man who had later gently chafed her hands and arms to warm them, who had then, with kisses and caresses, brought her to the peak of ecstasy and held her tenderly afterward—that man had not been testing her. He had been with her, genuine and real. Joanne told herself this over and over, but still a tiny thread of anxiety remained. The night together had been so marvelous, yet what if it had cost her her place on the team, robbing her of her dream....

After dressing in her black slacks and a dark blue blouse, Joanne made one final check of herself in the mirror, then walked out of Bryant's guest room, her head high, her step quick and energetic. Today was the thirtieth. She'd arrived in Seattle almost four days earlier—four days that had surely been the longest days of her life.

She found Bryant in the kitchen, settled in at the nook, sipping hot coffee and reading the morning paper. As she walked in, he glanced around. Smiling, he stood up and walked over to greet her. After holding her close for a moment he pressed a kiss on her brow.

"Good morning, darling," he said. "I hope you slept well."

"Yes, thank you. I did."

Bryant drew away. His hands clasped her loosely by the arms as his dark eyes gazed steadily into hers. "Are you still of a mind to return home this morning?" he asked.

Joanne glanced away, trembling slightly. More testing? Was he or was he not playing games with her? Her eyes circled back and caught his. Frowning, she said, "Yes, I really think I'd better."

Bryant's gaze became even more intense. "You aren't in the mood to turn your back on the world, forget everyone else and hide away here just with me for another day or two? I could phone my office, tell them I won't be in, cancel the luncheon date I have, the dinner date I have for tonight, all appointments tomorrow, tomorrow night's date—"

Joanne burst out laughing. "Enough, enough! No, I don't want you to do that, and I wouldn't feel right changing my plans, either. But thank you for asking."

Bryant released her arms, caught up one of her hands, raised it gallantly to his lips and kissed it. "You don't think, then, that the world is well lost for love?" he asked softly, his eyes meeting hers.

Love. Was Bryant saying that he loved her?

Joanne's pulse skipped. She felt a catch in her throat as she answered lightly, in keeping with his tone, "Not today, I'm afraid. I really must go home, and I don't want it on my conscience that I dragged you away from all your appointments. But thank you again."

Sighing Bryant released her hand. "As you wish. If I can't persuade you to stay, can I at least offer you some breakfast?"

"Thank you, yes." Smiling, Joanne walked by him to seat herself at the kitchen nook.

They shared a leisurely breakfast of hotcakes with mounds of butter and mouth-watering maple syrup. The conversation stayed light and friendly, yet over and over, as Bryant's gleaming eyes caught on hers, especially when he grinned or laughed, Joanne felt as if she were melting with joy. Twice it was on the tip of her tongue to say she'd changed her mind, she *would* stay after all, but each time she caught herself. She'd promised her mother that she'd drive down to San Carlos to see her, and she owed it to Scottie not to cancel their New Year's Eve date. Besides she wasn't sure how sincere Bryant's offer had been.

In a little more than an hour after breakfast, Joanne had all her belongings neatly packed, ready to be carried out to Bryant's car. During the drive to Seattle, neither she nor Bryant seemed to have much to say. They stopped by his office very briefly, then he drove her to the airport. They arrived a few minutes early and stood close together, Bryant's arm slipped through hers, but still neither one said anything of importance. As her flight was announced, Bryant caught up her hand and pressed it to his lips, his dark eyes gazing intently down into hers.

"Now or never, Joanne. You're sure you don't want to change your mind?"

Joanne's smile was quick but weak. "Yes, I'm sure."

His arms went around her, and he held her so close that Joanne's knees weakened, as did her resolve—almost. His lips found hers and softly, sweetly, he kissed her goodbye. As he released her at last, Joanne hurriedly picked up her carry-on case and walked away quickly, telling herself firmly again that she was doing the right thing. She hesitated once, glancing back, and saw that Bryant stood watching her, frowning. Seeing her wave, he smiled and waved back. With a sigh she turned and continued toward the plane.

BRYANT PHONED HER the next afternoon, a little before five. "Just wanted to wish you the very happiest of new years," he said. "I phoned this early knowing you were going out later. I hope you have a marvelous time."

"Thank you." Joanne's pulse raced at the sound of his voice. "You too, Jim." It felt strange to be calling him by his first name. "You're going to dinner tonight and on to your party with a beautiful female companion, no doubt?"

After a slight hesitation, Bryant said, "Well, yes, but I'll be thinking about you and missing you all evening, believe me."

Joanne laughed. "While I'll be thinking of you and missing you. Well, thank you again for phoning...and happy New Year."

She replaced the receiver and sighed, wishing for the hundredth time that she had given in to her weaknesses and stayed in Seattle.

TWO DAYS LATER Joanne heard news that enraged her. Her friend Hope from the Alpine Club phoned that evening and in the course of their talk asked Joanne how soon she was leaving for Washington.

Joanne felt the blood drain from her face. "What are you talking about? If you mean Washington State—Seattle—I just returned from a short trip there, but how did you hear about it?"

It turned out that that wasn't what Hope was referring to. She had run into Michael Ross, one of the climbers signed up for Bryant's team, and Michael had mentioned that the team was assembling in Washington State on January 4 for workouts on Mount Rainier, a mountain that had often been used as training grounds for Himalayan expeditions. Hope knew that Joanne planned to go on the expedition, so had assumed she would be heading to Washington State to meet with the other climbers.

Joanne was devastated, but she concealed this

from her friend. "Well, we're so busy at work right now," she lied, "I'm just not sure I can get away."

Though she'd spent almost four days with Bryant, winding up in bed with him, he hadn't told her of this meeting, hadn't even hinted at it. Apparently he still did not think of her as belonging and was planning to cast her aside. *Oh, that rotter!* Joanne thought, tears blinding her eyes. That he had made love to her while still plotting to dump her hurt almost unbearably. Somehow, some way, she'd pay him back!

She ended the call with Hope as fast as she could and with trembling hands dialed Bryant's home number. He'd given her the number while they were waiting for her plane that last morning in Seattle. The phone rang so many times without being answered that Joanne began to be sure that Bryant wasn't home, which left her feeling even more outraged and defeated, but finally the receiver was lifted and Bryant said, "Yes? Hello?"

"Bryant, it's me, Joanne." Her voice sounded breathless, she knew, but her mouth was so dry she couldn't help it. "When the phone rang so long—"

"I just this minute got home." Bryant's voice sounded cold and distant. "Give me half a minute, please. It's raining and I'm soaking wet. Or, on second thought, why don't you let me call you back?"

Because I'm not sure you will! Joanne

thought. "No, I'll wait, thank you. Just remember I'm on the line."

Bryant laughed, a brief hard sound. "Fat chance I'd forget." She could hear him place the receiver down.

In a surprisingly short time he was back, his voice sounding fuller, less strained. "All right, shoot."

Joanne caught her breath as best she could. "Well, the reason I phoned—"

"I know why you phoned," Bryant cut in.

"All right, why did I?" Joanne snapped.

"Because," Bryant said coldly, "one way or another you've just gotten word about the training sessions here on Rainier starting the fourth. I kept hoping you wouldn't hear but figured you would."

Joanne was so enraged she was near tears. "So why wasn't I told about it and invited?"

There was a slight pause before Bryant said, "You've already climbed Rainier twice."

"So what does that have to do with working out with the team?" she demanded.

There was a more pronounced pause before Bryant said, "Joanne, I thought it best not to invite you and that's that. I head this expedition, and if you're not willing to place yourself under my authority—"

As I placed myself in your bed, Joanne thought wildly.

"—you'd best just resign right now. It was my decision to make and—"

Joanne slammed the phone down, unable at that moment to do anything else.

Furiously she paced around her apartment, then picked up the phone and dialed Bryant's number again. Surely he would know it was she. Would he answer? Again the phone rang interminably before the receiver was finally lifted. "Yes?"

The moment she heard his voice, Joanne felt painfully tense once more. "Hi, it's me again. I was beginning to think you wouldn't answer."

"Sorry. I was in the shower. Joanne, I'm sorry about this problem, but I'm handling it the best way I know how. I told you right from the start there were problems with having you on the team. It shouldn't come as any surprise to you now, not when you had to resort to high-pressure tactics to get even this far."

Bryant's voice sounded fuller now, friendlier, but he also sounded very tired—tired of her? Joanne blinked back tears. *To get even this far*—how far was this, when she was being excluded from the training sessions due to start within days? Oh, how could he have made such marvelous passionate love to her and now plan to cast her aside?

"But I thought—" Joanne paused long enough to clear a huskiness out of her throat. She was pleased at how calm and even her voice sounded as she continued, "But I thought you'd come to realize that I'm a reasonably good, experienced climber. After Mount Shuksan you said as much. Do you recall what you said? You said that my father was right, that I'm one hell of a good climber.''

"Of course I remember." Bryant's voice sounded cold and distant again. "But what does that have to do with this? I happen to know that some of my best men would be adamantly opposed to having you on the team. I'm not about to have you up here with us and risk losing any one of them. If that upsets you, if you don't care for the way I run things, let me remind you, you are perfectly free to pull out.''

Of course, Joanne thought, *and that's just what you want.* "Sorry," she responded icily, "but I'm in this for the duration, no matter what." After a slight pause she added, her pulse racing wildly, "Well, what if I should just happen to arrive at Rainier on the fourth or fifth for a little climbing on my own? That way—''

"You pull any such stunt and you'll regret it," Bryant warned. "I give you my word on that. And right now I'm hungry and tired. Good night, Joanne." He hung up his phone.

Joanne replaced her own receiver. She would go anyway, she thought. Why not? Legally she was part of the team and needed to work with the other climbers, get used to them. Once she was actually there—what could he do? Feeling hollow and cold, Joanne walked tensely toward her bedroom. Her mind was made up, and nothing could swerve her from her course.

AFTER SHE WOKE in the morning, Joanne began to waver. Although she didn't approve of Bryant's decision, maybe he knew what he was doing in not letting the other climbers know she had joined them. After she dressed she walked thoughtfully out to the kitchen for breakfast. She tried to push aside all emotional considerations and think the matter through logically. If one or more of the other climbers would pull out immediately were they to know of her.... Suddenly, as she poured her coffee, Joanne's blood chilled. Maybe it wasn't that at all. Bryant had never backed away from his original threat to wring her out. Maybe he still figured he could do so. If that was it....

Joanne climbed onto a stool at her serving bar. On the other hand, Bryant's story held water, fit in with everything he'd ever told her. If he had leveled with her last night, if what he'd said was true, then she'd probably better swallow her hurt pride and let the whole thing ride. But if that wasn't the real reason, if Bryant was shutting her out now as a delaying tactic because he fully intended to shut her out for good.... What practical recourse would she have if she suddenly heard from Hope that the expedition had already flown out on its way to Nepal and Dhaulagiri? Bryant had told her that they'd be flying out in mid-February and that he'd let her know once the exact date was set. What if both statements were lies?

Joanne lowered her coffee cup. She felt sick.

Maybe that's why Bryant had taken her to bed: with the hope and expectation that it would so weaken her emotionally she wouldn't be able to fight back. Wouldn't *know* enough to fight back, wouldn't even recognize his sneaky method of wringing her out. With her heart involved, she'd feel that she *had* to trust him—it would simply hurt too much not to—and before she knew it, the team would fly off, without her. Was this what he had in mind?

She slid off the stool and walked tensely over to the sink to empty out what was left of her coffee. At the moment she was too overwrought to eat or drink anything. *If you thought, Mr. Bryant, that you could defuse me with a little attention, a little lovemaking....* Joanne felt hot tears flood her eyes. It hurt, but regardless of how it hurt, she wasn't going to let Bryant win.

By the time she'd jogged to work, taken a quick shower and dressed in her office clothes, she felt calmer. From her very first glimpse of James Anthony Bryant at Penny Palmer's party—she'd known she was up against a formidable foe. That didn't mean she couldn't win. Up to now she'd done all right, and all she had to do was steel herself, keep her eyes wide open and her defenses high to continue to do all right. Possibly she should carry out her threat to fly up to Rainier to join the team, possibly not. Ted would know; she'd discuss it with him as soon as she had a chance.

The opportunity came sooner than expected,

but immediately her hopes were drowned under an unexpected avalanche. Ted phoned her from his home. He was on his way to the airport for an emergency flight to Los Angeles and wanted her to leave at once for Sacramento to keep an appointment there to take some depositions. She'd have to figure on being in Sacramento the better part of a week. On the drive back, he wanted her to swing by Santa Rosa for an additional deposition.

"This all came up so fast," he told her, "which is the basic problem, of course. Emergencies have a way of doing that, tripping one up right when it's least expected—but I'm counting on you to step in for me. Can you, Joanne?"

Joanne immediately swallowed the dismay she felt and answered reassuringly, "Of course, Ted, I'll be delighted to. Just give me the names and phone numbers and I'll be on my way."

"Thanks, Joanne, I really appreciate this."

In less than an hour Joanne was on her way. It was a cold and drizzly day. She had rented a car and as she drove she tried to keep her spirits up by not thinking about the expedition, Mount Rainier and especially not about Bryant. After this emergency was taken care of, after she returned from the capital and Ted returned from L.A., she'd surely get a chance to discuss her problems with him. Though Bryant had quite possibly lied to her about a mid-February departure, the team wasn't apt to leave before the end of January at the very earliest. She still had close to a month to resolve the issue and force Bryant to live up to his agreement that she was a full-fledged team member.

Joanne ran into snags after she reached Sacramento and didn't get away from the capital until late in the afternoon on January 10. She spent the night in Santa Rosa, then found herself up against a further delay and had to spend a night there also. She arrived home early the following evening.

On her arrival home she phoned Scottie, as she'd agreed to do, and he drove over to take her out for dinner. Though Joanne felt pleased with herself over the work she'd accomplished, she also felt tired, and underneath the fatigue was a touch of panic. While she'd been taking endless depositions, the other expedition members had been getting to know one another, climbing together, becoming a team. For the first time she felt a deep-down certainty that Bryant would defeat her, that she wouldn't be going to Nepal to join the assault on Dhaulagiri after all.

"What's the matter?" Scottie asked her softly as they waited for their dinners to arrive. He reached over to press a hand on one of hers. "I know you must be tired, but you seem very dispirited too. Want to talk about it?"

As Joanne glanced up, she felt a mist sting her eyes. In one way she wanted to confide in Scottie, tell him how worried she was, but in another way she dreaded doing so. She was afraid of becoming or sounding emotional, afraid that Scottie might guess that she'd allowed herself—stupidly, foolishly—to become emotionally involved with Bryant. She felt so tired and distressed that if she tried to talk about it, her voice might break. She might even dissolve into tears.

She squeezed Scottie's hand and smiled across. "Nothing's the matter," she lied. "It's just that I'm tired, as you said, and my mind is still fretting over some of the delays and problems I encountered. Besides, I'm hungry. Once our dinners arrive—"

Just as Joanne said this, the waiter stepped to their table and poured the wine Scottie had ordered, a domestic Chablis. Joanne lifted her glass and Scottie, smiling, murmured, "To your climb," clinking his glass lightly against hers. Joanne tried to echo, *Yes, to the climb,* but couldn't quite manage the words. Scottie seemed not to notice.

As they ate their tender steaks Joanne tried to put her worries aside so that she could be a friendly and receptive companion. Scottie was telling her about his work. He'd been offered a promotion, one that would bring him a sizable raise, but the new job entailed moving down to Los Angeles, so he had already just about decided to turn it down.

"Oh, Scottie, is that wise?" Joanne protested. "When we first met, you told me that you had come to San Francisco simply to give the city a try and you weren't at all sure you wanted to live here for the rest of your life.''

Scottie's light blue eyes gazed steadily across at her as his hand again pressed on top of hers. ''Yes, I remember. But I shouldn't have to mention that a few things have changed since then. Now I feel I could live here forever very happily.''

Joanne sipped her wine, feeling dismayed. ''Scottie, are you sure?''

It was a moment before he answered, then his lips pulled apart in a sad little smile. ''You mean, am I sure you mean more to me than my job? Joanne, there's no contest. You know you do.''

''But, Scottie, you know what my plans are. If all goes well, I'll be leaving next month for Nepal and will be gone for four months, if I return at all,'' she ended weakly.

Scottie's hand squeezed hers. ''Don't talk like that. Of course you'll make it safely back. If I thought otherwise, even for a moment, do you think I'd stand calmly by while you finalize your plans? And in the long view of things, what in the world is four months? I'll miss you like the devil, of course, but before I know it, you'll be back. And as you come off the plane, I most certainly want to be here to meet you.'' Scottie shook his head slightly, as though just that moment deciding. ''That's it, no way will I take that job. No move to L.A. for me.''

Joanne gathered her energy to speak out, to

make her position absolutely clear once again. She drew her hand back as her eyes sought his. "Scottie, dear, please listen. You know how I feel about you, you're a close and dear friend. But that's all. It will never be anything else. And friends don't have to live in the same city or see each other every day. What I'm trying to say is that I hate for you to turn down this job. It sounds like a marvelous opportunity and if you had good sense you'd grab it. Maybe down in L.A. you'll find some other girl and fall in love."

Scottie's blue eyes had darkened as she talked and looked bleak. "But I'm in love with you," he said softly as she finished.

Joanne glanced away in frustration. *Yes, but I'm not in love with you!* she almost shouted. Scottie knew that. How many times did she have to remind him? She turned back to meet his gaze. "Scottie, I know, but I'm not in love with you, as you know."

His blue eyes lightened again and lost their sad look. With a smile he reached for her hand again and patted it, as though she were a confused little girl. "Sweetheart, I know. But nevertheless I'm sticking. Where there's life there's hope, you know."

Joanne opened her mouth to say that no, in this case there was no hope, but she remained silent. Maybe by the time she returned from the expedition, Scottie would realize that to nurture a love for her was futile.

When Scottie drove her home, he found a spot at the curb where he could park and walked her inside and up to her apartment. He came in for a nightcap and they sat on her sofa together, sipping their drinks, talking. It was a quiet, pleasant, companionable time. About twenty minutes later Scottie rose with a sigh, pulled Joanne to her feet, pressed a quick good-night kiss on her lips and left. Joanne carefully locked the door and went in to her bedroom to get ready for bed.

When the buzzer shrilled, she felt momentarily frightened, then told herself that of course it was Scottie coming back. Maybe he'd lost something or forgotten to tell her something. That wasn't like him, but at eleven o'clock at night it surely couldn't be anyone else.

Joanne walked to the door, stood for a moment undecided, then asked, "Yes, who is it," fully expecting to hear Scottie's voice.

"Jim Bryant," came the response.

Bryant? Joanne's head instantly whirled. Her fingers shook as she hastily unlocked the door and pulled it open. Bryant stood there, dressed in a dark blue suit, carrying a briefcase. He nodded to her with an unsmiling face. "Hello, Joanne. May I come in?"

Why was he here? Joanne's heart pounded. Momentarily it crossed her mind that she should refuse, should say, "No, Mr. Bryant, you can't come in!" To come to her apartment after eleven at night, to face her with that look—that was bad news, for sure. She'd never seen him with a briefcase before. Did it contain papers that could eliminate her from the team? Joanne pressed a hand to her throat in distress.

"I asked if I could come in," Bryant repeated, his voice softer, a slight smile curling his lips.

"All right—I guess," Joanne muttered, and motioned for him to do so.

As he walked across her living room, she shut the door and forced in several deep breaths, trying to calm herself.

"This is very nice," Bryant commented, "comfortable, with a lived-in look." After a slight pause he added, "I don't suppose you'd have a cup of coffee around you could spare me?"

"All right," Joanne said coolly, "but first give me some idea of why you're here. Needless to say I most certainly wasn't expecting you."

He watched her thoughtfully a moment, then his broad face broke into a grin, reaching out to envelop her and caress her warmly. He walked over to her, put an arm around her and pulled her toward him. "Because I've missed you, of course." He kissed her forehead, then drawing away, added, "And also because I have some things for you, your flight reservation, a few other things. I got in fairly early this morning and have been trying to reach you ever since. Your office said you'd be back sometime today, but then when I called just before five-thirty the receptionist there said you had gotten home but weren't coming in, so I started calling here instead. Still no answer. Half an hour ago I almost gave up, but then I decided to drive over to wait for you here. And here I am.''

"And if I hadn't come home all night?" Joanne said.

Bryant backed away a few steps, his dark eyes narrowly fixed on her. He shrugged. "Then I would have left in the morning and gone to the airport to catch my flight home—feeling very frustrated. But you *did* come home and I did catch you in, at last.''

"Had you come a few minutes earlier, you would have caught my friend here with me. As it is, you must have passed him in the hall or on the stairs.''

"No, I didn't pass anyone. I must have just missed him.'' Bryant laughed. "Great timing on my part, wouldn't you say?''

Joanne smiled, then laughed briefly too. "Have a seat," she motioned toward the armchair, "while I fetch the coffee.''

"You wouldn't by chance have something to drink instead?" Bryant asked.

"White wine. Would you rather have that?''

"Yes, thank you, I would.''

In her kitchen Joanne took down two clean wineglasses, put the glasses and wine bottle on a tray and carried it out. Bryant had ignored her offer of the armchair and had seated himself on the sofa. He'd cleared the end of the coffee table and had placed his briefcase on it, zipping it open. Joanne felt her pulse race happily at the sight. Her flight reservations. Then Bryant had no plans to cut her off after all.

She placed the tray on the table then slid down onto the sofa beside him. Bryant picked up his glass, gestured toward her and sipped. A moment later he set his wineglass down and faced her.

"I don't suppose you've had sober second thoughts and changed your mind about wanting to go?" he asked, scowling at her.

"No, no way. The fact is I want to go more than ever. It would break my heart if I couldn't go now."

Bryant sighed. His unsmiling face looked tired and strained. He pulled a flight packet out of his briefcase and set it down on the coffee table before Joanne. "All right, here are your tickets. Departure date has been set for February 19. I assume you're taking care of getting a passport?"

"Yes, of course."

"All right." As he sipped more wine, his manner became even more somber. He pulled a Xeroxed sheet out of his briefcase and handed it to her.

"Here's a list of our commercial sponsors. The starred items at the top of the page are those that you are expected to supply for yourself, and we ask that you buy the sponsor's product whenever feasible."

"Of course." Joanne glanced briefly at the list without surprise. This wasn't new to her. She'd grown accustomed to sponsor lists from the expeditions her father had arranged. Companies that manufactured equipment required in mountaineering customarily donated certain items to an expedition in exchange for endorsements to be used in their advertising. In Nepal the hired guides and porters had to be supplied, so the free equipment went to them, while the volunteer climbers were ordinarily expected to buy their own, which Joanne was fully prepared to do.

Bryant handed her three additional sheets stapled together. "Here's some papers I want you to look over. Our food, cooking and medical supplies are currently in storage at a warehouse here in the city. The address is right here." He tapped the top of the first sheet. "These supplies have to be broken down from the cartons they came in, sorted and packed into other cartons to be airfreighted over. All members of the team who can make it are gathering this coming weekend to tackle the job, which is going to be a big one."

"And I'm invited to come help?" Joanne asked expectantly.

Bryant glanced around at her with a resigned little smile. "You're invited to come help. The fact is we need all the help we can get."

"And I'll be there as what? A climber? Or simply as a friendly San Franciscan interested in helping the expedition along?"

Bryant's narrow eyes darkened momentarily. He sipped from his glass, then set it firmly back down. "I've been debating that, but I think the time has come to confront the situation head-on. If the whole thing blows up, it blows up. Better here than in Kathmandu or halfway up Dhaulagiri."

Bryant's eyes looked so somber, his expression so concerned, that Joanne felt her heart catch in sympathy for him. He had spent two or three years arranging this climb, and had obviously given his whole heart to it, yet he seemed sincerely to feel that her presence on the team constituted a very real threat, seemed to fear that after all his endless work and devotion, the expedition might explode in his face—just because of her.

"You really—" Joanne's throat was suddenly so choked her voice came out thick. She swallowed carefully and tried again. "You really think there's any danger of that, that it might all blow up?" She couldn't manage the final words, *just because of me*.

Bryant swung to face her. How tired and gray his face looked! Joanne longed to cradle him, to draw his worried-looking face against her breasts, to soothe and comfort him. He leaned back against the sofa.

"God, I hope not." Bryant lifted one hand and pressed it against Joanne's cheek, his touch sending an immediate tingle through her.

He shuddered lightly, tiredly, then his soft

lips broke apart in a smile. "No, I don't think so. Maybe I'm kidding myself, but I honestly think I can hold it together. There'll be fireworks—I know a few of the men well enough to be sure of that. But one way or another I'll hold it together." Smiling softly, he leaned forward to kiss her.

Joanne moved closer and slid her arms around his shoulders. The pressure of his lips increased, and momentarily his arms went around her. Then as the kiss ended he released her again. Leaning back, his face turned toward her, he smiled at her.

"You look very tired."

"I am. I haven't had more than six hours' sleep over the last three days." He reached for his wineglass and drained it, his eyes shining over the rim of the glass. "Could I have a refill?"

"Of course." The bottle on the tray was almost empty so Joanne rose, picked up both glasses and walked quickly into her kitchen. Her head whirled with confusing thoughts. The Bryant here tonight seemed like the quiet, friendly, affectionate man she'd gotten to know in his home. She could feel the happy glow in her cheeks as she refilled the two wineglasses and carried them back to her living room.

To her surprise Bryant was no longer sitting tiredly on the sofa. He had switched on the floor lamp and turned off the overhead light. Soft music flowed from the stereo, before which he knelt. Her pulse racing even faster, Joanne walked over to stand behind him. He swung around, smiling, then rose quickly and took one of the wineglasses from her.

"To a successful climb."

After they'd both sipped wine, Bryant took Joanne's glass from her and set it beside his on the coffee table. One arm went around her and he pulled her close, leading her into a dance step.

They moved slowly and sensuously to the soft music flooding the room. Bryant put both arms around her waist, and Joanne wound her arms around his shoulders, pressing close against him. As they passed the floor lamp, Bryant switched it off. The room was lighted only by light filtering in through the window.

"This is nice," Bryant said. His lips strayed kisses along the graceful curve of her neck, then with his tongue he outlined the delicate shape of her ear. Joanne shivered with the intense pleasure that went surging through her. Bryant drew back slightly, his eyes catching hers. "You're not cold, are you?"

"Oh, no," Joanne whispered.

Bryant pulled her against him again, and his large strong hands moved down her back, holding her even closer. His mouth found hers and his lips had never felt softer or more eager for possession.

As the kiss ended, Joanne sighed with contentment, resting her head on his shoulder.

"I've been so worried." She laughed softly, remembering her fears. This man who now held her—there was no way she could fear this man.

"What about? Because I didn't include you in the team workout?"

Joanne lifted her head and nodded. "You told me—remember—that you'd wring me out and toss me aside. I thought that's what you were doing."

Bryant stopped moving. The light from the window cast odd patterns across his face. "I was terribly angry when I said that. I was in a rage."

Joanne grinned. Again she was trembling. "Oh, I know. I understood that. But at the same time you've never retracted it."

"I retract it now." He pulled her close and his lips met hers, with a fierce hard passion that sent wild tremors through Joanne. Her hands lifted to press against his cheeks as his tongue thrust exploringly into her mouth. He held her tightly then slowly released her. In front of the double window the light formed a square on the floor. Bryant took a cushion from the sofa, dropped it onto the illuminated square, then pulled Joanne to the floor, her head on the cushion. He sat beside her, out of the light, smiling down at her.

The moon had risen, sending shafts of light through the window. Bryant nodded toward the sky, smiling.

"Do you suppose this is the same moon we saw from my place outside Seattle?" he asked.

Joanne laughed. "I doubt it. This one looks smaller but fatter."

Bryant bent over her, nuzzling his face against her throat. "That moon drove me crazy; it bewitched me. This one may, too."

Joanne's heart filled with excitement and joy. She lifted his head to kiss him and whispered, "Be my guest."

He undressed her slowly, sprinkling kisses along each inch of uncovered flesh. As his hands closed over her breasts, he kissed her mouth, then her ear, then her throat. Joanne shivered with pleasure.

"No, I'm not cold," she whispered quickly. "Just excited. I love your touch."

"And I love what I'm touching," Bryant said, his voice hoarse. "Your skin is so soft, so smooth—how incredibly beautiful you are."

When he had removed the last of her clothing, he drew back, kneeling beside her. As she turned toward him, he put his hand on her arm. "No, don't move, please. Just let me look at you for a moment." The moon had risen even higher, sending a brighter splash of light into the room. Joanne watched as his eyes caressed the gentle curves of her body, her softly sloping shoulders and firm rounded breasts, the barely perceptible dip of her abdomen, which seemed to catch and hold the silvery light, and the smooth silken thighs. Her breathing quickened beneath his probing gaze, and a quiet moan escaped Bryant's lips.

Slipping off his jacket, he draped it across her breasts and arms. "I'm afraid you are getting cold now."

Joanne smiled up at him, her voice thick with desire. "Then you must warm me up."

He shed his clothes quickly and soon he lay beside her, his strong warm flesh sending waves of liquid fire through her. Joanne closed her eyes, giving herself up to the intensity of her joy. Bryant gently kissed her closed eyelids. With the same gentleness he stroked and caressed her until she ached with readiness and cried out softly for him to hurry. She knew that this man—this excitement, this joy—was what she'd been yearning for all her life, and now he was here, with her, as close as a man and woman could be, and life was too good to bear.

"Oh, Jim," she cried, and then the explosion came, a million stars exploding behind her eyes. Still Bryant held her, tenderly, cradling her, keeping her warm. The moon rose and disappeared from their view, pulling its light away, and they lay in darkness, holding each other close, softly sharing a good-night kiss.

CHAPTER SEVEN

BRYANT SPENT THE NIGHT with her. Sometime before dawn they moved into Joanne's bed.

When Joanne woke in the morning, Bryant was gone. She found a note propped against the lamp on the nightstand.

Joanne—you're beautiful—I adore you. Woke early—couldn't get back to sleep—so I left for the airport. I'll phone you later today from Seattle. Hope to see you next weekend. Take care.

J.A.B.

Joanne smiled, reread the note, then let it drop and rolled onto her back. Bryant's first words of love: *I adore you.* She sighed. She'd so much rather he had said he loved her. *Love* held commitment. Still, remembering the night before, she felt warm and happy.

Joanne sighed again, gazing idly toward her bedroom window. Even though the blind was down and the drapery drawn, the morning light crept in. At last she understood the strange sensations she'd experienced over the past few months. She was in love with James A. Bryant. He was the man she'd been yearning to meet for years without even being aware of it, and she could not now imagine a time when she would no longer love him. Joanne's soft smile died away as a frown crept over her face. But how did Bryant feel about her, apart from finding her physically attractive? Was there any chance at all that he was falling in love with her as she was with him? *I adore you.* Joanne threw the bedcovers back and rolled out of bed. *Darn you, James Bryant, why couldn't you have used the word love?* He hadn't even signed the note, "With love," which would have been the natural thing to do. Maybe that was his way of telling her not to raise her hopes.

Shaking her head, Joanne snatched up his note and reread it, but the same words stayed stubbornly on the paper, friendly caring words, but no hint of love.

It was two that afternoon before Bryant phoned. She'd been out of the office all morning, worried that she'd miss his call, yet when she finally made it in a little after one, she felt terribly taken aback that he hadn't yet phoned.

"Ellie, are you sure? Did anyone call who didn't leave his name, saying he'd phone back later?"

"No, no one."

Joanne left the reception area and walked down the hall to her desk hastily checking her mail. Inwardly she was trembling. Surely Bryant had made it home safely. He must have been swamped with work and was waiting until he'd have the time to talk before he called.

When at last she heard his voice over the wire, Joanne felt relieved but annoyed. "Jim, I've been dreadfully worried. Why didn't you phone this morning, if only to let me know you'd made it home all right? It's after two now. You can't imagine all the frightening fates I've been imagining for you."

Bryant laughed. His laughter sounded deep, warm, delighted. "Maybe that's why I waited, because I wanted to hear you say that. Or maybe I waited because I knew you wouldn't be in the office until two anyway."

Joanne's pulse raced. "How did you know? You didn't know any such thing. Did you?"

"When did you get in?" Bryant countered. "I was told you'd get in at two, and if you'll please note, I was so impatient to talk to you, I picked up my phone and dialed about twenty seconds ahead, figuring I'd catch you the first moment I could."

Joanne's tension drained away. She rested back in her chair, smiling. "And who told you I wouldn't be in till two?"

"Some man. I tried your home a little before eight, you weren't there, so I phoned the office. A man picked it up and said you were scheduled to be gone all morning, try about two. So how have you been?"

Joanne laughed. "Except for worrying about you, I've been fine."

"I miss you," Bryant said.

"I miss you, too," Joanne murmured.

"I not only wanted to tell you that but I also had something extremely serious to discuss with you."

Bryant's voice hardened as he said this. Joanne's smile died instantly; tension gripped her again. She sat forward, grabbed up a pencil and held it painfully hard. "Okay, shoot."

"I can't quite see the whites of your eyes."

"Look harder," Joanne said, her voice dry.

"All right, now I can." After a slight pause, Bryant went on, "Joanne, I've never been with a woman as beautiful as you were last night. Everything about you—I can't tell you how perfect you were. How perfect you are: round, warm, soft, yet without an ounce of spare fat on you. But we're headed toward a high-mountain climb. Haven't you ever heard of the Facts of Fat? Climbers come home skinny, but they start out fat—overweight—with a padding for the lean times ahead. High-altitude living is debilitating. You've got to have some extra weight to fall back on. The way you are now, if you lose the ten to fifteen pounds you're almost sure to lose, there'll be nothing left of you. It's time you started fattening yourself up for the kill— the killing days ahead. Do you hear me?"

Joanne didn't answer at once. She drew in her breath, then slowly let it out again. "And that's it? That's the extremely serious matter you had to discuss with me?''

"That's it.''

Joanne's face broke into a broad relieved grin. She laughed. "What about you?" she challenged. "You're as lean and trim for your height as I am for mine. Last night I felt your—''

"Lady, please!''

Joanne laughed harder. "I ran my hand over your abdomen and marveled at how taut and trim you are. And your hips and thighs. Your arms, your shoulders. From tip to toe, in fact. I couldn't find a bit of flab anywhere. I should be the one telling you about the Facts of Fat.''

"Then why aren't you?" Bryant said. "And even more important, are you going to do something about yourself instead of all this concern about me? You only have a month left, you know.''

"I'll eat like a little pig," Joanne promised. "By the time we fly off, I'll be so round and chubby you won't even recognize me. Who in the world is that blimp, you'll ask. Will that satisfy you?''

Bryant answered softly, with a sigh, "Yes, that will satisfy me. Though the fact is I adore you just as you are right now.''

Joanne's pulse quickened. "I adore you, too." Just then her other phone rang. "Jim, I'm sorry, but can I put you on hold?''

"Sure. Go ahead.''

When she was able to return to the call, she had only a few seconds free. "Sorry again, but I've got to run. What time should I get to the warehouse on Saturday?"

"Whatever time suits you."

"Five or six in the morning is not too early?"

"Three or four's not too early. Starting Friday evening, we'll be working around the clock. I'm hoping to get down by ten or so Friday evening, though I may not make it. But I'll see you on Saturday."

"Great. See you then."

"I adore you, Joanne."

"Me, too, Jim." She blew him a kiss and with great reluctance punched the key to return to her other call.

IF ONLY she could have broken her date with Scottie for Friday night, but unfortunately there was no way she could: it was his birthday, and they'd made plans to celebrate weeks before. Friends of theirs who lived in Oakland were having a small party, and she and Scottie were invited for dinner prior to the party. It was a social obligation she could not duck.

Scottie picked her up at the office early Friday evening, as planned, and drove them over the bridge to Oakland. Joanne had showered at the office—Ted's office had a private bath attached, and he had told Joanne she was always welcome to use it, which she frequently did—and after showering she had changed at work into a dark blue dress. It was off the shoulder, with a soft clinging bodice and flared skirt. It occurred to her that except for the first evening they'd met, Bryant had never seen her really dressed up. He'd seen her in office clothes, climbing clothes, informal wear—and of course, Joanne thought with amusement, wearing nothing at all.

Bryant had said he was flying in tonight, or hoped to. She wondered if he would phone her apartment and find her gone. Or would he even phone? After the talk two days before, she hadn't heard from him. She'd thought about phoning him but hadn't, and had spent her evenings hoping he'd call. And now she had to spend the evening with friends, people she'd known and cared about for years, but at the moment they seemed virtual strangers, obstacles that prevented her from going home, changing into work clothes and heading down to the warehouse to help with the sorting and packing of supplies, a job she longed to get at whether or not Bryant showed up. Joanne took in a deep breath and let it out with a sigh. Scottie glanced around at her with a soft friendly smile.

"Tired?" he asked.

Joanne faced him, doing her best to smile in response. "A little. It's been a long week."

"How's everything going with the trip? Any more problems with Bryant?"

Joanne tensed. "Well, no. Not at the moment."

"Has he changed his mind, do you think, about what he said to start with? You know, his threat to twist you apart and push you aside."

"To wring me out and toss me aside," Joanne murmured. "Yes, he's retracted that threat, said in anger, and I now have my flight ticket along with the sponsor list and supply list."

Scottie's smile broadened. "Good, I'm glad. I love you so much I want the trip to be everything you want it to be."

"Thank you, Scottie."

Love. Scottie loved her, or at least thought he did. He could say the word and mean it. Adore. Bryant adored her, or said he did, but what did that mean? *I adore you, lady; allow me to hold you and do as I please with you.*

A stinging mist of tears crept into Joanne's eyes and she swung her head away to stare unseeingly out the window. Was she really in love with Bryant, or was she simply infatuated with him? Infatuation—who needed it? Up until their night together in Bryant's home, she hadn't even liked the man, and certainly hadn't trusted him.

She turned around to look at her friend. With Scottie everything was so calm and secure. With Bryant—Joanne swung her eyes away again. With Bryant everything was so frantic, uncertain, insecure—and so intensely exciting, causing so many doubts and such painful yearning in her. Was that really what loving was all about?

The party broke up a little after midnight and Scottie drove Joanne home. In spite of her promise to Bryant Joanne had found it difficult to eat. It wasn't that the dinner wasn't good. Patti, the hostess, had prepared the chili dish that was her specialty and a favorite of Scottie's; it was spicy and delicious. The birthday cake, served with ice cream later during the party, was layered with cream and topped with thick chocolate, and was about the best that Joanne had ever tasted. Still she had trouble finishing her slice.

All evening she felt drawn to quiet corners where she could be alone with her thoughts. This was symptomatic of her disease, she told herself wryly—adolescent lovesickness. One way or another she had escaped the infection until now, and to succumb at her age was more than a little ridiculous, like coming down with chicken pox or measles. But such childhood diseases were rarely fatal. Her case wouldn't be fatal, either. *Take two aspirins, spend the day in bed, and you'll snap back and be fit as a fiddle.* Joanne smiled to herself. As long as she spent the time in bed *alone*. Or maybe—if she had company—she'd recover even faster. She chuckled softly to herself.

"What's so funny?" Patti asked, appearing at her elbow. When Joanne simply shook her head hopelessly, making no attempt to explain, Patti took her arm, clasping it hard. "Joanne, snap out of it, please. You haven't seemed yourself all evening. Is something the matter? You're not sick, are you? Oh—oh, no, not you! You haven't fallen in love, have you?''

When Joanne shrugged without offering any other response, Patti gripped her by the shoulders and gazed intently into her eyes. ''Oh, of course that's it!'' she said emphatically. ''You've got all the classic symptoms. Poor Scottie. Does he know?''

Joanne shook herself free, extremely annoyed. ''For heaven's sake, Patti, I'm not in love. And besides, what do you mean 'poor Scottie.' Scottie and I are best friends and always will be.''

Shaking her head in dismay, Patti turned and walked off.

Joanne frowned, watching her friend walk away. The sooner she left for Dhaulagiri, the better, she thought. Maybe once she was gone Scottie would finally realize that they could never be more than friends, and she would no longer have to deal with these pangs of guilt and her friends' silent accusations.

She was glad when she and Scottie were back in the car and on their way home. Scottie came upstairs to her apartment with her but didn't stay long. ''I can tell how tired you are,'' he remarked in explanation.

The moment she locked the door behind him, Joanne felt suddenly energized, a feeling she had the grace to feel ashamed of. She checked her telephone answering tape and found, to her delight, that Bryant had phoned at ten-twenty. He said he was heading toward the warehouse and would be working there until midnight or so. He gave her the warehouse number in case she wanted to phone. Her pulse pounding, Joanne checked the time. A few minutes after one. Bryant had said that a crew would be working all night, so why not call?

She dialed the number, let it ring twenty times, but no one answered. Sighing, she dropped the receiver back down. She had half considered changing her clothes, catching a cab and going down to join the work crew as late as it was, but when no one answered the phone she dropped the idea. Abruptly she felt tired again and headed for bed.

She set her alarm for six, and by six-thirty Saturday morning was in a cab on her way to the warehouse. The weather was cold and foggy, but this had no effect on her spirits: she felt warm and energetic. Arriving at the address she'd given the cabby, Joanne climbed out, paid the driver and walked excitedly down the sidewalk checking for an entry door. The warehouse was a huge building, windowless, gray and dirty, in the most disreputable part of the old industrial area. Joanne found a door and tested it. It wasn't locked, so she opened it and stepped inside.

She found herself facing a narrow path between huge mounds of stacked cartons. There was little light. She strode forward cautiously.

"Hi. Anyone here?" she called out, and then heard a man's voice from deep within the bowels of the building. She continued on until she found herself entering a wide cleared area. A large light bulb dangled overhead above the dirty paper-strewn floor of the old warehouse.

A group of men were squatting and sitting in front of some cartons. One man jumped up and came striding over to meet her. He was of average height, black haired, dark eyed, about thirty-five, Joanne judged. He wore low boots, tight faded jeans and a black sweater that clung closely to his lean wiry form.

"Hi. I'm Robert Freeland," the man introduced himself. He carried a cup of coffee, which splashed a bit as he walked over. His dark eyes narrowed, quickly surveying her. "You looking for someone, beautiful?"

Joanne felt her breath catch. Apparently Bryant hadn't yet told these men about her. "Yes, I'm looking for Mr. Bryant. I'm a friend of his, come down to help sort and pack."

Hearing this, the other men let out various low whistles and catcalls. Freeland motioned them to be quiet and extended his right hand to her.

"And your name?" he asked courteously. "Mr. Bryant didn't mention that he had any lady friend in the area who'd be down to help, but all hands are welcome. As you can see—" he motioned toward the cartons stacked in every direction "—we face a monumental task. Don't let what you see now mislead you. We've been working all night and just now stopped for a few minutes' rest."

Joanne smiled. "I was sure of that. Mr. Bryant isn't here?"

Freeland smiled back. He had an odd crooked smile that Joanne found charming. Already she liked this man and instinctively trusted him. "No, he isn't. He was here from about ten last night until three this morning, but then he knocked off to go get some rest. We expect him back around eight o'clock. Would you rather leave and come back then, or can I put you to work myself? I'm the deputy leader of the expedition, Bryant's right-hand man. I'm also in charge of this sorting and packing job. When Bryant's here on this job he takes orders from me; I don't take them from him." Freeland grinned.

Joanne smiled back. "I'd be happy to have you put me to work."

Freeland thrust out his hand again. "Good enough." He emptied his coffee cup, squeezed it flat, tossed it into a nearby trash barrel and snapped at the circle of men. "Okay, men, up and at 'em again. And from now on watch your language. We've got a lady aboard."

Oh, no, Joanne thought. Why did men always feel they had to act differently when a woman joined them? As long as they felt that way, felt they had to clean up their act, watch what they said, what they did, it was understandable that they resisted feminine invasion.

"I'll put you back here working with Andy Howell," Freeland told her. "He's a nice friendly lad with a clean mouth and gentlemanly ways. Come on, Andy, hop to it," he yelled over his shoulder as he led Joanne down a narrow pathway between cartons toward the rear of the warehouse.

Andy Howell looked about nineteen but said he was twenty-four. He was from the east coast and had arrived in San Francisco the day before. Like Joanne, he had climbed in almost every part of the world except the Himalayas and was jumping with excitement at the chance to tackle Dhaulagiri, the sixth highest mountain in the world and, because of its treacherous weather conditions, one of the most challenging climbs. Mount Everest, the highest mountain on earth, had been conquered in 1953, seven years before anyone set foot on the top of Dhaulagiri.

He was talking excitedly about the upcoming trip when suddenly he interrupted himself, flushing. "I'll bet you think I'm crazy, don't you? People who aren't into climbing can't understand why it's so exciting to people like me. Take my girl friend back home. Ever since I got accepted on this expedition, we've done nothing but fight about it. Christa can't see why I want to go traipsing off to the other side of the world to eat lousy food and freeze my butt off— excuse me—freeze my tail off, risk pulmonary edema or getting swept away in an avalanche, and for what? Just to say I've been there and maybe even make it to the top, if I'm lucky.'' Andy grinned, shaking his head. "To sane people like Christa it just doesn't make sense. You have to be sort of crazy to do it, I guess.''

"I guess,'' Joanne agreed.

Freeland had them doing an easy but monotonous job. The food, cooking and medical supplies had arrived in large containers from the manufacturers. Once the climbers were on the mountain, they planned to rely on airdrops, which the American team had used in its successful assault on the mountain in 1973. For the airdrops to work, the supplies had to be repacked in smaller cartons for daily use. Joanne and Andy were working with the cartons donated by one of the expedition's sponsors. The cartons had come in flat, and she and Andy were assembling them into boxes, using muscle power and industrial staples. Each box when packed would contain a day's supply of food, plus cooking utensils and incidentals.

After a while Andy quieted down and the two worked silently together. Joanne found herself frequently checking her watch. Had Bryant arrived yet? Would Freeland mention to him that she was there? If he knew, would he come looking for her? How long would it be before the men were informed that she hadn't introduced herself with true precision? While she was a friend of Bryant's who had come to help, she was also one of the climbers, a fact she hadn't mentioned. Would there be an explosion when the men found out?

Eight o'clock—the hour of Bryant's expected arrival—came and went. Nine. Nine-thirty. A whistle blew through the huge drafty warehouse. Andy pushed in one more staple, wiped his perspiring brow with his arm, and told Joanne that the whistle signaled break time.

"Why don't we go join the others and have some coffee?" he suggested. Joanne nodded. They walked single file up the narrow path between cartons, Joanne in the lead, until they reached the cleared space in which everyone was gathering. Glancing around, her pulse racing, Joanne didn't see Bryant. She counted quickly and saw that there were nine men there. Nine men and herself.

Freeland strode over, grinning. "How's it going? Can I get you some coffee? There's a box over there you can use to sit on. I've told all the guys to keep off it, that it's for you."

Joanne felt dismayed. She didn't want to be treated this way, as someone deserving special consideration. If Freeland kept it up, the men would resent her even more than they would have otherwise. It didn't matter as long as they thought she was just a friend pitching in to help, but when they learned the truth.... "Thank you," she murmured to Freeland, and walked over to sit on the upturned box he'd motioned toward.

Andy walked over to stand beside her, as

though in some way bonded to her, a knight in shining armor set to defend the helpless maiden against all dragons or other fiends. Joanne sipped coffee from the cup Freeland had poured for her and which Andy had carried over. This was dreadful, she thought, sitting with downcast eyes. That morning when she'd first walked in, she'd heard the men talking and laughing together during their break. Now there was little talk and no laughter. As she glanced up, she saw that several pairs of eyes were fastened on her. As she scanned the faces she did her best to smile. Most of the men responded but with fleeting smiles that barely creased their faces. Oh, well, surely it would improve as the men got used to her and found she was willing to work hard without asking for favors. Possibly she should draw Freeland aside and suggest that he start treating her as one of the guys, as just another climber. Joanne dropped her eyes to the dirty floor again, sighing. If only Bryant would get here and straighten everything out.

JOANNE WAS BACK WORKING hard with Andy, assembling cartons, when an eerie silence fell. She still hadn't seen Bryant and had no way of knowing whether he was in the building or not. She checked her watch and saw it was a few minutes past ten. Andy finished a staple and glanced up, looking puzzled. Neither had mentioned the background noise that had accompanied their labors, and Joanne wasn't even sure she'd been consciously aware of it. But when the noise stopped suddenly, the silence was frightening.

"I wonder what's up," Andy remarked. He pulled a piece of toweling out of his back pocket and mopped the rolling sweat off his face. "For some reason everyone's stopped working. You don't suppose word's just reached here that the expedition is off?"

Joanne felt a huge lump in her throat. "Oh, no, I don't think that. Surely it's not that." She peered down the narrow pathway between the stacked cartons.

A man was striding toward them. When he stepped out into the cleared space where she and Andy were working, Joanne saw in shock that it was Bryant. She hadn't recognized his walk. His broad face was somber. He did not even greet her but instead spoke to Andy.

"Howell, Freeland's holding a meeting up in the main area and wants you to join them."

"What about?" Andy's tense voice cracked like an adolescent's.

"Join them and you'll find out."

Andy started off, then stopped and glanced back. His boyish face looked white. "The expedition isn't off, is it?"

Bryant's lips split apart in a harsh smile. "That's not up to me, Howell. That's what you men are set to decide with the vote you're about to take."

"Oh, no," Andy murmured, and disappeared up the path.

Joanne's insides were churning. She put her arms around herself, pressing her abdomen. Bryant walked over to stand beside her. "Is that really what's happening?" she asked him.

Bryant's dark eyes circled down to meet hers. His lips broke into a grim smile as one hand came up to press her cheek. "Would I lie to you, beautiful?" The smile died and he turned his eyes away. "Yes, that's what's happening." His voice sounded cold now as he strode to the far end of the cleared space, as though to put as much distance between himself and Joanne as he could. "When I arrived, Freeland told me you were here. I said fine, and mentioned that, as we're still a couple of climbers short, I'd signed you up recently to join us. Freeland froze and said that in that case he was backing out. No way would he stick it out with you on the team."

Joanne's knees almost gave out. "Freeland?" She'd liked and trusted the man on sight and had felt accepted by him.

"Freeland. So we walked outside, hashed it around for a while, and he changed his mind—I think. Other men around had caught on to what the discussion was about, so when we came back in we found they'd knocked off work to confront us. Freeland waved me away, said he'd run the discussion himself, give the men a chance to voice their feelings in the matter and then vote without my being there to inhibit them.'' Bryant sighed. "So now you know as much about it as I do.''

Joanne sank down to a squatting position. There was no place to sit, no upturned box such as Freeland had gotten for her to use during the break. She stared through dry eyes at Bryant, who stood with his back to her as he gazed down the narrow dark path. He had put his heart and soul into this expedition, had worked on arrangements for almost three years, and now it was in danger—because of her. Because she'd resorted to legal blackmail to get her own way. Did he hate her now? No matter how things turned out, would he hate her from this moment on? How could a man stand idly by and watch his most cherished dream explode in his face? Yet that was precisely what Bryant was being forced to do right now. As her legs began to hurt, Joanne lowered herself to sit on an unassembled carton that lay flat on the floor.

"Bryant—Jim—I suppose that right this moment you truly hate me, don't you?''

Bryant didn't answer at once. He moved his shoulder in a gesture of annoyance, then muttered, "I am feeling angry, yes. At you, at myself, at those men out there, at the whole damn world." As his voice died out, he lifted his wrist to check his watch. The seconds limped past. Joanne stared. Bryant continued to gaze at his watch, then suddenly he lowered his arm.

"Okay, that's it. They've had ten minutes,

which is long enough. I'm going out there to settle this thing.''

Joanne's tension increased tenfold. She jerked forward, as though to rush over and stop him. Freeland had asked him to stay away, and his intrusion might make everything worse. "Oh, Jim, do you think you should?"

Bryant's dark eyes flashed around momentarily to meet her gaze. "Yes, I should."

"But, Jim—"

"It's my expedition, dammit. I'll see you." With that Bryant took off, striding rapidly up the narrow aisle.

Joanne sank back into a sitting position on the carton. She hugged herself, feeling suddenly cold. She'd never in her life felt so alone. Through tear-blurred eyes she checked her watch and found that she had to blink repeatedly to clear her vision before she could read the watch hands. At a few minutes past ten all work had stopped. It was ten-thirty-five now. Joanne bit anxiously at her lip, combating a wave of nausea. How much longer would it take to decide her fate, and the fate of the expedition?

If those men opposed to her presence won the vote and the expedition was canceled, would Bryant ever feel the least fondness for her again?

If the vote went the other way and the expedition was still on, would Bryant forgive and forget, or would he continue to feel angry and resentful?

If this expedition foundered, would she ever come even this close again? Would she ever make it to the Himalayas, her most cherished dream?

Joanne jumped to her feet and strode anxiously over to the dark narrow aisle. She could see the lighted area at the end where the men were and could occasionally hear the rumble of voices without being able to distinguish a word. She lifted both hands and pressed them against her mouth. Oh, why didn't they hurry up and get it over with? How much longer could this go on?

It was a few minutes past eleven when Joanne spied a man starting down the dark path toward where she stood. She caught a glimpse of his face and felt certain that it was Andy. He was moving quickly and evenly, with a calm purposeful walk. Joanne backed out of his way so he could step into their lighted working area. She stared at his face, trying to read some sign, feeling unable to breathe.

"Well, it's still on." Andy's face looked white, but his eyes were relieved. "Some of us had sense enough to see it would have been crazy to throw it all away at this point, not to mention that it doesn't make sense to object to someone just because of her sex." After a slight hesitation, he walked over, smiling, and thrust out his hand. "Welcome aboard, mate."

"Oh, Andy!" Joanne couldn't control herself. She threw herself against her gallant young knight and gave him a fierce hug. At least she had one friend on the expedition.

JUST AS THE NOON WHISTLE BLEW, Bryant came striding into their cleared space. Earlier he had been dressed in a dark blue business suit, but now he wore jeans and a loose sweat shirt. He carried a brown paper bag in one hand, a box lid with three cups of coffee in the other.

"I'd like to join you two back here for lunch, if you don't mind. We caught a catering truck outside a few minutes ago so I bought three sandwiches, some chips and some nuts. Ham and cheese, egg salad or tuna salad. Which will you have, Joanne?"

"It really doesn't matter. I like all three. Andy?"

"Well, if you really don't care, I'd prefer the ham."

Bryant gave it to him, Joanne took the egg salad, which left the tuna for Bryant. "Thank you. I wound up with my first choice," he remarked with a smile.

Joanne and Andy had just dragged out a new batch of flat cartons, which were at a comfortable height for sitting. They sat in a row, Joanne in the middle, and talked very little as they ate. Andy did mention, in an obvious attempt to make conversation, that he'd heard Freeland say it took more than seven tons of food to feed an expedition of this size and that the cartons alone, these sheets of unstapled cardboard they were assembling into boxes, weighed at least a ton.

"Imagine the fortune it's going to cost to air-freight this stuff over," Andy exclaimed, shaking his head. "But Bob Freeland mentioned, Mr. Bryant, that you weren't willing to risk sending anything by ship, that too many things could go wrong if you went by boat."

Bryant nodded. "Right. That's the decision we made, Freeland and myself. Going by air is costlier but less risky."

After this, conversation died once again.

Joanne wasn't sorry to see the end of the lunch break and Bryant's departure. Had she had a chance to be alone with him, to talk privately with him, she would have welcomed it, but with Andy there she felt constrained and was sure that Bryant did, too. His manner toward her was courteous but formal, and whether this was for Andy's benefit or because he still felt angry toward her, she didn't know and couldn't guess. It was a relief to have him leave and to get back to work.

"Mr. Bryant seems like a nice enough guy," Andy remarked as they worked. "I've heard it said that he runs a pretty tight crew, that he won't put up with having his authority questioned and that he's the wrong guy to cross. But that's the type of man you need to head something like this, it seems to me. Otherwise it can get pretty screwed up, and I feel that at heart he's a fair enough man, don't you think?"

"Well—I guess so," Joanne agreed. Her heart pounded as she added, "I really don't know him that well yet." *And quite possibly never will,* she thought.

For the three-o'clock break, she and Andy went forward into the main area. Joanne tensed as she followed Andy into the light. She had felt so friendly toward Freeland that morning, had felt such instant instinctive trust. She tensed even more as she saw him notice her, cut short what he was saying, and come striding over to greet her, a taut smile on his face.

"Miss Patton, I heard tell you misled us this morning. You're not just a friend of the boss's who dropped in to help, you're one of us." He stopped before her, lifting one hand to push back a cap on his head. His gaze dropped to her feet, then traveled slowly back up to where his eyes again met hers. His smile became crooked and rather friendly. "I'll level with you, lady. I was anything but thrilled when I first heard, but rather than call everything off, I took your side, rallied everyone I could to my way of thinking, and now everything's the way it was, except no more kid-glove treatment. Whatever language the men want to use, that's their business, and that box over there, the one you sat on earlier, happens to be mine. I brought it in for myself, and from now on I'll use it. From now on, if you're one of us, you're one of us, understand?"

Joanne nodded, smiling. "I understand."

After eyeing her intently for another moment, he put out his hand. "Okay. Welcome to the team, Joanne."

With gratitude and relief, Joanne slipped her hand into his. The worst was over.

There were twelve people in the group now—two other women besides herself, Joanne noticed with pleasure—but there was no sign of Bryant. The men talked and laughed freely together, as though she were already accepted and forgotten. One of the other women walked over to say hello.

"I'm Bob's wife, Edie," the woman said, "and that's his sister, Mellie. I heard that you're Joanne and that you're going with them."

"Yes. How do you do, Mrs. Freeland? Edie."

The woman looked momentarily startled, then she laughed. "No, I'm not Mrs. Freeland. I'm Bob Lansing's wife. That's my husband over there, the tall skinny one with the red shirt on."

Joanne glanced over. "The one who's never heard about the Facts of Fat?" she suggested, sipping her coffee.

Edie Lansing laughed again. She was a short stocky woman dressed in loose black pants and an oversized man's blue cotton work shirt. "That's the one. Every time before he leaves on one of these climbs I stuff all the food down him I can, but he gets so excited and nervous he can't eat and loses weight while I—wouldn't you know it—gain."

The two laughed together.

At the end of the break, Freeland walked over to Joanne again. "I'm breaking you and Andy up and switching you to harder work," he told her, a challenging glint in his eye. "Bob Lansing and his wife will take over assembling the boxes. Andy's going to work up front with Jack Goodson, and you come with me."

Joanne was pleased with this chance to show Freeland what she could do, while at the same time she kept her fingers crossed that she'd be able to pass the test he was obviously planning to subject her to.

For the next three hours she and Freeland shifted huge heavy cartons around, carried cartons from one end of the warehouse to another, piled them one on top of another and in general used muscles that Joanne had never even known she had. Fortunately she'd been taught years before, by her father, to lift anything heavy with her legs, not her back, and her legs were strong. After twenty minutes of working with Freeland, she was sweating profusely. After an hour she was panting for breath. At the end of three hours she was delighted to hear the whistle signaling the break she'd begun to think would never come.

"Dinnertime," Freeland sang out. They carefully lowered the carton they were carrying onto the pile where Freeland said it should go, then Freeland stood for a moment looking at her, grinning. To Joanne's relief, he tossed an arm around her shoulders and muttered, "In my book you're one okay lady. No wonder Bryant signed you up."

Joanne smiled in delight. Now she had two friends—maybe even three, if she could count Bryant.

When she was back in the cleared area, Joanne's heart leaped at the sight of Bryant. He was talking to Bob Lansing. As he absently glanced Joanne's way, a flase of recognition crossed his eyes, but he didn't break off to come speak to her. "We take an hour's dinner break," Freeland said, walking over to her side, his dark eyes twinkling. "That is, if you're up to coming back and working some more."

"Thanks. I'll be here," Joanne assured him.

As she started rather reluctantly down the passageway to the street, she ran across Andy. His boyish face lighted up and he reached out to clasp her arm. "Hi. How you doing? I was looking for you. There's a guy out on the front sidewalk says he's a friend of yours. Scott something. Wants to know if you're free to come out to speak to him."

Scottie. "Thanks, Andy." Joanne nervously sped up her step.

Scottie greeted her with a quick hug.

"For Pete's sake, how long have you been hanging around out here?" Joanne asked, unsure as to how she felt about having him there.

"Not long. I had to work until five, as I told

you. I just thought, as hard as you're working, I could at least come down and drive you home. You must be beat. My car's down here.''

As they started walking toward it, Joanne mentioned that she had only an hour.

"You're not going back?" Scottie said with open astonishment.

"Of course I'm going back. We have an incredible amount of work still to do; we've made barely any headway at all. I'll probably work until midnight or so, if I can hold up till then.''

Scottie's lips became set. He wound his arm through hers. "Then I'm going back in to work with you. Now don't argue with me, Joanne, I am.''

"But—Scottie, you're not dressed for it. You'll ruin your suit!''

"Nonsense. It's an old suit anyway. I'll leave the jacket in the car." He smiled winningly at her, and Joanne, as nervous as the idea made her, could not think of any further basis for objecting. Besides, there were enough people working that the chance of Scottie and Bryant meeting was slight—she hoped.

As luck would have it, when she returned with Scottie to the cleared space in the middle of the warehouse after dinner there were only two men there—Bryant and Freeland. Her heart racing, Joanne led Scottie over to introduce him.

"Mr. Freeland, this is a friend of mine, Scott

Rowland. Jim, you remember Scott, don't you?
He was with me at Penny's party the night we
met.''

An instant flash of awareness ran through
Bryant's eyes. He smiled, rising to his feet, and
put out his hand. "Of course, Scott. Nice to see
you again.''

"Nice to see you, too, Mr. Bryant. Jim.''

"Scottie's come in with me as he wants to
help.''

With a grin, Bob Freeland thrust out his hand
and caught up Scottie's. "Hey, that's nice of
you, fella. Believe you me, we can use all the
help we can get, and more.''

Bryant emptied his coffee cup, crumpled it
and tossed it into a nearby trash barrel. To
Joanne, his eyes looked extraordinarily dark
that moment. "If you mean that, Scott, I'll put
you to work right now. Come with me.''

Scottie shot Joanne a look of surprise, then
with a little shrug and a smile he followed
Bryant down one of the dark corridors.

Joanne did not see either one of them again
until the ten-o'clock break that night.

She worked with Freeland again, lifting, carrying heavy cartons until she was bathed in
sweat. At moments she suspected that Freeland
was indulging in make-work, shifting boxes
from one end of the warehouse to another just
for the sport of it. "Once these paths broaden,
we can bring in dollies to move stuff for
us,'' Freeland remarked, with his appealing

crooked smile. "But for tonight it's good for us. It'll harden our muscles, make better men out of us, right?" He grinned with delight at his joke.

Joanne decided in time that what they were doing wasn't just make-work. A team began breaking into the cartons of freeze-dried food they had moved, assembling estimated daily rations into a mound, then packing them into the newly assembled cartons. The packers worked with lists: so many packets of stew, so many packets of soup, and so on. Little by little the packed cartons were mounting, while the piles of original boxes were dwindling. Order was emerging out of chaos. There was still an enormous amount to do, but some progress could be discerned.

After a brief break at ten o'clock work continued until midnight, at which time the whistle blew and Freeland told everyone to quit and rest. He would be bedding down in a cot in a small office at the back of the warehouse. "And I'm taking the phone off the hook, so don't anyone try to phone me," he said. "You know we don't answer the phone anyway." He mentioned that there were a dozen easily accessible sleeping bags for those who might want to spend the night right here on the job. Scottie walked over to Joanne as Freeland was bawling out this information.

"We'll sleep better if we go home," he whispered into her ear. "We can come back as early as you like in the morning and work all day.''

As she fell into bed some forty minutes later, Joanne felt too exhausted to worry, or even to care much that she hadn't had a single chance to talk to Bryant alone all day.

CHAPTER EIGHT

WHEN JOANNE AND SCOTTIE ARRIVED at the warehouse at a few minutes past seven Sunday morning, they were approached by a woman who'd been standing on the sidewalk near the entrance. She was a pretty woman in her early thirties, her dark hair parted in the middle and drawn back tautly into a bun. There was something rather Madonnalike in her appearance, except for the anxiety screaming from her eyes.

"Hello. I'm Beth Freeland, Bob's wife. Would you please tell him I'm here and ask him to come out to speak to me?"

"Of course, we'd be glad to," Scottie said, with his instinctive warmth and courtesy.

"But why don't you just come inside with us?" Joanne suggested. She pulled the door open, smiling. "This is open; you could have gone on in by yourself."

The woman drew back, looking momentarily even more anxious. "Oh, no, thanks. I don't want to go in. But please give Bob my message, if you will."

Freeland wasn't in the cleared space when Joanne and Scottie arrived there. The warehouse seemed older, dirtier and more disordered than ever. No one else was around, but the large coffee maker was plugged in, bubbling away, and the aroma of coffee filled the air. After Scottie poured them each a cup, he and Joanne started down one of the passageways to the small office in the back of the warehouse.

They found Freeland there, sitting at a small cluttered desk.

"There's a very attractive woman out front asking for you," Scottie said, his blue eyes smiling. "Name of Beth. She said she's your wife. And she'd like you to go out to speak to her."

To Joanne's surprise, she saw an immediate look of fear, of near panic, flash through Freeland's eyes. He appeared to be a tense, tautly wound-up man by nature, but that moment he visibly tightened even more. His eyes dropped onto the desk top, and for the first time in all the hours that Joanne had watched him in operation, he seemed to waste time and energy nervously pushing papers around.

"Well—thanks for telling me. But do me a favor, will you, Scott? Go out and tell her that I'm not here and that there's no point in her hanging around as I'm not expected in today. Please."

Obviously upset by this request, Scottie glanced around uncertainly at Joanne. A gentleman by nature, he wasn't used to lying, especially to worried women.

"Go on, please!" Freeland snapped, in the

face of Scottie's hesitation. "It's cold out there. The weather report is for rain. You want her standing out there freezing, maybe getting soaked and catching cold?"

"We could suggest she come inside," Scottie said. "Or you could go outside to speak to her since she asked. She is your wife, Mr. Freeland."

"So she's my wife!" Freeland yelled furiously at Scottie. "Will you go out there and do as I say or do I have to ask Joanne?"

With a sigh Scottie gave in, turned away and left.

Joanne and Freeland were in the cleared space a few minutes later when Scottie returned.

"Well, your wife asked that I give you this message," Scottie began.

Freeland waved his hand imperiously. "Forget it. I don't want to hear it. Both of you, come this way and I'll put you to work."

"Your wife says she doesn't for one minute believe you're not in here," Scottie snapped, his voice rising in almost the first display of angry defiance that Joanne had ever heard from him, "and she's going to wait outside until you have the decency to go out to speak to her, even if it takes all day."

"So let her," Freeland muttered, leading the way down a passageway, irritably gesturing for them to follow. "She can wait out there till hell freezes over for all I care."

Joanne and Scottie were put to work packing

cartons for shipment. Ten cartons were set up in a ring around the work area, to be packed at one time. It was easy physical work but required concentration and carried a heavier worry load. Little mistakes didn't matter very much, but big mistakes could be costly, as Freeland had warned. They had a posted list of what was to go into each carton, and after getting their first cartons packed, both Joanne and Scottie had a nervous impulse to unload a box and make sure they hadn't missed anything. One day soon the team would be high on the slopes of a treacherous mountain, dependent upon one of these cartons for the day's nutritional needs. Joanne sent up a silent prayer that she and Scottie wouldn't forget to pack anything essential.

Freeland dropped in on them about twenty minutes after they'd started and told them with a crooked smile, his eyes sparkling, to stop working in slow motion. "Speed it up, for Pete's sake. Yesterday Bob Lansing and his wife packed at five times the rate you two are making. Stop doodling around here or I'll bust you two up and throw real work at you."

By noon it was possible to see the first results of all the work done. The entire east side of the warehouse was stacked with cartons that had been packed, labeled, sealed and were ready for shipment. Freeland had organized the work into a smooth assembly-line operation. There was no wasted motion. For hours Joanne and Scottie had been packing, moving rapidly, automatically, no longer weighted down with worry that they might make mistakes. The weather had warmed and the interior of the warehouses had become hot and humid. Perspiration gleamed on Joanne's face and ran down the sides of Scottie's. They worked together rhythmically, in complete harmony, and Joanne felt her fondness for her friend deepen with every moment. How generous he was to spend his one free day down here sweating it out for her and the team.

They worked until midnight that night and went home exhausted. Again that day Joanne hadn't had even one moment alone with Bryant. In fact, she had scarcely seen him.

As Scott drove them home, he remarked that he liked and respected Freeland. With a tired grin, he said, "The guy really knows how to get work out of people, a born leader. Of course, I like Bryant, too. When we were working together, he seemed like a nice enough guy."

Despite how tired she was, Joanne tensed. "So—did you two have much of a chance to talk?"

"Oh, a little. You know how it goes. Mostly we just worked, but I did have the chance to mention that I was happy to see you go off on this expedition because I figure that when you get back maybe you'll have gotten climbing out of your system to where you'll be ready to settle down and marry me."

Joanne's stomach lurched. "And what did Bryant say to that?"

"Not much. As I recall, he didn't say anything at all. We were working very hard, you know, and talked very little. However, he did mention once that you were an excellent climber, one of the best, if not the best, on the team."

Scottie had to return to work on Monday. Joanne went into her law office in the morning, but by noon had finished all essential work for the day and went down to the warehouse to pitch in for the afternoon. She was filled with a sense of anticipation as she walked down the sidewalk toward the entrance. Now that Scottie wasn't with her, and many of the other team members had returned to their homes and regular jobs, possibly she'd have the chance to work with Bryant. She knew he'd be there, for she'd heard him tell Freeland that he would.

As she approached the entry door, she noticed that Beth Freeland was there again. Mrs. Freeland glanced up to smile at her, the same anxiety glistening in her eyes.

"Hi."

"Hello, Mrs. Freeland." Joanne slowed her step, then came to a stop beside the woman. "I'm Joanne Patton," she remarked on impulse. "One of the climbers." She put out her hand.

Beth Freeland shook hands. "Oh, so you're Joanne. Parke Gilford—one of the other climbers—told me about you. Congratulations on making the team."

"Thank you." Joanne pulled the door open,

then hesitated and let it close again. "Look, Mrs. Freeland, it's none of my business, but you're not going to wait out here all day, are you? Why don't you just come inside? You're right that your husband's in there, but for some reason he refuses to come out to speak to you."

Beth Freeland's worried face suddenly looked even paler. "We're separated. I don't know whether Bob told you or not. Have been for almost a year, which was entirely my fault. I told Bob he'd have to choose between me and climbing, and you can see which he chose." Her wide-set eyes filled with tears. "But after twelve years of it, I felt I couldn't take it anymore, the loneliness, the worry—especially the worry. Bob was always off on climbs. He was never home."

After a slight hesitation, Joanne said gently, "Well, if you couldn't cure him of mountaineering, why didn't you give it a try yourself? If you can't lick 'em, join 'em," she ended with a soft little smile.

"Oh, I tried. And Bob was so patient and loving with me at first. But—but I have this fear of heights, you see, and I just wasn't able to overcome it. On one climb, in the Alps, there was a sudden blizzard, and one of the climbers fell into a crevasse and I panicked. Bob kept yelling at me, telling me what I should do, but I froze and couldn't move. It almost cost the man his life, Bob said, and after that he would never climb with me again. Women are too emotional and undependable, he says; in a crisis they fall apart.''

"So that's why..." Joanne murmured to herself.

"Why what?"

Joanne smiled. "Never mind. But thank you for telling me what you did. It makes me understand some things more clearly.''

Beth smiled too. "I'm glad. Frankly I was surprised when I heard there was a woman on the team. I didn't think Bob would ever agree to that. But then Parke Gilford explained it to me, the guarantee that Jim gave Bob and the rest of the team that you were only going with them as far as base camp and then would oversee the camp while the other climbers went on to the summit. I guess that's why Bob and the others accepted you.''

Joanne's ears rang. Her head felt light as the blood instantly drained away. "What? What did you say?'' She shook her head to clear it, to stop the whirling.

"I said—''

"Never mind. I heard. Jim Bryant guaranteed that I wasn't going any higher than base camp. Thank you, Mrs. Freeland, for letting me know. I'll see you.''

Still in shock, Joanne pulled the door open and stepped inside. She strode down toward the cleared area. As the initial shock died away, anger moved in. She found Freeland in the packing area, overseeing the labeling of some cartons.

"Mr. Freeland, I'd like very much to speak to Mr. Bryant. Please tell me where he is."

Freeland looked surprised at her tone but merely shrugged. "He's toward the back, over where the canned stuff is stored."

"Thank you."

Bryant was working with Andy Howell, lowering to the floor heavy cartons of beer. He was on top of a stack of six cartons, working a pulley rope around the carton he knelt on. In the dim light Joanne stared up at him. He wore jeans but was bare chested. Perspiration glistened on his face and across his shoulders. Her heart constricted momentarily at the sight of him, but she quickly regained control.

"Mr. Bryant—Jim—I'd like very much to speak to you."

Bryant glanced down at her, a startled look flashing through his eyes, then his face settled into grimness. "All right, in a minute." He finished what he was doing, lowered himself over the side of the stack of cartons to the floor and grabbed his shirt to slip it on, as though unwilling to face her less than fully dressed.

"Andy, if you wouldn't mind, could I have a minute alone with Mr. Bryant, please?"

The young blonde flushed lightly, but muttered "sure," and wiping the sweat off his brow, he turned and walked away down one of the aisles.

"All right, Joanne, I know what you're in a fury about." Bryant spoke in a patient but patronizing voice that infuriated her even more. She had to fight to retain any control at all.

"You betrayed me!" she hissed. "You knew how I felt about being stuck in base camp, that I had no interest in that at all, and you led me to think—"

"I led you to think *nothing*!" Bryant cut in, sounding as furious as Joanne now. Veins stood out at his temples, and his sweaty face was flushed red with anger. "Follow me, Miss Patton, I've got something to show you!" He led the way across the rear of the warehouse to the small cluttered office.

From the desk Bryant drew out a batch of papers. Joanne saw at once what they were: the applications submitted by the climbers to join this team. Bryant grabbed the top application and thrust it in front of Joanne. His finger tapped a paragraph printed near the bottom of the page.

The paragraph read:

I agree that if I am accepted on this expedition that I will put myself under the leadership of James A. Bryant, that I will not question his authority on any question of substance, furthermore that if my personal ambition clashes with what is perceived by Mr. Bryant as the good of the team, I will suppress my personal ambition for the good of the team.

Under this was her signature.

Bryant's dark green eyes blazed. He spoke harshly between clenched teeth. "No one asked you to submit this application, no one forced you to sign it. But you did sign it, you did submit it and you will now abide by what you signed."

"But—but—you're not being fair! I'm as good a climber as any you've got, you told Scottie so! Why should I be the one team member discriminated against before we even begin?"

Bryant yanked the application form out of her hands, shoved it under the clip and tossed the pile back into the open desk drawer. He slammed the drawer shut.

"You know perfectly well why, and I don't want to hear another word about it. Now go back to work."

Joanne swayed momentarily, torn between the desire to stand her ground and the need to turn and run out of there before her fury got out of control and she burst into tears. The latter impulse won.

She left the small cluttered office in a rage, tears of fury splashing into her eyes. She'd been right about Bryant from the first: he was not to be trusted. He had teased her along, manipulated her, made a complete fool of her, then had turned on her without remorse. For weeks he had pretended to be giving her a chance, had pretended to be impressed by her skills, had even put on a show of caring for her. Yet at the first sign of trouble he had sacrificed her on the altar of expediency. He was a hollow man, a man without honor, devoid of all decency, and she would never, ever again feel anything for him but contempt.

As THE EXPEDITION FLIGHT DATE NEARED, Joanne found herself unable to sleep. In spite of her best efforts to kill off her rage at Bryant, on some deep level she remained furiously angry with him. She knew this wasn't good for her and repeatedly reminded herself she had two options: she could remain a member of the team and adjust to the conditions imposed, or she could drop out and do her best to forget about it. But feeling constantly agitated about the situation, making herself sick with anger, was the worst possible way to treat herself.

Though she knew this with her head, her heart stayed in its tumultuous state. She couldn't sleep, she had a hard time eating. With each new day, she grew more tired, nervous and irritable. At work Ted Myers did his best to reason her out of her wrought-up mood, and whenever she saw Scottie, he did his best to calm and soothe her. But neither Ted nor Scottie, despite their good intentions, were able to help. *It's up to me to cure myself,* Joanne kept reminding herself, night after night as she lay sleepless in bed. *I can't go on this way much longer.*

But the days crept past and nothing changed.

January gave way to February, and soon the flight date was less than ten days away. Joanne found in dismay that she was dropping weight daily. She was nervous and edgy. She tried very hard not to give even a moment's thought to Bryant, to erase him entirely out of memory as though he didn't exist, and to a large extent she succeeded in this. But the success was costly—it kept her in a taut agitated state.

On this particular evening she returned early from having dinner out with Scottie, showered and got ready for bed. As tired as she felt, surely she would sleep. But this was what she told herself every night. She'd climb into bed feeling so weary she was certain that this night would be different, but it never was. Once she was in bed in the dark, sleep fled from her.

She was turning down the bedspread when her buzzer sounded. It was only a little after nine, but still the sound of the buzzer startled and frightened her. She knew it wasn't Scottie, he had phoned her from his apartment a few minutes earlier.

"Yes, who's there?"

"Bryant."

Joanne's heart leaped to her throat. After a minute she answered, "Go away. I have nothing to say to you."

There was a brief pause before Bryant said, "But I have things that I'd very much like to say to you."

"That's your problem. Just go away."

Joanne swung around and started back toward her bedroom.

Bryant pounded on the door. "Joanne, open this door!"

"No!"

"Do as I say!"

"Drop dead!"

"The expedition's in danger of being canceled, and I need your help."

Hearing this, Joanne wavered. *The liar!* He was probably just saying this to get her to give in. She walked unsurely back toward the door and stood near it. "Are you telling me the truth, Mr. Bryant?"

"Joanne, please, just unlock the door."

Fighting down a sudden trembling, Joanne relented.

The moment she slid back the bolt lock, Bryant opened the door and stepped inside. His arms went around her and he drew her close. Though she hadn't wept over any of this before, Joanne began to cry. Her head rested on his shoulder while tears overflowed her eyes. One of Bryant's hands pressed the back of her head. "Sweetheart, I know," he said softly. "I know, I know."

He swept her up into his arms and carried her over to the sofa, where he put her down. He sat down beside her, his hands tightly holding one of hers as he assessed her with a worried frown.

"Darling, you look so thin, and you've got

dark circles under your eyes." He shook his head in dismay.

Joanne felt her tears dry up as renewed anger came sweeping in. She jumped up from the sofa and moved a distance away. "And what else do you expect? After what you did—" Her voice choked off as fresh tears threatened.

Bryant sighed. He sat leaning forward, elbows on knees, eyeing her with concern. "You still feel angry, naturally—"

"Not only angry!" Joanne flared, swinging back around to glare at him. "Betrayed! Do you understand what I'm saying? Not just attacked and robbed by some impersonal crook, but *betrayed*."

Bryant sighed again, his eyes dropping as he stared at his clasped hands.

Nothing further was said for several minutes. After glaring at Bryant's bowed head for a time, Joanne turned and strode swiftly into her kitchen. She turned the flame on under her coffee pot, then allowed it insufficient time to heat before grabbing up one cup and pouring coffee into it. She swept back out to the living room, sipping the lukewarm coffee.

"I'd offer you a cup, too, Mr. Bryant, if you were staying, but unfortunately you're not. Please go now."

Bryant was no longer seated on the sofa. He had risen during her absence and now stood over in front of the double window on the spot where they had made love. Joanne wondered whether Bryant remembered that, if that was why he had gravitated over there. Was he trying to defuse her anger by stirring up memories? Well, it wouldn't work. No way.

Bryant glanced around, smiling. "Thanks, but I don't care for coffee anyway, and if you want me to leave—"

"I do." Joanne forced herself to take another sip of the tepid liquid, then she placed the cup down on the end table by the sofa. "I'll show you out."

She walked quickly toward the door. With a sigh Bryant crossed the room and came up beside her. She pulled the door open, but Bryant didn't step through it at once. Instead he stood gazing solemnly, intently down at her.

"I'd apologize for what I did, Joanne," he said quietly, "except that any such apology would be meaningless. Given the same circumstances, I'd do the same thing again. I understand how you feel and I'm sorry. But what would it have profited you or me or any of us if the expedition had blown apart? Would you rather that had happened? Possibly you would have, but that's where we differ. As I told you beforehand, I was determined to hold it together, any way I could."

Joanne's eyes flashed up. "Even if it meant sacrificing me, obviously."

Bryant's face became impassive. "Yes, even though it meant sacrificing you, which is not to say I wanted it that way. I simply did what I thought was best."

Joanne's eyes flooded with stinging tears. "If someone has to be the sacrificial victim, why not Joanne?"

Bryant's face tightened and a muscle rippled along his jaw. "I didn't single you out; the men did."

"My gender did," Joanne snapped bitterly.

Bryant sighed. His large strong hand touched her shoulder, then ran down her arm, sending a tingling through her. "Yes. But as long as the expedition's still on, and you're a member, we still have something. Can't you see that? Maybe not as much as you wanted, as much as you hoped for, but *something*. Isn't something better than nothing? I never promised you anything more than you have now."

Joanne's eyes were swimming with tears as she stared up. She tensed against the tumult of emotions roaring through her and did not trust her voice enough to speak.

Bryant leaned down and pressed a soft kiss on her cheek. "Thank you for letting me in and talking with me. And do try to put on some weight, you look dreadfully thin. Have you been that distressed about me and what happened?"

Joanne nodded, blinking back her tears. "Yes. Precisely."

"Oh, damn." Bryant glanced away, then returned his eyes to her face again. His hand came up to press against her cheek as his eyes enveloped her with care and concern. "I know you're tired and don't want to discuss this any further tonight, but can I phone you tomorrow and possibly take you to dinner tomorrow night? If we could hash it out some more—one way or another we've got to get you back to eating and sleeping well so you'll fatten up."

A flicker of hope sprang out of Joanne's desolation. If they could discuss it some more, "All right, fine," she said. "Call me tomorrow."

A slight smile curved Bryant's lips. "All right. Till tomorrow night. And try to push aside your anger at me enough to get a good night's sleep."

Catching up her hand, he gave it a little squeeze, then stepped through the door. Before Joanne had closed it behind him, he turned back, his face shadowed. "Oh, one other thing. While I was working with your friend Scott, he mentioned that once this expedition is over he hopes to marry you."

Joanne tensed slightly, but managed to keep her eyes on Bryant's. "So?"

Though a look of annoyance crossed his face, Bryant's voice remained quiet and friendly. "So? Is it your plan to marry him?"

Is that any of your business? Joanne couldn't bring herself to voice this thought, for in her heart she suddenly hoped fiercely that it *was* Bryant's business. "No, I don't. And I've told Scottie that time and time again, but I can't seem to keep him from hoping."

"I see." With a relieved look Bryant swung

away and strode rapidly away down the corridor.

For the first time in weeks, Joanne fell asleep almost as soon as she climbed into bed. She slept soundly all night. When she woke she felt rested, newly energized, and almost insatiably hungry. Tonight she'd see Bryant again; they'd go out to dinner and talk. And after dinner— well, maybe after dinner, when Bryant brought her home.... Joanne smiled to herself, her cheeks flushing. Though she still felt keenly disappointed about the climb, the restrictions imposed on her, she was no longer angry about it. Bryant was right: something *was* better than nothing, and things could change. There was always that hope. Once they were actually over there, mounting their assault, the situation might change.

Joanne had a busy day. Eating lunch at her desk and taking no breaks, she managed to clear up all pressing matters by five. She left the office early and arrived home forty-five minutes later. Bryant's call came right on the dot of six. His voice sounded rushed.

"Joanne, sweetheart, I'm terribly sorry, but I had to fly home this afternoon—an emergency came up at the home office. For months I've been so caught up in the expedition that I've neglected everything else and it caught up with me today. Please believe me, I had no choice. I've got two dozen things I've got to straighten out, or I won't be free to fly out on the nineteenth. Please say you understand."

"I understand," Joanne said dully, disappointment a knife blade cutting through her. "Of course I understand."

"Good. Now I've got to run. I'll phone you later tonight, if that's all right."

"Sure. Fine."

Joanne listlessly dropped the phone. All her plans, her high hopes. Obviously Bryant cared less about being with her than she did about being with him. For all she knew he might have several close women friends at home in Seattle—or even worse, one woman. Joanne blinked back tears. Why hadn't she held onto her anger against him? It had protected her like a shield. Now she felt exposed, vulnerable. Why had she ever allowed herself to fall in love with a man like that?

She fixed herself a quick dinner then relaxed for an hour in front of the TV set. As the cutting edge of her disappointment dulled, so did her feelings of vulnerability. If Bryant could survive happily without seeing her, she could do likewise without seeing him. Love might be a sickness, but it wasn't an incurable one, or at least her case wasn't incurable. She'd strengthen her defenses and make sure of that.

Bryant phoned her back a few minutes after ten. Joanne was already in bed reading. She wasn't unfriendly, nor did she exude an overflowing warmth. When Bryant asked her at one point what was bothering her, she lied and said nothing, she was tired, that's all. The conversa-

tion faltered and died. They said their good-
nights and each hung up.

Joanne did not see Bryant again until the
team assembled at the airport on February 19
for the flight to Nepal.

CHAPTER NINE

Six members of the team were flying out from San Francisco, including Bryant. Others were leaving from New York, Chicago, Miami, Los Angeles and a couple from cities in Canada.

When Joanne walked into the airport at 8:40 on the morning of February 19, she felt amazingly calm. After Bryant's brief visit earlier in the month she had managed to come to terms with her love for him. In consequence she had been sleeping soundly, eating voraciously and had regained almost all of the lost weight. As she went striding into the airport, she knew she looked rested and well.

Scottie had driven her there, but once they'd checked her luggage in, she had insisted that he not wait to see her off. With a sad smile Scottie had kissed her goodbye, then left.

Now, walking toward the designated gate, Joanne began to feel a bubbling excitement, undimmed by any fear or hurt. She no longer felt angry toward Bryant. As far as the expedition went, she was ready to admit he had been right. She *had*, willingly and eagerly, signed that form putting herself under his leadership. She did believe that on a difficult climb personal ambition should be submerged, when necessary, for the good of the team, so she had little justification for her earlier feelings of having been betrayed.

As far as the climb went, she was basically back to square one. That very first day in his hotel suite, Bryant had offered her exactly what she had now: a chance to be on the team and to climb as high as base camp. When he'd made this offer, she'd had it on the tip of her tongue to accept just before he'd snatched the offer back. If all she'd been able to achieve was to retrieve that offer and accept it, at least she hadn't been left wholly out of it. And base camp would be set up on an altitude around nineteen thousand feet, which was no mean climb in itself. Mount McKinley, in Alaska, the highest mountain in North America, was only 20,320 feet, just over one thousand feet higher than she would be in base camp. In her heart she still wanted to try for the summit of Dhaulagiri more than anything in the world, but she wasn't going to let this wish spoil the entire climb for her. One way or another she'd persuade Bryant to give her a chance.

Bob Lansing was already there when she arrived at the gate area. His wife and sister were there, too, seeing him off. A few minutes later Bryant came striding up.

At the sight of him, Joanne's pulse quickened. He wore a dark blue suit with a lighter blue turtleneck sweater and moved with that marvelous power and grace that always made Joanne feel breathless. The reddish tint of his dark brown hair was more noticeable than usual, and health and strength seemed to radiate from him. Yet his face looked tense. As he saw Joanne, recognition momentarily flashed through his eyes, but he didn't smile. He continued to look far more worried than pleased. Arriving at her side, he threw an arm around her shoulders and gave her a quick squeeze.

"Hi, beautiful. You're looking marvelous, much better than the last time I saw you. You'll be sitting with me."

"But—what about Freeland?" Joanne had conditioned herself to the fact that Bryant would surely sit with Freeland so they could discuss any details about the team operation that still needed to be worked through.

Bryant ran a hand over his hair, a nervous gesture Joanne had never seen him make before. "Freeland's already in Kathmandu. He flew out right after we shipped the supplies and has been over there to receive and store them. I just got a call from him this morning. He went some time ago to check on our permits, and there's been a snag. He's been trying to straighten it out, but the bureaucrats over there, like bureaucrats everywhere, are hung up on petty details. Because Freeland didn't apply for the permits—I did—and they are in my name, not his, they won't deal with him. If the damn mess isn't straightened out, we might find ourselves cooling our heels indefinitely in Kathmandu instead of climbing.''

"Oh, no.''

Bryant's dark green eyes caught on hers and suddenly his broad handsome face broke into a grin. "Oh, yes. But that's par for the course, isn't it? Did you ever go on a single climb with your father that didn't have its share of last-minute slipups and foul-ups?''

Joanne grinned. "You're right. Not a one.''

As Bryant's grin died away, the worry again gripped his face. "Neither have I. So this is no different. Each time you figure this is the time you'll be so careful, so precise, that everything will go smoothly, but it just never does.''

Lansing, who had left for a few minutes with his wife and sister, reappeared and walked over to greet Bryant. Courtland Mitchell and Michael Ross came striding in together, laughing and talking. A few minutes later John Naylor arrived, completing their group. The gate opened and they boarded their plane.

The first leg of their flight was to Tokyo, with a stop in Honolulu. After a brief stopover in Tokyo, they would proceed to Hong Kong, where they would catch a flight to New Delhi. Arrival in New Delhi was scheduled for 2:50 A.M., and at 8:15 the next morning they would catch a Royal Nepal Airlines flight to Kathmandu, arriving at 9:40 A.M.

"Are you a good air traveler?" Bryant teased Joanne as they settled down in their seats.

"I am an *excellent* air traveler," she responded, delight streaming through her. They were on their way, on their way to the most magnificent mountains in the world, the Himalayas.

For the first few hours Bryant seemed steeped in worry and was not in a talkative mood. He frequently caught up her hand in his, held it for a few minutes, then released it again. As always when flying, Joanne found it easy to lean her head back and doze off. Almost before she knew it, they were in Honolulu, where they could deplane and stretch their legs.

During the hour layover in Honolulu, Joanne had no chance to be with Bryant. Lansing and Courtland Mitchell cornered him and began earnestly discussing technical aspects of the climb. Joanne found herself walking along beside John Naylor, a stocky man of medium height, with thick graying hair and beetle brows over small bright eyes. Joanne had heard that John, who was forty-two, was the oldest man on the trip but possibly the least experienced and skillful of all the climbers.

"So how does it feel to be off on the grand adventure at last?" Naylor asked her.

Joanne glanced rather curiously around at him. Ever since that morning when the team members had first heard she was going along and had voted on whether or not to cancel the trip, Joanne had wondered who had voted for or against her. Every time she found herself talking with any of the other climbers, the question would pop up. She tried to push it out of her mind, but still it surfaced with every new encounter.

"It feels just great," she said, smiling. "How does it feel to you?"

"Frightening," Naylor said, shaking his head. "Half the time I ask myself what in hell I'm doing here. The truth is I get dizzy climbing a twelve-foot ladder."

"Then why *are* you here?" Joanne asked curiously.

Naylor's eyes circled around to catch hers. He shrugged. "Who knows? My wife called to say she thought I was crazy when she heard about it."

"Called to say?"

Naylor's weather-beaten face seemed to flush. "Ex-wife, I should say. She divorced me last year, the minute our last kid left home. This left me pretty shaken up, at loose ends. I'm a house painter by trade. I did quite a bit of mountaineering years ago when I was young. We lived in the northwest, then when I was fifteen I left for Alaska with my dad. He loved to climb and we went up McKinley, both the South Peak and the North Peak, then we moved back to Washington. After my folks reconciled, we went climbing all through the Cascades." Naylor paused, sighing. The skin of his face was edged with white under the dark tan. "But all that was years ago and I didn't ever enjoy it much. I guess you could say I'm here because my dad used to love climbing and because it's a stupid way to grab for my lost youth.''

Naylor's glance had fallen, but when he lifted his eyes again there was an amused glint in them. ''When they reach middle age and their marriages break up, a lot of men go chasing after young girls. I don't have it in me to do that. So I guess I've come chasing after this mountain instead. Do you suppose she will let me catch her?''

''Who knows?'' Joanne answered, and joined in Naylor's brief burst of laughter.

When they were once again in the air and she was seated next to Bryant, Joanne asked him, as quietly as possible, about John Naylor. Naylor was seated directly in front of them, but he was away from his seat, so he couldn't overhear.

''Was John Naylor with the group that trained on Rainier?'' Bryant nodded. ''So how did he do? He seems so uncertain, not to mention downright unhappy.''

Bryant looked surprised. ''He did extremely well. Seemed to have adequate knowledge of and experience with every aspect of climbing over ice and snow. He seemed tough and unbreakable, with a greater stamina than some of the younger men. And he most certainly did not express the least fear or uncertainty. I had him tagged as one of our very best men.''

As Naylor was returning to his seat, Joanne

decided not to pursue the subject, yet her curiosity about the man had been aroused. She would simply have to wait and see for herself how he operated on the mountain.

At last, after endless hours in the air and interminable, dreary hours waiting in airports, they arrived in Kathmandu. Although Joanne had been seated beside Bryant for the entire trip, they had had surprisingly little chance to talk. Surrounded as they were by other team members—Bob Lansing and Courtland Mitchell across the aisle from them, John Naylor and Michael Ross directly in front—they avoided discussing anything personal, and the superficial conversations they had about flight conditions, weather and the prospects for a successful climb tended to die from their own lack of substance. It was a relief to arrive at their destination.

Freeland met them at the airport with bad news. Two climbers had dropped out at the very last minute. One climber on his way to the airport in Miami had been broadsided by another car. Both he and his wife had been injured, though neither one seriously. Another climber had phoned from Chicago to say that just before boarding his scheduled flight he'd asked himself why he was going, hadn't been able to come up with any compelling reason and had therefore decided to pull out. Two down, with no way in the world to replace them.

After Joanne had forced her way onto the

team, Bryant had been able to sign up three other climbers, so that at peak strength the team had had eighteen members. Two of these had dropped off before Christmas. Bryant had tried, unsuccessfully, to replace them, to bring the total back up to eighteen, but had been ready to go with sixteen. He had always felt that sixteen was an absolute minimum. Now they were here, ready to go, with only fourteen climbers.

"Suits me fine," Freeland said as he walked with Bryant and Joanne out of the airport. "I never did see this craving for a big team. The more people you take the more problems you've got, in my view. I'd be happy to lop off a couple more. Can't have too few to suit me."

Joanne could see from Bryant's worried eyes that he did not share Freeland's view.

The two represented opposing camps in the mountaineering world, she had observed. Her father had dubbed the two opposing views the Sleeks and the Plumps. The Sleeks wanted a taut streamlined expedition, with as few climbers as possible. This kept supply and personnel problems to a minimum and allowed for maximum flexibility and maneuverability. Spectacular results had sometimes been obtained by these small inexpensive expeditions, on occasion by a single climber accompanied solely by a local guide.

The Plumps were made nervous by such lean unpadded operations. With the sickness or in-

jury of one man, the entire climb might have to
be canceled. They preferred greater manpower,
even though this inevitably brought with it
ponderous logistics problems.

For an assault on treacherous Dhaulagiri, or
for any Himalayan climb, success would almost
certainly depend on sufficient manpower, regardless of the supply problems this entailed.
Glancing around at Freeland, Joanne sensed
that he knew this, too, and that his comments
to the contrary were simply his way of dealing
with adversity, whistling to keep depression
away.

Their luggage in hand, they left Tribhuvan
Airport and hired a small bus to take them into
the city. As they drove, Joanne gazed around in
delight. To the north she could glimpse Himalayan peaks rising majestically into the sky,
gleaming white against the purest of blue skies.
The Kathmandu Valley was almost forty-five
hundred feet above sea level, she knew, and at
the same latitude as central Florida. The summer monsoon season brought heavy rain to the
basin, which made possible extensive irrigation
and rich fertility. On this February day, the sky
was clear, the weather crisp. Joanne felt a growing excitement, an irrepressible delight. She
glanced around to share her delight with John
Naylor, who was seated beside her.

"I hadn't realized it would be this warm. And
to have everything look so green and lovely—I
can hardly believe it."

"Another garden spot of the world, like California," Naylor grunted.

Joanne laughed, then turned back to the window so as not to miss anything. She had never been in the Orient before, and as their bus entered the bustling city of Kathmandu, she was enchanted.

"I can't believe how Westernized everything looks," she exclaimed to Naylor. "American automobiles, people dressed in western clothing."

Bob Lansing, seated behind her, tapped her on the shoulder. She swung around to face him. His long narrow face looked a little less thin now that his chin was covered by a stubby beard.

"You're right about the Western influence, but I've traveled extensively all through the Orient, and, believe me, this is one of the least modernized cities I have seen in all of Asia. Wait until you have a chance to see the main square, with its pagoda-style Hindu shrines, and all the Newar women hawking their produce— you'll love it."

"Newar?" Joanne echoed.

"The people believed to be the original inhabitants of the Kathmandu Valley." Lansing leaned forward to explain. He spoke quietly though his eyes sparkled excitedly. "We've all heard of the Sherpa mountaineers and the Gurkha warriors, but few people have heard of the Newars. They ruled here until two centuries ago, when the hill tribes from the Gurkha region came down and conquered the valley, making Kathmandu their capital. But the Newars still clung to their identity, their language and their religious rituals, and currently they make up at least half of the population of Kathmandu. They are farmers, traders, craftsmen. Glance around and you'll see them everywhere, in their bright native dress.''

As the bus took them through narrow crowded streets, Joanne saw women in long, bright, wraparound skirts, with broad shawls around their shoulders. The men wore full-cut pants of a soft-looking material with long-sleeved shirts and broad ties looped around their waists. Some women were dressed in saris. Joanne found it all new and fascinating and felt an ever-growing delight to find herself here in the tiny Kingdom of Nepal, half the world away from her home.

The bus drew up before the Kathmandu Guest House, where the expedition would be staying overnight or until Bryant could get their permit situation straightened out. As they were climbing out of the bus, grabbing their bags, Joanne felt a hand clasp her arm and glanced around to see Bryant beside her.

''Freeland has arranged for us to stay in the basement here, where we can set up our own kitchen and cook our own food. Lansing has the room assignments Freeland made, so check with him as to which room is yours. I'm going to wash up and then head out to do what I can about this permit mix-up, and Freeland's going with me.'' Bryant paused, gazing intently at her, then added, almost in a whisper, ''If I were you, I'd grab a few hours' sleep. I wish I could. I'll see you later.'' He touched her arm for a moment, then turned and followed Freeland inside.

Her room was small, sparsely furnished but adequate. The bed, as narrow and hard as it was, looked incredibly inviting, but Joanne resisted the temptation to crawl into it. After opening her one suitcase and taking out a change of clothing, she took a sponge bath from the large basin in the room, dressed, and headed out into the corridor to see what she could do to help prepare a meal. Surely everyone was famished by now. She certainly was.

With both Bryant and Freeland gone, Lansing seemed to be in charge. A minikitchen had already been set up in the largest room, the room Freeland and Bryant were sharing. Freeland had obviously been preparing his own meals since his arrival. In a corner near the two-burner stove, supplies were neatly stacked: the dried food, packaged nuts, chocolate bars, tea bags, sugar, powdered cream, cups and plates. On the other side of the burner was a case of beer. Once the menu was decided upon—beans with crackers, meat spread, candy and nuts for dessert—it was simple to prepare. As each man, drawn by the talk and laughter, stepped into the room, Lansing strode over to hand him an open beer and tell him to find himself a spot. Soon

the room was full and Joanne was dishing up
steaming hot beans into stainless-steel pie pans
and passing them to Lansing to distribute. The
mood of the group was high, excitement con-
tagious. Everyone was laughing and talking.

The meal was satisfying if not exotic, and
Andy Howell helped Joanne clean up. On the
expedition itself, Sherpas would handle the supplies and do all the cooking, but Joanne was
happy to do it for the time being.

As they finished cleaning up, Andy asked
Joanne if she'd like to go out sightseeing. "Just
for an hour or so, sure." As weary as she felt,
she was too excited to try to nap. As she and
Andy were leaving the guest house, they ran
across John Naylor and Courtland Mitchell.
Mitchell looked about twenty-five, had light
brown hair, a pleasant face, and was, judging
from what Joanne had seen so far, the team's
practical joker. With a grin, Mitchell threw an
arm across Andy's shoulders and drew him
aside, whispering excitedly to him. Joanne
found herself walking with Naylor.

"These footloose young tomcats," Naylor
muttered, an edge of envy in his voice. "Mitchell's been scurrying around the hotel trying to
learn, through grunts and sign language, where
he can go for some fun and games and he thinks
he knows. He can't wait to go looking for action."

Joanne eyed her companion uncertainly for a
moment, then murmured, "Well, from what

you said you're a single man too. Feel free to join them if you like. Don't worry about me.''

Naylor's weathered face seemed to darken in embarrassment. ''I'm too old for that kind of nonsense. Besides, at the moment I'm beat. A ten-minute walk and then I'm going back to hit the sack.''

Andy Howell glanced back at Joanne with an uncertain look. Mitchell was leading him along, one arm still over his shoulder. Joanne couldn't tell whether Andy hoped she would rescue him from Mitchell or whether he wished that she would free him of the social obligation he had taken on when he'd invited her to go walking with him. Joanne sighed. Were things going to be this complicated all the time? She slowed her step, then stopped.

''Andy?''

Andy stopped walking, too, and his eyes shot around. ''Yes, Joanne?''

''I'm more tired than I thought. I'm going to head back.''

Andy broke free of Mitchell's hold. ''All right, I'll walk you back.''

As he reached her side, Joanne murmured, ''You don't have to, you know. I'll be perfectly fine.''

''I *want* to,'' Andy said firmly.

John Naylor glared unhappily at Andy, then at Joanne. He half turned, as though to return with them to the hotel.

''How about you, Naylor?'' Mitchell called,

his young face frowning. "You want to come along with me?"

"Sure, why not?" he replied grumpily, following Mitchell.

By then Joanne and Andy were walking away, back toward the hotel.

"I think I'll go to my room and write my girl, Christa, a letter, then maybe I'll sleep for a while," Andy explained to Joanne.

Feeling a surge of affection for her young friend, Joanne put her arm around his waist and gave him a hug. "Good idea," she said. "I think I'll do the same."

Once in her room, Joanne drew out the notebook she'd brought. There was no one she felt any urge to write to at the moment, but she planned to do what her father had always done on expeditions: keep a daily journal. Propping the notebook on her knees as she sat on the edge of her hard narrow bed, she wrote for three pages: the trip, the arrival, the guest house, the room she found herself in. She started to add the tidbit about Courtland Mitchell, John Naylor and Andy, then suddenly felt too tired to bother with it. She put the notebook aside and stretched out on the bed. Where was Bryant now? Was he getting the permit problem straightened out? He'd said he would see her later. Would he come to her room when he got back?

Thinking about Bryant, how hungry she felt for the feel of his arms, the soft pressure of his mouth on hers, Joanne drifted off to sleep.

It was dark when a knock on her door awakened her. She jerked to an upright position, momentarily confused as to where she was. Oh, yes, Kathmandu, the guest house, her room in the basement. There was a second rap on her door, a bit harder and more insistent. Joanne's pulse raced. *Bryant*. Surely it was him. She threw herself off the bed and hurried over to unlock the door, ready and eager to pull it open to welcome him.

Oh, my God, she thought as she saw who was there. "Mrs. Freeland, what in the world are you doing here?"

CHAPTER TEN

BETH FREELAND'S LOVELY FACE looked even more anxious than it had back home. "May I come in?"

"Of course. Please do."

There was only one chair in the room, a whitewashed, straight-backed, wooden one. Joanne offered it to her guest.

"Thank you. But close the door, please. I don't want anyone else to know that I'm here."

"But why *are* you here?" After Joanne closed the door she walked over to sit on the narrow bed.

Beth Freeland let out a long pained sigh. Tears shone in her anxious eyes. Her fingers fiddled nervously with the buttons of her dark blue jacket. "If you think about it a moment, I'm sure you could figure it out. I'm just so worried. I have this terrible feeling—a premonition—that something will happen to Bob, that he won't survive the climb."

Joanne felt a chill breeze through her. "Oh, no."

Beth's worried eyes, nervously circling around, met Joanne's. A fleeting smile crossed her soft pale lips. "Don't take that to heart, please, Miss...I'm sorry, I've forgotten your name."

"Patton. Joanne Patton."

"I'm Beth."

"Yes, I remember, Beth."

A tremulous smile played across Beth's lips. Momentarily it almost erased the deep anxiety her face held. "As I said, Joanne, don't take my words too seriously. I always feel that way, every time Bob goes off on one of these climbs. That was our worst problem. I couldn't seem to control how I felt. I was sure that each time he left, that would be it, I'd never see him again, so of course I'd cry and beg and carry on like a madwoman, trying to get him not to go. Bob got angrier and angrier about it, more and more fed up with me, while I grew more and more incensed at what I saw as his lack of consideration for me. If he'd loved me at all, wouldn't he have listened to me and stayed home?"

After a slight pause, in which she smiled again, Beth added, "But then each time he came home safely, proving me wrong, until finally I had to face that I wasn't having psychic premonitions at all. I was simply the victim of my own neurotic fears. That's one of the things I want to tell Bob, to explain to him. I'm learning to deal with my irrational fears, and I feel that from now on, if he'd give me another chance, I could handle it much better than I did before."

"And that's why you're here, just to tell your husband that?"

Beth's smile made her Madonnalike face even prettier, shy and soft. "Well, yes. That's one of the reasons."

"But couldn't you have written him instead?" Especially, Joanne thought to herself, when he refused even to speak to you? All this way, halfway around the world, to track down a man who might not even agree to see her.

"Well, yes, I could have, I suppose." Beth straightened her shoulders back and lifted her chin. "But one of my grandfathers died, my mother's father, leaving me a few thousand dollars. When the money came, a totally unexpected legacy, I asked myself what was the one thing I'd most enjoy giving myself, and as soon as I asked the question I knew the answer: a vacation trip to the Orient. I've always wanted to see the Orient, especially Hong Kong and Tokyo. So while I was here I thought why not hop over to Kathmandu to see Bob? To me it made perfect sense."

"I think that's marvelous," Joanne replied.

Beth's smile suddenly faded as a new worry gripped it. "I arrived here yesterday, timing my arrival for one day ahead of the expedition, but, Joanne, at the airport this morning, when I watched all of you come off the plane, I didn't see Bob. One of the men back home told me the flight date. I thought I had it all figured out, and obviously I did, for I saw you come off the plane and Jim—Bob and I have known Jim Bryant for years. And I recognized a couple of the other men, but I didn't see Bob. I was there watching from the first passenger off until the last, and I didn't see my husband." Beth was tense again. "Didn't Bob come with you?"

Joanne answered quickly, "No, but he's all right. He was already here in Kathmandu. It seems he flew out right after that weekend we worked in the warehouse. He's been claiming and overseeing the supplies as they came in. Had you followed us out instead of watching for the other passengers, you would have seen your husband greet us."

Beth let out a long sigh of relief. "So that's it. I was stunned, just worried sick. I couldn't figure out what had happened. All I could think was that Bob had taken ill just before the flight or had had an accident, something terribly serious, for it would take a life-threatening situation to keep him away from a climb like this. He'd have to be strapped down or dead. I know that man."

Joanne laughed softly. "Well, it was nothing like that at all. He's here and he's fine. He's sharing a room with Bryant at the far end of the hall. It wouldn't surprise me if he were in right now. All you have to do is walk down there to find out."

Beth's face paled. "Oh, no. You saw how he was in San Francisco—he wouldn't even come out to speak to me. After I left the airport this morning, I returned to my room and just sat there all day, worried sick. All I could think to do was to leave, fly out and return home to try to find out what had happened to him."

"You say you've known Jim Bryant for years," Joanne remarked softly. "Couldn't you have made contact with him and asked him about your husband?"

One of Beth's hands flew up to press against her mouth. "Oh, no! That's the very last thing I'd do, let Jim know I'd flown clear over here just to speak to Bob. Jim knows me—knows how I've always acted when Bob was leaving—and he has no sympathy for me whatsoever. I'm sure he wondered why Bob stuck it out with me as long as he did. I respect and admire Jim, I even like him, but he's not a soft or understanding man when it comes to climbing. Then I thought of you. I remembered you from the warehouse and saw you get off the plane with the others this morning, and I decided to come over to speak to you, hoping I could get here to see you without being seen by Jim—which I managed to do. I thought as a woman you'd be more understanding, maybe even sympathetic."

Tears filled Beth's eyes, and she drew out a tissue to wipe them away, her pretty face flushing. "I love my husband, I'm concerned about our future, and all I want to do is talk with him for a few minutes before I leave Nepal to return home. Can you understand how I feel?"

Joanne rose quickly and stepped the few feet

across to put her arms around Beth's shoulders. "Of course I can. And if there's any way I can help—"

As she drew back, her voice died away, leaving the sentence unfinished. She remembered San Francisco, how indignant she had been with Bob Freeland that he wouldn't even go out to speak to his wife. But if Freeland still felt that way, if he still didn't want to see or speak to Beth, did she, Joanne, really want to become involved? She felt a natural sympathy for the woman, but at the same time her position with the expedition had enough problems without risking more. The last thing she needed or wanted was to antagonize Freeland, the deputy leader of the team, Bryant's right-hand man. Freeland already objected to her presence. It would take so little, she was sure, to have him come stomping down on her, making her position even more tenuous. Sitting down again on the bed, Joanne thought, *This is all I need.*

"If you mean that," Beth said eagerly, her eyes shining with tears, "there is a way you could help. I was thinking about it as I came over. You could ask Bob to please come here to your room because there's some problem you need to discuss with him—without letting him know I'm here, of course. He'd have no reason to be suspicious. I'm sure that the last thing he'd ever imagine is that I would unexpectedly have enough money to fly all the way over here to see him."

Joanne was dismayed. Lie to Freeland, deceive him, lead him into a trap. "But—but, Beth, would that really do any good? If he's set on not talking with you, he could turn on his heel and walk out again the moment he saw you were here." *While I'd be on his blacklist for sure.*

"That's a chance I'd have to take," Beth answered quickly, her face now eager and alive. "But I honestly don't think that will happen, Joanne. I wouldn't have flown all the way over here if I thought that. He wouldn't see me that weekend at the warehouse partly because he knows how he still feels about me, that he still loves me. He was afraid I had come there to plead with him to back out of this trip, and he didn't want to be torn apart. But now that he's here, in Nepal, now that he's already on his way, there's no reason to have those fears. I feel so confident that he'll talk to me now, that in his heart of hearts he'll even be glad I'm here."

If only I could feel confident too, Joanne thought, gazing worriedly across her room. Beth Freeland now looked radiant, all anxiety flown, while Joanne felt infected with anxious gloom. "Well—"

"*Please*, Joanne. If only you'll help me, I know it will work out just fine."

There was a rap on her door and Andy Howell's voice called cheerfully, "Freeland just rang the dinner bell, Joanne. Are you awake?"

"Yes, thank you, Andy, I'll be right along."

A few minutes later, as Joanne entered the makeshift kitchen, the first man she saw was Bryant. Her pulse raced excitedly at the sight of him, as it always did. He was standing near the beer cases, talking earnestly with Greg Reed, one of the expedition's two doctors. He wore black slacks and a black pullover and looked incredibly attractive, tall, lean, powerful, his broad face tanned and glowing. As she walked in, his dark eyes traveled across the room to welcome her and a smile of recognition—and of love, she wondered—flickered across his lips, but he didn't break off his conversation.

Freeland was already dishing up stew. A platter of crackers covered with meat spread was sitting on a card table a few feet away, and there were open cans of warm beer.

"Hi, Joanne, help yourself." Freeland flashed her his charming, slightly crooked smile.

"Thank you, Bob." Joanne's pulse raced. She took a pie pan of stew, moved out of the way of Courtland Mitchell and Michael Ross, who had come up behind her, and stepped over toward Freeland. She wasn't at all sure she wanted to do this, but how could she not? "Say, Bob—" her heart pounded even harder "—a problem has come up that I'd like to discuss with you, so I'd appreciate it if you would stop by my room sometime later this evening, all right?"

"Hey, hey!" Freeland said, lifting his eyebrows flirtatiously. He leaned close to say, in a stage whisper, "At your service, lady. Anytime, anyplace."

Joanne laughed, her pulse still racing. "It's nothing like that." As she turned away from Freeland, aware that her face was flushing, she saw Bryant's eyes on her. She smiled quickly, and Bryant's lips parted in a half smile back.

Andy Howell stepped up to Joanne's elbow. "It's so crowded in here. Want to join me out in the hall? I can bring the chair from my room and maybe you could get the chair from yours."

"Sure. Fine."

She held Andy's platter for him while he went to fetch his chair. When he came back, he offered to go for hers. "Thanks, Andy, but I've got two good legs, you know. I'll go for my own." She declined his offer to hold her platter. Quite possibly Beth Freeland was hungry. She carried her stew down the hall, and on the way passed John Naylor.

"What's the matter, princess? You're too good to eat with the rest of us?" Naylor's expression was as sour as his voice.

Joanne tossed him a slight mocking smile but passed by without answering.

At first Beth said "Oh, no," she wasn't hungry and wouldn't dream of taking Joanne's dinner, but when Joanne said that in that case she'd throw it out since she wasn't hungry either, Beth changed her mind and accepted the offer. Joanne told her that she had given Bob the requested message. "Right now, of course, he's busy with dinner, so I'm sure it'll be an hour or more.''

Beth's eyes flashed with a momentary worry. "Well, if you don't mind my staying here...?''

"No, of course not," Joanne lied. She asked Beth to move to the bed so she could have the chair. "They'll wonder what happened to me if I don't come back.''

When she rejoined Andy, he asked her what she'd done with her dinner. "I always wake up hungry during the night so I'll have it then," Joanne answered.

"Cold stew?" Andy asked, astonished, but Joanne merely shrugged.

She tried not to eye Andy's food, but the aroma of the thick beef stew sent fierce hunger pangs through her. As Andy finished, he rose to his feet. "That was good for starters, but I'm going for a refill. Can I get you anything, Joanne?''

"Well, I—well, maybe just a bit of the stew with a couple of crackers. I find I'm hungrier than I thought.''

"Gotcha.''

He returned with a full platter for each of them and commented that if she found she couldn't eat it all he was sure he could finish anything she left. With a smile Joanne took it from him and ate every bite.

"You know," Andy remarked as they ate, "on the climbs I've been on the worst grumbling has always been about the food. Beef stew.

Chicken soup. Meat spreads. Crackers. Always the same tasteless stuff, never any variety. But as far as I'm concerned, it's always tasted great." He glanced around with a grin. "I guess I'm just not what you'd call a gourmet eater. When I'm hungry, any old thing tastes good to me."

Joanne laughed. "Me, too."

After they finished eating, they sat for a few minutes talking, then Andy rose and placed his dirty platter on top of hers. "You take the dinnerware back and I'll return both chairs," he suggested.

Joanne hastily handed the platters to him. "Thanks, Andy, but I'll take my own chair back." She picked it up and started quickly off down the hall.

After she'd left the chair with Beth, she returned to the large room at the other end of the hall wanting to offer to help clean up. But Greg Reed and Courtland Mitchell were already busy washing and drying platters, and her offer was declined with friendly smiles. Freeland stepped up behind her and clasped her shoulder with his hand.

"We're out to prove we're not male chauvinist pigs," he told her with his crooked smile. "Just because we've got a woman with us doesn't mean we can't take turns cooking meals and doing the dishes, even though it *is* women's work."

"Says who?" Joanne countered, smiling back.

"Says I," Freeland answered. "Didn't you just hear me say so?" He leaned even closer to say, "I'll drop by your room as soon as I get everything cleared away here."

Joanne tried not to be too obvious as she moved back a bit. "All right." Turning to leave, she saw Bryant a few feet away, standing between the two Canadian climbers, Claude and Charles Mandel. He was sipping a beer, and eyeing her.

She walked over to him, feeling that familiar sense of breathlessness he always caused in her. "Hello, Jim. How did you do on the permit problem?" A smile trembled on her lips and would have come fully to life had Bryant returned it.

He didn't. With a sober expression he gazed steadily across. "I spent the day working on it but made little apparent progress. Back tomorrow for more of the same."

"You will be able to straighten it out, won't you? There's no chance that it's going to stop our climb, is there?"

Bryant's lips parted in a grim little smile. "Only over my dead body. Yes, I'm sure I can get it straightened out. It takes time, that's all." His eyes stayed steadily, soberly on her as he spoke, an odd intensity in them.

Joanne felt even more uncomfortably breathless. She wished she dared reach over to touch him, his arm, his hand, but with the Mandel brothers standing right there, eyeing her curiously, she felt constrained from making any such move. If only she could see Bryant sometime later, alone, but there was no way she dared suggest that, not with various members of the team standing around within hearing distance. With a self-conscious little smile, she said, "Well, I'm glad to hear it's going to work out," then turned and walked out of the room.

Once back in her own room, she settled down with Beth to wait for Freeland's arrival.

As they waited, Beth talked about her marriage, how she'd met Bob Freeland, their courtship, the problems they'd had. "But we always loved each other, that was one thing that never changed." Beth's face was flushed with a lovely color as she said this. "Even when everything was bleakest, I always knew Bob loved me, that I was the only woman in the world for him, just as he was the only man for me."

She laughed. "That was one of our problems, I guess, why we fought as often and as hard as we did. I loved him so much I was always frightened of losing him. So in the end I gave him the ultimatum—me or the mountains—and we had this fierce fight, and I ordered him out of the house and told him that was it, I was getting a divorce." She frowned slightly. "But I haven't ever filed for one and I never will. All I want from him is another chance."

The first hour passed this way, then Beth quieted down and said little more. At a few minutes before eight, an hour and a half after Joanne had returned to her room, Beth asked her whether she was sure Freeland hadn't gotten suspicious. "Are you sure you didn't give anything away?" she inquired worriedly. "Without meaning to, I mean."

Joanne was equally concerned but for different reasons. Surely he had only been teasing when he'd acted as though he saw something sexually inviting in her request. But why else would he postpone coming so long? Was he waiting for everyone else to settle into his room for the night, for Bryant to climb into bed and fall asleep? Jim had been on the go all day after an exhausting trip. Surely he would retire early. Did Freeland have some crazy idea that Joanne really wanted to start something up with him?

At a few minutes past nine there was a knock on the door. Beth's eyes lighted up with both relief and fear. Joanne, who had been sitting on the edge of the bed, jumped to her feet and walked quickly over to the door, calling out, "Coming." Her pulse threatened to burst. Would Freeland be furious at her and make her life as miserable as possible for the rest of the trip?

"No hurry," a man's voice called back. *Bryant's voice.* Joanne's right hand flew to her throat. *Oh, no.* Beth's face drained white. She ran noiselessly across the room and pressed against the wall on the far side of the door, out of sight. She shook her head beseechingly at Joanne, pleading with her eyes that Joanne not let

her be found here by the one man she most
dreaded seeing, Jim Bryant.

With a trembling hand Joanne opened the
door halfway, and then stood in the entrance.
"Yes, Jim?" She tried to make her expression
and voice as calm as she possibly could, while
her heart thudded wildly.

Bryant eyed her for a moment, then moved
his gaze away to glance idly up and down the
hall. There was no one in sight. "May I come in
for a minute, please?"

Joanne's knees threatened to give and her
pulse was racing so furiously she half feared she
would faint. "Well, I—it's getting late, Jim,
and I'm feeling dreadfully tired, and I know you
must be, too, so maybe—maybe we could see
each other in the morning instead."

A shadow moved into Bryant's dark eyes. "In
the morning I have to get up early and leave immediately to go do battle with the Nepal authori-
ties once again. I won't have time in the morning
to make social calls. Naturally you're tired and
so am I. Too tired to have anything in mind except a very brief visit, just a few minutes of your
time, so, please, may I come in?"

A mist stung Joanne's eyes. She ached to
throw the door open wide, to say, *"Oh, Jim,
yes, of course!"* to have him step inside, shut
the door, shutting out the world, and put his
arms around her and hold her, if only for a moment. But how could she do that to Beth?

As Joanne hesitated, not answering, Bryant

said, in a cold hard voice, "Well, as you said, it *is* getting late. Please forgive my intrusion. Good night, Miss Patton." He offered her a very quick, mocking little bow, swung away and strode off down the hall.

Joanne closed the door, wanting to cry.

Twenty minutes later there was another knock on the door. Joanne and Beth had spent the intervening time sunk in silent gloom. As Joanne heard this second knock, she tensed painfully. Walking toward the door, she said, "Yes, who is it?"

"Bob Freeland."

Beth's face drained white. Again she hurried over to stand near the wall, out of sight. Joanne pulled the door open and motioned Freeland in. He stepped in, flashing his crooked smile, his eyes dancing. As Joanne shut the door he swung around to face her. As he did so, he saw his wife.

Momentarily Freeland looked dumbfounded. Then he walked over to his wife, grabbed her by the shoulders and shook her, more in frustration, it seemed to Joanne, than in anger.

"What on earth do you think you're doing here?" he demanded, his voice low and hoarse.

Beth didn't answer. Her face paled as her eyes pleaded for understanding. Freeland released his hold and stood staring at her in exasperation.

Joanne pulled her bedroom door open. "Well, I'll leave you two alone," she murmured, anxious not to intrude.

Freeland acted so swiftly Joanne could scarcely believe it. He moved sideways to push the door closed again and caught her eye. "Oh, no, you don't. I don't want anyone wondering why you're out there wandering around."

Joanne's cheeks warmed. "But—surely you two want to talk—"

"We can talk right here."

"But—"

"No buts."

Beth had seated herself on the bed and Freeland moved beside her. Joanne had no choice but to take up a position by the door in the only other chair available.

Freeland kept his voice very low as he talked urgently and rather irritably to his wife, leaning in close to her. Joanne tried not to eavesdrop, but it was impossible. Beth said very little, but every once in a while her voice would rise. They seemed to be rehashing the same old argument that Beth had said caused their marriage break-up, with one difference: Beth was now insisting that she wouldn't again try to keep her husband from going on climbs if only he would reconcile with her.

Their voices dropped so low for minutes on end that Joanne would almost forget they were there. Finally Freeland stood up and walked away from the bed. He motioned for Joanne to move away from the door, then he opened it, stepped out into the hall and glanced up and down.

"It's all clear," he said, stepping back into the room. "Come on, Beth, I'll take you to wherever you're staying and we can finish this discussion there."

Beth climbed off the bed. Her face was calmer now, and no longer reflected such intense anxiety. Before leaving she walked over to give Joanne a hug, and her eyes seemed bright with hope. Freeland took her arm and pulled the door open, then he fixed Joanne with a stern eye, warning her not to say one word to anyone.

"I don't know what's going to happen with Beth and me, but I don't want to be ragged for the rest of the trip about this. I mean it, Joanne. Not a single word to anyone. If this leaks out, I'll know who to blame and I'll make you pay for it, which believe me I have the power to do."

"I believe you. And don't worry, I won't say a word. Just be careful that no one sees you leaving here."

Joanne quickly closed the door behind them. She waited two minutes, then quietly opened her door. Seeing no one, she stepped out of her room. Bryant and Freeland shared a room, but for now Freeland was gone. She'd go see Bryant even if it meant waking him up. Without giving away the Freelands' secret, she would somehow explain away her earlier behavior and smooth things over.

As she approached Bryant's room she noticed that the door was open and light spilled out. She could hear voices, two males voices, neither of which was Bryant's. One belonged to Greg Reed, one of the expedition's doctors. He had an extremely deep, full voice that was unmistakable. Slowing her step, Joanne listened more intently. The other male voice belonged, she thought, to Orin Thatcher, the other team doctor. Greg Reed was a surgeon from Florida, an attractive man in his late thirties toward whom Joanne had felt immediate liking and trust. He fit her idea of what a doctor should be. Orin Thatcher, an internist from Cincinnati, was tall, almost completely bald, moon faced, and seemed to have struck up an immediate rivalry-friendship with Courtland Mitchell. Each man seemed intent on outdoing the other as the team's practical joker and cutup.

She listened carefully, and soon she detected Bryant's rich smooth tones. The three men seemed to be discussing what medical supplies were available. There would be no chance for her to talk with Bryant tonight. With a sigh Joanne turned around and walked back to her room.

When she joined the others for breakfast in the morning, she learned that neither Bryant nor Freeland was there. Freeland had phoned Bob Lansing, given him instructions, and Lansing was temporarily in charge. Expedition supplies were currently stored in an unused hangar at Tribhuvan Airport. All team members were to spend the day at the airport sorting supplies. A bus would take them there right after breakfast. Lansing would give more detailed instructions once they were on the job site ready to work.

The work in the hangar was slow and tedious but not strenuous. All the boxes so carefully packed in the warehouse in San Francisco had been stenciled with code numbers to identify contents. Lansing had the mimeographed sheet with the key to each code. The supplies were to be divided into three groups: one for portage by the team once they departed from Pokhara for the start of the climb; one for airdrop number one, which was scheduled to take place at French Pass at 17,300 feet; the third group for airdrop number two, which would occur, if all went according to plan, at the base camp established around nineteen thousand feet. With proper distribution the team would have a reasonable amount and variety of food at all times, including cooking utensils and medical supplies.

Bryant was following the example of the 1973 American expedition to Dhaulagiri headed by Jim Morrissey, which had successfully employed airdrops. Without airdrops it would have taken more than seven hundred porters to carry the supplies. Even if that number of porters had been available, the proposed route was far too hazardous to expose untrained porters to its dangers. Without a long porter train, the team would be far more independent and could move more rapidly and with greater flexibility.

Using airdrops entailed risks, of course. The

weather might turn so treacherous as to make the drops impossible. Even if the drops proved possible, there was always the chance of high breakage and low recovery. The team could find itself stranded at nineteen thousand feet without food or equipment. But simple logistics made the climb impossible without airdrops.

The workday began slowly for nothing was sufficiently organized. Lansing had his two lists—the one decoding the stenciled numbers on the cartons, the other dividing the cartons into the three groups—but he didn't seem to know how to direct activity into profitable channels. For the first couple of hours almost everyone lounged around waiting for direction. Joanne had teamed up with Andy Howell, but when Lansing finally put them to work, they found themselves moving cartons first to one place, then back again to the original place. *If only Bryant were here,* Joanne thought in frustration, *or Freeland.* But both were busy elsewhere. Around eleven that morning she found herself standing across from Greg Reed. As Reed's eye caught hers, she saw that he felt as frustrated and dismayed as she did. With a grim little smile, he went in search of Lansing, and then little by little he took charge himself. That afternoon everything began to fall into place, and by evening the team was rolling. They worked until midnight, then on the bus going back toward the city, Greg Reed rose and announced that they would almost certainly have to return in the morning to complete the work, so no one was to make other plans.

By late afternoon the following day, the job was done. Every carton had a stenciled letter, A, B or C, along with a number indicating priority, 1, 2 or 3. The cartons were stacked by group, with breaks between. Greg Reed walked around to shake everyone's hand to thank them for their work and congratulate them on a job well done. Team members laughed, sang and joked on the bus taking them back to their rooms at the Guest House. Word had come through that afternoon that Bryant had cut his way through the red tape and had secured their permits. More than a year earlier he and Freeland had arranged to hire an experienced and respected sirdar, or head Sherpa, and an assistant sirdar. Both men, devout Buddhists, had consulted with a lama in Kathmandu and had been told that two days hence would be a propitious day to fly to Pokhara for the start of the climb. All systems were go for a flight out in two days.

When that was announced, the team cheered. After months of hoping and planning, after a flight halfway around the world, the great adventure beckoned. Joanne and Andy cheered together, then impulsively hugged. At last, at last.

The night before, they had returned to the Guest House so late that Joanne had gone to her room without seeing Bryant. He would be asleep already, she had reasoned, or others would be dropping in to consult with him. In any case, Freeland would be there with him. Going to bed, she'd wondered about Beth, whether she was still in Kathmandu or whether she'd already left. She wondered with even greater curiosity how things had gone between her and her husband after they'd left the guest house and been alone. Freeland would tell her what had happened at some point, Joanne supposed. But if he said nothing, she most certainly wouldn't ask. The last thing she wanted was to fall out of Bob Freeland's good graces.

When the team returned to the Guest House after its second day of sorting supplies, Joanne was relieved and pleased to see Bryant. When she entered his room in answer to the call for dinner, his eye caught hers and he bowed his head in recognition but did not walk over to speak to her. Courtland Mitchell stood beside him and engaged him in conversation. Joanne felt dismay that Bryant's glance was so cool and distant, but she could hardly blame him. This was the first time she'd seen him since he had asked permission to enter her room when Beth Freeland was there, and she had reluctantly told him no. She *had* to see him alone as soon as possible to attempt to straighten that out.

While Bryant's manner seemed cold and formal, Freeland, who was also there, greeted Joanne with a warm crooked grin, his eyes beaming with friendliness. As he dished up her chicken soup, he asked how she was.

"I'm fine, Bob, thank you. How are you?"

"Never better." He winked, then added, "Tomorrow's a free day for us. Everything all taken care of, and we fly out the following day. It would be a pity for you to leave the city without at least seeing the main square. I've been here for weeks, have picked up some of the local patter and know my way around pretty well. How'd you like to hire me as a tour guide for the day?"

Joanne tried not to appear hesitant. She had hoped against hope that Bryant would be free, too, and that somehow she'd get the chance to spend at least part of the day with him. At the same time, the last thing she wanted to do was offend Bob Freeland, who seemed to be overflowing with friendliness toward her.

"Thank you, Bob. That's very kind of you."

"You accept?"

"I accept."

Joanne went to bed a couple of hours later feeling particularly lonely. She hadn't been able to work up the nerve to go down to Bryant's room and ask to speak to him alone. But surely fate would give her the chance before too much longer.

The next morning she and Freeland started out right after breakfast. From what she'd heard, Bryant had already left the house. He was gone even before she woke up, apparently. As she started off with Freeland, she tried to shake off her slight depression so she could enjoy the sights. What Freeland had said was certainly true: it would be a shame to leave Kathmandu without seeing more of it than she had. But, still, where was Bryant? By now it was hard to feel much of anything except an aching loneliness for him.

The main square was as colorful as Freeland had told her it would be. Western automobiles were parked at the steps of pagoda-style Hindu shrines, while worshipers, their heads tilted back and their eyes closed, sat cross-legged on the dirty overgrown steps. Children played in the square, running in and out, with high gleeful laughter. Men and women displayed boxes of farm produce for sale, while wood sellers set up shop alongside.

"Many residents of the city come to one of these shrines at least once a day to pay their respects," Freeland told her. "For years Nepal closed its doors entirely to Westerners, and even when it opened them again in 1951 to begin a program of modernization, it still resisted Western religion. Any proselytizing for Christianity is strictly illegal. These people take their Hinduism seriously—or Buddhism, as the case may be—and also their astrology. Neither of our head-Sherpa guides would take one step up the mountain if he hadn't first gotten word that it was safe to do so by his lama and was in accord with his stars."

Joanne was fascinated by what she saw but still couldn't completely shake off her loneliness and depression. Freeland seemed in fine spirits, though, so she decided to ask him whether his wife was still in the city.

He shook his head, his eyes darkening. "No, I put her on a plane out of here yesterday. The day before that, while I had the team out working at the airport, I showed her around a bit, then off she went. Crazy woman," he added, "wasting all that money dashing over here to see me—because of some stupid premonition that I might not make it out of here alive. She's had that same premonition every time I've gone on a climb."

"Yes, so she told me."

Freeland grinned. He threw an arm momentarily around Joanne's shoulders. "But between you and me, I'm still here, right? Still alive and kicking. As I will be after we climb Dhaulagiri. I'm too mean and ornery for any mountain to kill."

"So are you two getting back together?" Joanne asked.

"Who knows?" Freeland growled, in a voice that said clearly he did not wish to discuss the matter.

Late that afternoon they returned to the Guest House. As they walked down the hall, they ran into Bryant. His eyes traveled over Freeland's face, then Joanne's. "Hello, you two," he greeted them, then strode by with no further word.

Dinner was being served an hour later, so Joanne worked up her nerve to approach Bryant.

As usual he was engaged in conversation with two of the climbers, but Joanne walked up to the group and stood her ground. Noticing her, the men—Parke Gilford and Michael Ross—cut off their conversation and after a moment drifted away.

Joanne's heart raced. She lifted her eyes to meet Bryant's. "Jim," she said softly, "there's something I'd very much like to discuss with you. Could you please drop by to see me sometime later this evening?"

Rebellion flashed through his eyes, and anger threatened at the corners of his mouth, but after a moment he nodded yes.

"Thank you," Joanne murmured. She didn't move away at once, but a few moments later, when Courtland Mitchell walked over and addressed himself to Bryant, she excused herself softly and left.

In her room she washed and changed clothes, putting on her black pantsuit, the only nonhiking or climbing clothes she had with her. She combed and brushed her fine black hair and carefully pinned it back, then for the first time in days applied a light lipstick to her lips. She settled down in her one chair, picking up a paperback to read, and tried to calm her racing pulse waiting for Bryant's knock.

She'd left her door open. It was over an hour before Bryant finally appeared. "Is it all right if I come in?"

Joanne rose, feeling rather shaky in the legs.

"Of course. Please do." She motioned him toward a seat on the bed, the only other place to sit. He sat leaning slightly forward, his knees spread. His expression was cool and distant, his eyes unfriendly.

"All right, what did you want to see me about?"

Joanne had it all worked out. She had been practicing in her head for the last hour the question she wanted to ask.

"Well, I wanted to ask you this, Jim: if I can win over the other men on the team, Freeland and the others, to where they have no objections to my trying for the summit, will you drop your own objections and give your okay?"

There, she'd gotten it out word perfect. Still her mouth felt dry and nervous and her head spun slightly. Bryant sat looking steadily across at her. His hands were drawn into fists, and he was pressing one against the other. His face was so shadowed and so deeply sunburned that the light sprinkling of freckles across his cheeks seemed to have disappeared. His hair looked darker, too, with less of the reddish tint.

"And do you think you can win the men over, especially Freeland?" There was open mockery in Bryant's voice.

Joanne moved nervously forward in her chair. "Well, I—don't know, of course, but I think that yes, possibly I can. If I can get Freeland on my side, I think the others would follow or at least wouldn't grumble too much. He seems to have everyone's trust and to be very popular.''

Bryant gazed steadily across for several moments, then his eyes dropped and he stared down at his hands. Unclenching them, he pressed them against his thighs. In time his dark eyes came up to challenge her again.

''And just how far are you going to win Freeland's approval?''

Joanne felt herself jerk slightly at the question. She blinked nervously. ''What do you mean?''

A look of scorn flashed through Bryant's eyes. ''The question seems clear enough. How far do you plan to go—how far have you already gone—to win Bob Freeland to your side? I know that trying for the summit means a great deal to you. I'm sure you see Bob as an obstacle in your path. A few nights ago during dinner I heard you ask him to drop by your room. When I came by myself, you kept the door half closed and wouldn't invite me in. It seemed obvious you had other company. Freeland was out all night. I hear that the two of you spent today sightseeing, and I saw you returning together with my own two eyes.''

Bryant paused for a moment, his gaze intent upon her. After a moment he went on, his voice cool and hard, ''I'm finding it very hard, Joanne, not to add all of this up into something I would find extremely distasteful. So now I'll ask you straight out: just how far have you already gone to win Bob Freeland over?''

Joanne stood up quickly, her face flushing red. "Not that far. It's nothing like that. Please believe me. I can't tell you exactly what happened, but I swear, Jim, it was absolutely nothing like that."

Bryant, too, rose. The room was so small that only a few feet separated them. His eyes seemed to burn her already flaming face. "Will you give me your word?"

"Oh, yes. I swear."

Bryant stepped toward her, causing Joanne to tense. She couldn't tell from his expression whether he meant to embrace her or strike her. He did neither. Instead he stepped on by her, through the open doorway and into the hallway. Joanne watched in dismay. Did he believe her or didn't he? Bryant glanced both ways down the hall, then turned around and reentered her room. He stopped just inside the door, gazing soberly across at her.

"I heard someone call my name. Mitchell's down at the end of the hall, and when he saw me he waved for me to join him, so I'll have to leave now. As for what we were discussing—"

Joanne felt as though she couldn't breathe. "Yes?"

Bryant stared at her for a moment, then his eyes dropped and he shook his head. "I want to believe you, but in all truth I'm finding it a struggle. With so much evidence right smack in front of my face—'' He shook his head even harder, then his eyes lifted to meet hers. With a quick pained-looking smile he said, ''Unfortunately we can't discuss it anymore right now, but I'll give it more thought, believe me.'' With that, he spun on his heel and left her room. Joanne could hear his swift stride receding down the hall.

It wasn't until a couple of hours later, as she was settling down to sleep, that it occurred to Joanne that Bryant had not even acknowledged much less answered her question about trying for the summit.

Joanne's eyes popped open as this thought struck. She had been so upset by Bryant's suspicions that all considerations regarding the upcoming climb had been swept from her mind. Now she lay on her back, staring at the dark, wondering. Did she dare corner Bryant to ask him the same question again? Joanne bit her lip. Yes, of course she did. No matter what Bryant suspected, no matter how much evidence seemed to be piling up against her, she knew she was completely innocent. Before too many more days had passed, she would challenge Bryant once again.

CHAPTER ELEVEN

AT LAST, after months of planning, working and hoping, they were on their way. First they flew the short distance to Pokhara. The cartons to be airdropped later were carefully stored in a mud house near the airstrip there, then everyone piled into a truck Freeland had secured and drove to an overnight campsite. For sentimental reasons, camp was set up by Pokhara Lake, close to where the American expedition had camped in 1973. The sirdar and his assistant guarded the camp while the expedition cook set up a kitchen with freight containers and boxes and served a dinner of rice and beans. The mood of the camp was festive, with excitement palpable in the air. Joanne found herself talking almost nonstop with Andy Howell and laughing over nothing.

After dinner they walked along the edge of the lake, and Joanne couldn't pull her eyes away from the majestic White Mountain, Dhaulagiri, as it faded into night with the last rays of the sun. If all went well, one day soon she might be standing on that glorious peak. Correction: if all went well, she *would* be standing up there, looking down on the world, on all of creation. The thought made her breathless, and she continued to stare in the direction of Dhaulagiri, the Mountain of Storms, even after all light had vanished and she was staring into darkness.

Earlier Joanne and Andy had worked together, setting up tents for themselves on the rim of the camp. Their peaked low tents were built strong enough, it was hoped, to withstand the devastating winds of the high mountains. Many team members hadn't bothered with their tents. Some had elected to sleep in the back of the truck, while others planned to use sleeping bags in the open. Joanne had opted for a tent. That way if Bryant found time to come and talk with her, they could be alone.

She had been in his company all day of course, first on the flight from Kathmandu, then on the truck ride. They'd even exchanged a few words, though naturally enough not of a personal nature. In front of the other team members, Bryant was rather formal with her, which Joanne understood and approved. While some of the men were easy and friendly with her now, others eyed her warily and kept their distance. No one had been openly rude or rejecting, but she could tell by their expressions that several of the men still resented her presence. This festering resentment at her presence would only be exacerbated if it became known that she and Bryant had been lovers. The team would immediately jump to the conclusion that he had signed her up and brought her along because of their relationship. No one would bother to seek the truth, to learn that it hadn't been that way at all: first she had forced Bryant to sign her, *then* they had become lovers.

In any case, she wasn't sure herself what her relationship with Bryant was these days. For all she knew he might still assume that she was involved with Freeland. Still she hoped against hope, as she said good-night to Andy and went to her tent, that in an hour or so, after everyone had settled down for the night, Bryant would come to call. She missed being with him.

She had barely crouched down to enter her tent when she heard a man striding behind her. "Hey, Joanne, can I speak to you for a minute?" John Naylor pulled the tent flap aside and stuck his head in. With a slightly forced smile, Joanne waved him in.

"Sure, John. You wanted to see me about something?"

Naylor's step in was a little wobbly. He half fell, half plunked himself down on an upturned box across from where Joanne was seated cross-legged on her sleeping bag. "Brought you a beer." Naylor leaned forward to hand it to her. His dark-complected face had taken on an even deeper suntan since their arrival in Nepal. His eyes looked reddened, as though he had been drinking quite heavily. A week's growth of beard bristled on his chin.

"How are things going for you?" Naylor

asked sociably, then lifted his beer can and gulped from it without waiting for an answer. Joanne could sense his underlying tension, which the beer seemed to do little to dispel.

For the next hour she found herself listening to Naylor while he again poured out, in repetitious detail, his uncertainties about being where he was, his dislike of climbing and his fear of it, his impulse to quit the team even now and head back toward civilization and sanity.

"I'm going crazy, I can't eat or sleep. I keep asking myself what in hell I'm doing here," Naylor repeated tensely. "You seem like a level-headed woman, Joanne, a perceptive one. What do you think I should do?"

No matter how Joanne answered, Naylor gave her an argument. If she suggested that, feeling as uncertain as he did, he should quit the team, he would insistently list all the reasons he could not possibly do so. If she then flipped over and suggested that he should get hold of himself and stay, he would argue heatedly that he had tried and tried to get his head together, to accept his fate and go with the team, but it was simply impossible for him to accomplish and there was no point in trying any longer.

"Then quit, for heaven's sake!" Joanne hadn't meant to sound so testy, but it was late, she was tired and she ached for Bryant. By now Naylor wasn't saying anything new, he was simply repeating himself, endlessly, boringly, and she was tired of listening to him.

Her pulse picked up as she heard another step outside. She had lighted a lamp before so whoever was approaching would know she wasn't yet asleep. Bryant's voice called, "Joanne?"

"Yes, Jim, come on in," Joanne called back, indifferent to caution at the moment. Bryant lifted the tent flap, crouching down to enter. She saw the startled and dismayed look in his eye as he saw she had company.

"Sorry. I didn't know you had a visitor."

"Oh, that's all right. Don't go," Joanne said quickly. "John's been debating for an hour about possibly going to talk to you."

Bryant dropped to where he was balancing on his haunches. "What about?"

Naylor shot Joanne a resentful look, took a gulp from his beer can and muttered, "Nothing. Nothing important."

Bryant stayed about twenty minutes, then left, taking Naylor with him. Joanne was relieved to get rid of John but felt dismayed at Bryant's departure. Tonight was quite possibly their last chance to share a few minutes alone together, and Naylor's presence had made that impossible. It was now so late that Bryant wouldn't risk coming back, she knew.

She undressed, crawled into her sleeping bag and lay on her back, staring into the blackness. During a lull in the activities that morning she had written to Scottie, answering several letters of his. Again she had told him in as kind but straightforward a way as she knew how that he must stop nourishing hope that she would ever fall in love with him or marry him. So far she had apparently not gotten through to him, but maybe when he got her letter, which spelled it out clearly on paper, he would at last take her at her word and try to find someone else. At the very last minute, on impulse, she had concluded her morning letter with the admission that she had met someone else. "I'm in love with him, Scottie, for the first time in my life I'm in love, so please try to understand and forgive me. With love, hastily, Joanne."

Joanne thought of that letter now as she lay there, camped alongside Pokhara Lake in Nepal, the magnificent Dhaulagiri rising to the north. She thought of home, of her fondness for Scottie, of her love of mountaineering, then her thoughts wandered to the uncertainty of her position here as a climber. She'd hoped to have the chance tonight to ask Bryant the question she'd put to him the previous night: if she won the other climbers over, would he drop all objections to her try for the summit? If she could corner him long enough to ask him, would he give her a straight answer or find some new way to dodge and evade the issue? Joanne felt a slight stirring of anger. It wasn't that she was asking for any favors. She did not expect or want special treatment; all she was asking for was to be treated as one of the climbers on the team, with as much right to go for the summit as everyone else had. Let her skill and endurance, her good luck or bad luck, decide the issue, not her sex! That's all she was asking for, and it wasn't fair that Bryant wouldn't answer a simple question to let her know where she stood.

Thinking this, Joanne felt even angrier. Tomorrow, or if not tomorrow then the very first opportunity that presented itself, she would challenge Bryant again, and one way or another, no matter what kind of argument it stirred up, she would force an answer out of him.

Firmly resolved on this, she closed her eyes and settled down to sleep.

In the morning they broke camp, packed everything possible into the back of the truck, strapped on their backpacks and took off in small groups to walk through Pokhara. Campsite that night was on the Yagahdi River, where the entire expeditionary force assembled for the first time: Bryant, Freeland, and the other climbers; Ang Darje, the sirdar, Pamba Tenzing, assistant sirdar, Sangay, the expedition cook, five high-altitude porters, two kitchen helpers, twenty-five low-altitude porters plus fifty-six mules to carry supplies to the village of Tukche at the base of the Dhaulagiri massif. At Tukche, an elevation of 8,485 feet, the expedition would slim down to a climbing weight: no more mules or low-altitude porters, just the core climbing group, ready to mount an assault on the treacherous Mountain of Storms.

The early hiking days were pleasant. Team

members walked alone or in small groups, with the grouping very fluid. The first morning Joanne set off with Andy Howell, but within two hours Andy started having trouble with blisters on his feet, and soon he was limping. Even though he repeatedly stopped long enough to take off his boots to apply medication and fresh padding, nothing seemed to help very much. By early afternoon he began to act embarrassed and kept urging Joanne to go on ahead, not to let him hold her up. He'd really rather walk by himself, at his own pace, he insisted. Unable to be of any help to him, and reluctant to fall even further behind the main group, Joanne at last took him at his word and ventured ahead on her own.

During their second day of hiking, Freeland joined forces with Joanne for the entire morning. Ever since Kathmandu, he had been extremely friendly to her. His eyes would twinkle warmly as he spoke to her, and he frequently patted her on the arm, shoulder or back, as though to affirm that they were buddies now and that he deeply appreciated her ability to keep a secret. Joanne had instinctively liked and trusted Freeland from the first moment she'd met him, and the more she saw of him now the more she enjoyed his quick dry wit. As they were hiking together, he kept her smiling and laughing throughout by making caustic comments about the other climbers and unexpectedly romantic comments about the countryside they traversed.

It delighted Joanne to glimpse this softer poetic side of Freeland. She was especially pleased that he was willing for her to see it, and she instinctively knew that, too, was to be kept a secret between them. With the other climbers, Freeland was always a man's man, rough and ready, all hard edges and practical strength. With her, he let this image slip a bit to allow her a clearer understanding of the complex soul within.

One day Joanne found herself walking with John Naylor, one of the few men she tried tactfully to avoid. He hiked silently along at her side for a time, then when they stopped momentarily to rest, he motioned toward the Dhaulagiri massif, looming so close now, and asked her whether she was aware that while the 1973 American expedition had been successful, an earlier American expedition, in 1969, had ended in tragedy and failure.

"A sudden unexpected avalanche—" he snapped his fingers "—and seven men were swept to their deaths."

"Yes, I know."

"Those weren't the first deaths and they won't be the last. Only a crazy bunch of loonies would tackle a mountain like this."

Joanne didn't answer. Naylor hiked silently along again for several minutes before he added, in a deep matter-of-fact voice, "I have a feeling I'll be one more the White Mountain can add to its total. I know I'm crazy going in, but I don't think I'll survive long enough to worry about it.''

"John, that's morbid. If you're so worried about it, you can always stay at one of the lower camps. Not everyone has to go higher.''

Naylor's eyes swept around to challenge hers. His dark face was badly sunburned above his straggly beard. ''You're too young and untroubled to have the least idea how I feel. I'd sort of like to go out that way—zip and you're gone. I'm fed up with living anyway. What's the point of it? I think that's probably the real reason I joined up, figuring there's no better way to go than to be zapped in a sudden avalanche—whooey, away you go.'' One hand made a wide sweeping motion through the air, then he broke into a brief, all but soundless laugh. ''So if I go, sing no sad songs for me, okay? I wanted you to know so you could tell the others.''

On impulse Joanne reached over to catch his hard bony hand. ''I have a feeling you're terribly wrong. Bryant's got you pegged as one of the top men on the team, and I think he's right.'' She lifted her eyes to the highest summit in the range of mountains before them. ''Before very long,'' she said defiantly, ''you and I are going to climb the last few feet to that peak. I just have a feeling we will.''

Naylor laughed again, almost soundlessly. He drew his hand back. ''Sure we will.''

A half hour later the two reached the temporary camp set up for lunch. Gathering courage from her brief conversation with Naylor, Joanne approached Bryant and asked if she could please have a few words with him in private.

Bryant's face immediately tightened in annoyance, as though he knew what was coming. But with a resigned bow, he excused himself from the others and walked some twenty feet away with Joanne. "Yes?"

Joanne took a deep breath, then challenged Bryant with her eyes. "Jim, you still haven't answered the question I have. I feel that I'm slowly, one by one, winning the men over to my side. Regardless of their feelings at the start, they are learning to respect and trust me. If Freeland and the others drop all opposition to my attempting the summit, will you drop yours?"

Bryant directed his eyes away from hers and stood gazing off at the Dhaulagiri massif, so close to where they stood. A moment later he answered, without glancing her way. "No, I will not."

Joanne felt instant rage. He wouldn't even face her as he spoke! "And why not?"

"Because."

"Because why not? Don't I deserve a straight answer at least?"

Bryant's broad face remained turned away from her for a moment. Joanne could spy again, under his deepening sun- and windburn, the light sprinkling of freckles. At last Bryant faced her.

"All right. Here's my reason. We're not on a picnic here. Dhaulagiri is a tough mountain to climb. Regardless of any other considerations, I care too much about you to let you risk your neck up there."

Momentarily Joanne felt too startled to reply, then she snapped, "That's not your real reason. I don't believe you."

Bryant's dark eyes narrowed into angry slits. "If you're calling me a liar, we have nothing further to discuss." He started past her.

Joanne grabbed his arm to stop him. "All right, I'm sorry. But I just can't believe you'd do this to me and call it love. You know how I feel, how I've always felt. Why haven't I as much right to risk my neck as you have to risk yours?"

Bryant shook her hold off, his sun- and wind-burned face still flushed with anger. "And you know how I've felt, right from the very beginning. I did not voluntarily sign you onto the team, as you well know. I was ready to allow you to join us on the condition that you remained in base camp. In spite of all your fancy legal maneuvers, that condition still remains. And I see no point in discussing it further."

Again he started past her and again Joanne reached out to stop him. "Well, I do!" She was breathing hard now, with fury rampaging through her. "Are you trying to tell me that you're holding on to your condition simply as a means of proving to me that no one gets the better of James A. Bryant, ever? I can't believe you'd be that stubborn, that mean and inconsiderate, just to prove some meaningless point. What are you playing with me, some senseless game of one-up-manship?''

Bryant stared stonily at her, his dark eyes hard. "I'm not the one playing games. I'm not the one who thinks the world owes me whatever I want, that everyone should roll over and play dead so that I can indulge every last little whim. Grow up, Joanne. In my best judgment—and I'm the final authority here—you do not belong higher than base camp.''

"Because I'm a woman?''

Bryant's face flushed deeper. He glanced back toward the camp. "Keep your voice down! The men are beginning to wonder what we're arguing about. You knew what the conditions were before we left San Francisco, and I'll thank you not to bring the subject up again as I'm sick of discussing it.''

Again he started past, and this time when Joanne clutched on to his arm to stop him, he roughly shook off her hold.

"Just because I'm a woman!'' she hissed after him, beside herself with rage.

"Because I care about you, you spoiled little bitch!'' Bryant threw over his shoulder at her without breaking his stride.

Joanne was so furious she had a hard time settling down. She ordered herself repeatedly to eat her meal but had a difficult time choking it down. Bryant said he cared about her, but he didn't—he cared only for himself. Now that she clearly saw that this was so, she would never allow him near her again. He was arrogant, mean, dishonest and immovably stubborn. Finally she gave up trying to eat, set her platter aside and drew out her notebook to scribble a letter to Scottie. Maybe that would help her cool down. As she wrote, she was startled to see a shadow fall over her page. Glancing up, she felt her heart stop. Bryant stood before her.

His hand touched her arm. "Joanne, I'm sorry. I've got a hell of a lot on my mind right now, and my temper's not as controlled as it ought to be. I don't know myself why I feel the way I do. But I worry about you and feel frightened that something might happen to you. I tell myself that it won't, that you're a skilled experienced climber, but still I can't quite drive the nightmare away." He paused for a moment, then added, his voice even softer, "Can we possibly let the matter drop for now and discuss it again after we've made it up to base camp? I give you my word I'll consider every possible angle between now and then and do my best to be fair to you, to myself and to the team. All right?"

Joanne sighed in relief. "All right."

Bryant smiled. "Now I'll leave you to your letter." He gave her arm a slight squeeze, dropped his hold and swung away.

Joanne felt her anger die as she watched him

stride away. She too would drop all thought of their opposing views for now. A dozen things could happen between this rest spot and base camp to determine who tried for the summit and who didn't. In fact, chances were that neither she nor Jim would decide the question: in all probability, Fate would decide it for them.

CHAPTER TWELVE

SIX DAYS AFTER LEAVING POKHARA, the team arrived in Tukche.

During their six-day hike they had followed a well-traveled trail that had taken them along boulder-strewed paths, up hill and down. Outside the village of Tirkhe, the trail rose steeply up to Ghorapani Pass, an altitude of over nine thousand feet. In the Ghorapani forest they walked a muddy trail through blooming rhododendrons, orchids and mosses, which most of the team members found a refreshing change from the hot lowlands they had just left. The forest was cool and filled with delightfully gnarled old trees. Every step took them closer to their goal, the south face of Dhaulagiri, though often the weather was too rainy and gloomy for the mountain to be seen. After a precipitous descent from the small town of Chitre, they crossed the Kali Gandaki River on a steep suspension bridge, then walked north to Tatopani, a town known for its hot springs. At last they reached Lete, only half a day's walk from Tukche. After Lete there was a dramatic change in the scenery as they left the pine forests behind and entered upon high desert land. Along the way they had camped beside streams, near towns, or occasionally had been overnight guests in the rust-and-mud-colored homes of villagers. With every step the team's eagerness to reach Tukche and start the actual ascent on Dhaulagiri grew.

During the near-week hike the level of fitness of the various climbers soon became evident. Some, like Bryant and Freeland, seeming never to tire, strode along at a fast pace all day. Others kept up, or almost kept up, with varying degrees of difficulty. Still others lagged far behind and came huffing and puffing into camp late each night, dragging weary bodies along. With each new day Joanne felt herself grow stronger and more confident. Occasionally she hiked right behind Bryant and Freeland, matching them stride for stride. Other times, not wanting to antagonize anyone, she intentionally allowed more distance between herself and the two leaders but continued to keep up the pace at this more respectful distance. Her stamina was excellent, her spirit soared, she felt increasingly excited with each new dawn. She rarely walked with Andy Howell, for he continued to have great difficulty with his feet and seemed embarrassed if anyone noticed what a hard time he was having. Evening after evening he'd be the last team member to straggle into camp. For all his youth and apparent good health, their daily treks were a problem for him, while for Joanne, so far, they were no problem at all. As she settled down to sleep each night, she exulted in how well she was doing. Surely at least some of the men had taken note and were dropping any lingering resistance they might have felt to her presence.

At the various campsites along the way, Joanne felt that it would be next to impossible for Bryant to drop in on her at night, and not once did he do so. Porters patrolled the campsites, guarding against predators, and it would have proved embarrassing had Bryant been intercepted making an unscheduled visit. Joanne had expected it to be this way, and therefore she was neither upset nor disappointed. For now Bryant was too involved heading his expedition to risk a secret impromptu rendezvous with her.

At last they reached the charming old town of Tukche, with its flat-roofed buildings, cobbled streets and air of grandeur. For endless generations Tukche had been a major commercial center on the trade route between China, Tibet and Nepal. Everything in the town—the streets, the buildings, even the people—seemed roughened by its arid, windy, harsh weather. Just off the town square was an empty house that a smiling official of the town had offered for their use, and the team gathered inside its small square rooms. Grinning, Freeland walked over to Joanne, handed her a can of warm beer and remarked, "From here on the picnic is over.

This is where we separate the men from the boys.''

"So I've heard," Joanne laughed.

Freeland was called away, then about twenty minutes later he caught Joanne's eye from across the room and motioned for her to follow him. They walked through the house, stepped outside and walked some ten feet away before Freeland stopped and turned to face her. His face was tight, his eyes intense.

"I'm not a superstitious man," he began, his voice low, "and I know I'll make it through this climb."

"Of course you will," Joanne agreed.

"Nevertheless," he went on, "one never knows." He dug a folded piece of paper out of his inside jacket pocket. "So if anything should happen to me—"

"It won't."

Freeland's eyes flashed with impatience at this interruption. "I know it won't. Nevertheless if it does, I want you to do something for me. My wife's address is on this paper." He pressed the folded paper into Joanne's hand. "I want you to write her, tell her I love her and my plan was to go back to her. If I'd lived through the climb, I would have. Is that clear?"

Joanne smiled. "Of course. And I'm so glad, Bob, for both your sakes."

Freeland's mouth curved into an embarrassed smile as he brushed this off. He stepped quickly past her and led the way back inside. As they entered the house, Bryant stood only a few feet away. He'd been talking to Greg Reed, but his voice cut off as he noticed Freeland enter, then his gaze swept past Freeland to catch on Joanne. His face flushed momentarily with what seemed to be both anger and pain.

"There you are, Bob," Bryant said. "We were looking for you." He led the way out of the room, motioning for Reed and Freeland to follow him. Joanne watched them leave, trembling slightly at the remembered look on Bryant's face.

THAT NIGHT everyone bedded down early. Joanne settled into her sleeping bag after a refreshing bath. She wore clean hiking pants and a shirt, and was in one corner of a small back room on the ground floor. John Naylor slept nearby, the silence of the night broken by his frequent gruff snores. Andy Howell was also close. Joanne fell asleep quickly, but was awakened sometime later by a shake of her arm.

"Joanne?"

Startled, she stared into the darkness, then her heart began pounding furiously as she realized the man kneeling beside her was Bryant. He leaned down to kiss her cheek, then motioned for her to follow him. The next moment, stepping noiselessly away, he was gone.

Her pulse racing, Joanne crawled out of her bag, drew on her heavy jacket, pulled on socks and boots and followed him out of the room.

She stepped over the figures in an adjacent room, walked through the small kitchen and found Bryant on the back steps of the house.

He put his arms around her and kissed her. "Let's go up to the roof," he whispered into her ear.

Joanne glanced upward in dismay. A few feet away there were muddy steps leading up. "But—it's so windy and cold!"

"You're not game?"

Joanne hesitated, feeling on the one hand cold and sleepy, on the other excited, as always, by Bryant's nearness. "Well—"

Bryant's dark eyes seemed to drill into her. One of his hands rose to slip in under her hair and press against the back of her neck. "It's up to you, of course, but this is apt to be our last chance to be alone for some time to come."

In response Joanne stepped over to the mud steps and began climbing. Bryant followed behind her. The flat roof was dusty and bumpy. After Joanne stepped onto it, she turned back to watch Bryant. Under one arm he had a bedroll, which he unrolled and gestured for her to seat herself on. He sat down cross-legged facing her, and placed his flashlight between them.

"I stashed this roll alongside the house before I came to wake you." He leaned across the short distance between them and pressed a kiss on her cheek, then drew back, smiling. "What does this remind you of?"

"Your treetop hideaway," Joanne said softly.

Bryant's smile broadened into a grin. He reached across to run his hand through her gleaming hair, then leaned over to kiss her again.

As he drew back, his smile was gone. The shadow across his face seemed to deepen. "I've given a lot of thought to what we discussed in Kathmandu," he said.

Joanne tensed. "Freeland?"

"Freeland." Bryant's eyes swung away. There was a taut, pained look around his mouth. "Every time I see the two of you together, even if you only exchange a word or two, I feel as though someone was cutting my insides out with a rusty knife." His eyes circled back, resting intently on Joanne's. His hand pressed briefly against the back of her neck, then fell away. "I want to believe what you told me, with my whole heart and soul I want to—"

"Then do!" Joanne broke in urgently. "What I told you was the truth."

Bryant's mouth curved into an uncertain smile. "You'll still swear to it?"

"Yes. Without hesitation. I already have once and I will again. There is nothing between Bob Freeland and myself now and never has been, except that we're friends."

Bryant leaned toward her, and his mouth pressed hungrily against hers. Joanne moved closer and put her arms around his shoulders.

Her breath caught as she pressed her cheek against his. How she loved this man, and how glad she was that he'd come in to wake her! If only she could put his fears about Freeland to rest once and for all!

Bryant's lips began caressing Joanne's ear, sending shivers of excitement through her. He kissed her temple, then whispered, "I want to believe. I try to believe and I do believe. Then I'll catch sight of you talking with Bob. Instantly I'm reminded of the sequence of events, all the evidence, and unwelcome doubt rushes in to rip me apart again."

He drew back, then caught her face between his hands. "It's just that I can't bear the thought of sharing you, when I love you so much, Joanne."

He'd said it. For the first time, he'd said it. "Oh, Jim, and I love you, too!" Joanne cried.

She pressed forward against him with such force that Bryant, laughing, fell back on the roll. His arms slipped around Joanne and pulled her down on top of him.

For a time they lay like that, Joanne luxuriating in the feel of his strong arms around her, his large sturdy body beneath hers. She would happily have fallen asleep right there, so close to him, and felt momentarily dismayed when Bryant gently rolled her off him until she was lying on her side beside him. His hand pressed her cheek, then brushed back her hair.

"Look up at the sky, Joanne. You've never seen such a sky."

Minutes before, when they'd climbed up here, the night had been cold and overcast. It was still cold, but a wind had whipped up and blown the haze away. A million stars sparkled brightly above them. They seemed so near that Joanne felt she could reach out and touch them.

"Oh, Jim, it's beautiful!"

Bryant kissed her. "And so are you. Let me show you how much I love you."

Joanne's breath caught with excitement and joy. Her head rested on Bryant's arm. Her body felt warm and alive, desire quickening at Bryant's touch. Slowly, with great tenderness and care, he opened her jacket and slipped a hand in under her shirt. His fingers brushed across her nipples, which were already fully erect. He loved her! For the first time he had told her he did, and she loved him. He was her man, the one man she wanted to be with forever, not just tonight, but every night. Bryant pressed hot little kisses against the base of her throat while his hands—such strong warm hands—eased down to cup her rounded buttocks. She wanted to stay like this forever, close against him, loving him, seeing the stars sparkling so close overhead.

Bryant raised his head and his mouth found hers. Weaving her fingers through his soft thick curls, Joanne drew him even nearer. As the kisses ended she cried out with joy, "Oh, Jim, I love you, I love you so much!"

"And I love you. Oh, darling, my darling!"

Their lovemaking was tender and controlled at first. Bryant's body kept Joanne warm, his movements kept the warming blood pounding through her with such joy, such bliss. And then the stars overhead exploded, exploding even behind her closed eyelids. At last Bryant's embrace grew still, and with a deep sigh of utter contentment Joanne drew up to a sitting position, smiling at her lover.

"Thank you, sweetheart," Bryant whispered, nuzzling his head against her throat.

"Thank you, my darling," Joanne replied softly. They held each other gently for a long time until Bryant, sighing, drew back. Time to pick up the flashlight, roll up the bedroll and climb back down the mud steps.

In the morning they'd be on their way, up the Mountain of Storms.

THE MULE DRIVERS had been paid the day before, and the loads carried by the mules stored in the house for the high-altitude porters to carry up to the first campsite. From now on time became the crucial factor. Every high-altitude climb was a tug-of-war between the need to climb slowly enough for everyone to become acclimatized and the need to move swiftly so the supplies required could be limited. Climbing too quickly without acclimatization would almost certainly cause acute mountain sickness, with dizziness, shortness of breath and general malaise. Mountain sickness could lead to pulmonary and cerebral edema, which, if the victim wasn't immediately taken to a lower altitude and given oxygen to regularize breathing, could result in death. High altitudes had to be approached cautiously, with this very real danger of mountain sickness in mind. But every day on the mountain necessitated additional supplies, so a team that proceeded too slowly would soon find itself running out of food. Somehow a balance had to be struck. Dates had been set for the airdrops—March 25 for the first of three airdrops at French Pass at 17,500 feet; April 2 for the first of the drops at the base camp at 19,300 feet—and these dates, which had been determined in advance by Bryant and Freeland as the best of possible dates, had to be met. If they weren't, there would be a supply problem, the team would be forced to make a quick descent and the expedition would prove to be a resounding failure.

All light clothing was to be left behind, stored in the little house, and all last-minute qualms should be left there, too, Freeland announced. In a last-minute pep talk he told the team members that if they were having second thoughts and wanted to back out, this was their last chance.

Joanne glanced instinctively across the room at John Naylor, but though his face was grim he made no move to respond to Freeland's challenge. Apparently he was going to stick. For the most part, the climbers looked as happy and excited as Joanne felt, ready and eager to begin. Dhaulagiri loomed above them; they couldn't wait to have a go at her, to conquer her. Joanne's pulse raced excitedly. A moment later Bryant edged his way into the crowded room, and when she glanced around to look at him, he saw her and smiled at her, a smile full of love. How supremely happy she felt!

One by one, or a few at a time, the team members left the house, crossed the town square and started up the dusty trail through orchards and yak pastures toward their first campsite on the mountain, scheduled to be set up at twelve thousand feet. They carried what they could in heavy backpacks. The porters would carry the main supplies in successive stages up to the campsite. From now on they would rarely be completely together as a team. There would be advance parties ranging ahead, setting up camps, dropping down to pick up additional supplies. There would be the unavoidable dropouts, through sickness or accidents. The stronger would forge ever higher, those with physical ailments would stay behind. Few would make it all the way to the summit. By the time they established their base camp at 19,300 feet, many would no longer care to climb another foot. Eagerness, ambition, all sense of adventure would have died by then, frozen by the ice and snow, by the pain of weary bones chilled through. Joanne had seen it before and could only hope that she wouldn't be one of those physically or emotionally defeated before the challenge had been fully met, before she dragged her sore complaining body the last few feet to the peak. As Freeland had said, once the team was on the mountain slopes the separation process would begin. There would be those who would have the stamina and luck to make it and those who wouldn't. And regardless of past climbing experience, level of fitness or expertise, it was never sure beforehand who would fall into which group. Each mountain was different, had its own personality, slapped some back with cruel caprice, while allowing others to ascend successfully. Some would make it while others wouldn't, that was the only sure thing. *Please, God, let luck be with me!* Joanne prayed as she started up the steep trail from Tukche.

Although the distance was less than a mile it took the entire day to reach the first campsite, four thousand feet above Tukche. No one was as yet acclimatized and everyone suffered at least some dizziness accompanied by headache. The wind whipped across the site with such force that it was difficult to stay upright and every bone in every body was numb. Pitching tents became a fierce challenge, but at last, with ten people working together, one by one the tents went up, tied together, anchored with rocks. The noise level was deafening, the tents cracking in the frenzied wind. Joanne slept little that night and was sure no one else did any better.

From that night on the days and nights seemed to melt into each other. In two weeks the team had climbed to the base of Dhaulagiri; now the peak towered over them like a brooding white god, ready to slap them down in an instant if they angered or displeased her. On occasion Joanne was a member of the advance group, which forged ahead to pick out and set up a new campsite. Other times she descended to lower sites to help cart up supplies. Soon the snowline was far below them; they lived in a frozen white world. With every passing day the summit, though closer, began to look more formidable, less ready to welcome them. Climbing as part of the advance party to French Pass, at about 17,000 feet, Andy Howell fell, severely spraining his ankle, and had to be carried back down to a lower site. That ended his climbing. He would descend to Tukche with some porters.

Joanne had the chance to say goodbye to him and found, to her relief, that while he was disappointed he did not seem overly distressed. With a smile he remarked that at least his girl friend, Christa, could stop worrying about him now.

"She never did want me to come, you know. She thought I was crazy, and maybe I was. But, anyway, it's all over now, and Christa will be delighted to hear I'm on my way home."

Joanne kissed his cheek in goodbye and wished him well.

As they wound their torturous way up the slopes, some team members acclimatized so slowly that they lingered in lower camps. For those who remained healthy, Joanne among them, it was up, down, lift, carry, until the body screamed for relief and the mind rebelled. At French Pass the first airdrops were successfully completed, to the joy of all those still on their feet and functioning. The drive to the northeast col began in earnest, to the site where the base camp would be established at 19,300 feet. This date, too, was met, to everyone's jubilation. The col, a high pass between two peaks, was a wide level field of packed ice and snow. There base camp was established; there Joanne was supposed to stay, not to be allowed to try climbing the towering peak. Only a few would attempt this final assault, and if Bryant hadn't yet changed his mind, she would not be among those few.

For the airdrop, the small plane swept in low, the bay doors opened, and cartons rained from the sky onto the deep soft snow. A gigantic X had been carved out to guide the pilot and his helper, and the entire drop was right on target. After three drops the plane circled away to return to Pokhara for another load. That day the weather stayed clear enough for three trips, with three drops each trip. There were additional drops the following day, and by nightfall of the next day, April 4, all of the remaining supplies had been safely delivered, with no lost cartons and almost no breakage.

By then the entire team, Americans and

Canadians plus the sturdy reliable Sherpas, had moved up to base camp. Andy was the only climber who had been injured, but two others—Bob Lansing and Michael Ross—were having serious problems. Both rebelled against being taken back down the mountain by porters, but the team doctors, Reed and Thatcher, had forced them to agree that they would not attempt to go any higher. With three climbers effectively out of commission, the team had more than trimmed down to a lean fighting weight. It was more like a skeleton. Joanne knew that both Bryant and Freeland were worried that, after all the planning, money and effort that had gone into the expedition, it would now be defeated by numbers: too few climbers would remain healthy enough for any member of the party to make it to the summit. Disaster seemed to hover just overhead, ready to slam down on them and send them reeling back down the mountain in total defeat.

At the base camp elevation, acclimatization was not possible. Most people could acclimatize fairly readily at altitudes below fourteen thousand feet, if they allowed their bodies sufficient time to make the necessary physiological changes. As one climbed higher, with less and less oxygen to breathe while the effort expended in the climb was greater, acclimatization became more and more difficult. Between eighteen and nineteen thousand feet a critical elevation is reached, above which it is not possible to become completely acclimatized. Base camp was above this critical altitude, which meant that there would be a steady deterioration in health and performance for every member of the team for every day he remained this high. Some degree of breathlessness, dizziness and torpor would be a constant companion from now until the descent.

During the three days that the airdrops were being made, everyone had time to read the incoming mail, which had accompanied the airdrop, and to write letters to be sent down the mountain by the mail runner. Joanne received two letters from her mother, two from her brother, one from Ted Myers and three from Scottie. She read Scottie's letters last, in the order in which they'd been written. The contents of the third pleased her and greatly relieved her mind. Scottie wrote that he had again been offered the promotion, which would entail a move to Los Angeles, and in view of all she'd said and written, and after giving the matter a great deal of thought, he had decided to accept the transfer. Scottie wrote:

My job could never mean as much to me as you do, but that quite possibly has become an irrelevant comparison. I guess it's time I started dealing with reality and the reality is, obviously, that you don't love me now and never will—enough to marry me, I mean—so if I'm going to have to dream up

an entirely new future for myself, I figure I
might as well do so in the tinsel town of
Hollywood with the new affluence this promotion will give me. I'm still hoping to
make it back to San Francisco to greet you
on your return, but finalization of any such
plan will depend on getting more detailed
information as to when you'll arrive. I do
hope you are doing well on the climb and
enjoying it. When it comes to having a
dream come true, one always risks possible
disappointment, it seems to me. Hope your
experience with this expedition isn't disap-
pointing you. Take care, dear Joanne.

As always, Scott

Joanne scribbled off a note in reply, telling
Scottie how pleased she was to read of his decision to accept the promotion and also assuring
him that up to the time of writing she was not
the least disappointed in the climb; despite the
hardships she loved every moment. She would
write him later with more up-to-date information about their expected arrival date back
home, but he mustn't worry about being there
to greet her.

Once all the supplies were airdropped, the
team settled in for a few days of rest. Bryant's
plan called for further climbing to resume on
April 10 for those sufficiently acclimatized by
then to give it a try. This schedule was aborted
by storms. On the morning of the tenth every-

one woke from fitful sleep to be greeted by crashing thunder and winds so fierce that visibility was less than twenty-five feet. The temperature of the snow was measured at minus ten degrees Fahrenheit. Tempers grew short as team members were gripped by a new fear: if the weather didn't clear, time would defeat them. If they were going to reach the summit, they *had* to be on their way. They had only a little longer than a month before the deadline for beginning the descent so that they would be down and away ahead of the torrential rains of the monsoon. But for three days a blinding storm kept the team immobile in camp.

From base camp they were faced with two alternate routes to the summit. Previous expeditions that had successfully conquered the treacherous White Mountain had followed the same route, up the northeast spur. Bryant wanted to attempt a different route: the southeast ridge, a route that had been attempted before and each time given up as impossible. The ridge could be reached after a two-thousand-foot climb up an icy face dotted here and there by fallen rocks. As the storm howled outside, argument raged within between those who wanted to follow Bryant's lead and attempt the more difficult route and those who wanted to follow the easier route to be more assured of reaching the summit.

"If we had more men, we might attempt the southeast ridge," Greg Reed argued with Joanne. "But stripped down as we are, and with time running out, I say we should stop talking like idiots, face the reality of our situation, and take the only route that makes sense: the northeast spur."

Bryant was rarely present in the dining tent where the others gathered to discuss, argue and fight out the issue. He said very little, but everyone knew where he stood.

At last the storm abated—action could take the place of argument. Freeland ducked into the dining tent just after dawn on April 13 to announce that no final decision had yet been made. For today he and Bryant were going to tackle the icy face leading up to the southeast ridge route, while four others were to head up the northeast spur, carrying supplies for a camp to be established two thousand feet higher up.

As Freeland read off the names of those who were to begin carrying supplies, Joanne tensed. With each name he spoke she hoped to hear her own but knew she wouldn't. She was to be one of those left in base camp, to rest, wait and watch.

The day was bright, clear and breathtakingly beautiful. Joanne sat on an upturned carton, using binoculars to watch Bryant and Freeland. Soon they had crossed the snow bowl leading to the mountain's two-thousand-foot icy face. Both men were using crampons fitted to their boots. They carried alpine hammers, slings and hardware and were roped together. All of this equipment was necessary, Joanne knew, yet she also knew that the greatest resource any climber had was himself, his inner poise and intelligence. These traits were what made a great climber great. Physical strength was of less importance and the equipment even less.

With Greg Reed sitting alongside, Joanne spent the morning watching the climb. Bryant and Freeland were anchoring a fixed rope to the icy face at 150 feet per pitch. Although the distance from base camp was such that their figures seemed little more than ants crawling up a vast white wall, Joanne watched in fascination, caught up in the drama of what they were doing. With her head she thought that Greg Reed was probably right, that this preliminary effort up the southeast ridge was a waste of time. This team would find, as had each one before, that the ridge route was impossible. But with her heart she cheered Bryant and Freeland on, and she couldn't help but feel excited at the thought that possibly, just possibly, it would be decided that it *was* a possible route and they would make mountaineering history by taking it. Her heart exulted at the thought while her mind told her this was nonsense, that it wouldn't happen. In the end they'd have to go via the northeast spur just as every other expedition had.

The next few days followed much the same pattern. The weather was clear, so pairs of men worked on climbing the steep icy face to the southeast ridge, anchoring a fixed rope and hacking steps into the ice at the more difficult places, while others carried supplies up along the northeast spur route to establish a camp two thousand feet higher up. On the third day, two of the men scheduled to carry supplies felt too ill to climb, and Joanne was asked to join those carrying to the higher camp. The first slight break in Bryant's restriction! She was pleased to be active again, to be at least partially accepted as part of the team, but still would have much preferred to work on the southeast ridge route, climbing up the steep icy face. She thought about asking if one of the men scheduled for that would exchange assignments with her but decided against it. There was still almost a month of arduous work to be done before anyone would step foot on the summit. No use pushing her luck too soon.

Three pairs of men took turns climbing the icy face toward the southeast-ridge route. It was a rest day for Joanne when Bryant and Freeland again took their turn. As she sat on her upturned carton, watching through binoculars, she saw that they were making good progress. They made one final pitch up and attained the ridge summit. Before long they started back down, rappeling down the fixed rope. After a trek across the deep soft snow of the mile-wide bowl at the foot of the icy face, they came trudging into camp, their faces grim. Even under the heavy sun- and windburn, Bryant's face seemed flushed with anger while Freeland's looked ashen with fury. They strode into camp yards apart from each other, neither one glanced at the other, nor did they speak.

At dinner, Freeland and Bryant, as always, were seated across from each other at the table. By then their falling out had been sensed by every team member, and the meal began in a tense nerve-racking silence. Joanne, seated three places down from Freeland, had a clear view of Bryant's face. Halfway through the meal of beef stew with peas and biscuits, Greg Reed, seated at Joanne's right, his face expressionless, addressed the grim silence with a direct question:

"So tell us, Bob, what did you find when you reached the ridge? Is it a possible route?"

Freeland's eyes sparked fire as he glanced down to answer Reed. "No way. It's impossible. Cross it off. From now on, we concentrate on the northeast spur."

Joanne's eyes flew immediately to Bryant's face, as did everyone else's. Bryant's eyes narrowed, becoming red slits. He spoke softly but with deadly clarity. "Stuff it, Freeland. I didn't spend years of my time and thousands of dollars just to go up some route that's already been successfully climbed three or more times. I have not now and never intend to abandon my original plan, which is to attain the summit via the southeast ridge."

A stunned silence fell. The only sound was the

roaring of the wind whipping around the tent.
Staring at Bryant's face, the sound of his voice
still reverberating in her, Joanne couldn't doubt
that he meant what he said. But it was hard not
to believe what Freeland had said: that the
southeast ridge route was clearly impossible.
That was what all previous expeditions had
found. Having surveyed the route now, that was
what Freeland, the most experienced climber on
the team, had judged. For Bryant to persist in
the face of such a judgment seemed crazy.
Worse, suicidal. Somehow, some way, Bryant
would have to be dissuaded.

The rest of the meal was consumed for the
most part in silence. Peaches and cake for dessert, with hot tea. Muted sporadic conversations
broke out here and there down the long line of
diners. When Greg Reed, seated beside her, addressed her, Joanne swung her head around to
listen, but before she took in what Greg was saying, her attention was caught by a further angry
exchange between Bryant and Freeland. Her
head whipped around as she caught their words.

"There is no way you can stop me," Bryant
said, in a soft deadly voice.

Freeland's eyes again flashed fire. "Like hell
there isn't. You'll either listen to me, or I'll pack
up and start down the mountain in the morning,
taking everyone with me who'll go. And plenty
will. There's no way you could go up after
that."

Bryant's heavily bearded face tightened in

resolution. He leaned forward, still speaking in the same soft voice. "Enough will stay. Go ahead and leave if you like."

Freeland jumped up, looking as though no movement could adequately relieve his fury, as though even if he could plunge across the table and strangle his opponent, it wouldn't be enough. "Jim, you're crazy. You're out of your mind. I'll break up this team so quickly—you better believe I will. I'll leave you without a stove to cook on or anything to cook if you had a stove. If you're dead set on throwing your life away up here, I won't have it on my head, by God!" Freeland spun on his heel and stalked out.

Within minutes the entire tent was in an uproar. Joanne felt so tense and worked up she couldn't finish her food. Few others seemed able to eat, either, except for Bryant, who, grim faced and silent, continued until he'd finished. By then most of the men were on their feet, arguing, haranguing each other in small knots. Greg Reed pushed his way around Joanne and walked up to Bryant, clasping him by the shoulder. The two men exchanged a few words, but Joanne couldn't catch them. Reed left the tent. In minutes he returned, a step ahead of Freeland, who stalked in with reddened eyes lowered.

Reed raised his arms, calling out for quiet. Within moments the noisy uproar died down. "That's better," Reed said. "Obviously this difference of opinion has to be worked out, but let's handle it like civilized people. Everyone sit down again, and we'll listen first to Jim, then to Bob, then after that we'll reach some kind of resolution. Please. Sit down.''

Looking relieved, everyone returned to his place at the table. After a momentary silence, Bryant gulped down the last of his tea and rose to his feet. In that moment, it seemed to Joanne, he looked taller, stronger and more powerful than she had ever seen him look. His voice was calm and quiet.

''I have very little to add to what I've already said. As most of you know, it was my intention from the very beginning to attempt the southeast-ridge route. I organized this expedition with that in mind and wouldn't have spent my time and money otherwise. We attained the ridge today, and I do not feel my plan is unfeasible—''

''It's crazy!'' Freeland threw in, his voice rising in anguished rage.

Bryant's eyes fixed on Freeland's face. ''You've known from the first what I planned to do.''

Freeland jumped angrily to his feet, straining forward. ''I didn't know I was dealing with a madman,'' he cried. ''I wanted to go the ridge route, too, to be the first up that route, to make history. But, dammit, man, when we stood on that ridge today and reality moved in—I faced reality, Jim, and you must too!''

Bryant drew back, his broad face tightening in even more willful determination. "One man's reality isn't always another's. Someone, some-time, will go via the ridge, so why not now? Why not me? I've been working toward this for four years, and I'm not about to abandon it now."

"Just to make history?" Freeland sneered. By now his anguish seemed palpable. Joanne felt that, were she a little nearer to him, she could have reached out to touch it. "Well, you won't, you know. All you'll do is throw your life away, and there's nothing new in that. Half a dozen men—more than that—have already died right here."

Bryant stood silently staring across for a mo-ment, breathing deeply, then he remarked soft-ly, "It's my life, Bob."

Freeland's eyes took on an even wilder, more anguished look. He pounded the table with a fist. "But I won't help you. I didn't come all this way to help you kill yourself. If you don't drop this madness, I'll leave in the morning, down the mountain I'll go, taking more than half the men with me, you just watch. Once we've left, there's no way you could go on. If you persisted after that, it would be clear proof you're too much of an idiot to worry about!"

As Freeland's words died away, his deep gasping for breath filled the tent. Joanne drew her eyes away from his face, glanced across at Bryant, then looked quickly around at the other men. If Freeland followed through on his threat to break up the team, how many of the climbers would follow his lead, pack up supplies and follow him down the mountain? Bryant's plan seemed suicidal, but what should *she* do? Her eyes flew back to Bryant's grim, burned, heavily bearded face, and her heart beat so hard it was difficult to draw in breath. But surely, surely, there had to be some way to stop him and still hold the team together, to make the ascent to the summit up the northeast spur—if only that way could be found.

CHAPTER THIRTEEN

DEBATE RAGED NOISILY for an hour. Purposeful-
ly Bryant rose and started out of the tent. It
seemed as if a way had opened before him, as
though he had become a god or an untouchable.
No one spoke to him or attempted to detain
him. After he'd left Joanne ached to go after
him, to try to reason with him, but Freeland had
rushed around the table to grab her arm and
hold her there.

"It's madness," Freeland insisted, his reddened eyes that moment looking wild. "I know
I agreed to the southeast ridge plan at home, we
all did, but we were all having pipe dreams,
don't you see? The route had been declared impossible, but what did those people know? At
home we were giants, each of us was super-
man. We'd come over here, take one look and
somehow magically resolve all the problems and
make history by going that route. That was the
foolish dreaming of kids, Joanne, little kids
who'd never grown. But when I sat on that ridge
today, on that rotten ice, getting a firsthand
look—

"To try what Bryant wants to do would be

suicidal. He's a good man, Joanne, I love him—'' as he said this, Freeland's reddened eyes filled with tears and his hand compulsively squeezed Joanne's ''—and I don't want to leave the mountain without him. I don't want to give him to the mountain, another sacrifice, another corpse. So will you back my hand, Joanne, will you agree to break up the team and follow me down in the morning if we can't get Jim to change his mind, yes or no?''

"Bob, I—don't know yet.'' All Joanne knew at the moment was that she could barely breathe, and her head was spinning with worry and indecision.

Freeland confronted Greg Reed next, asking him the same question: would he break up the team and go down the mountain, yes or no?

Joanne started past them, wanting more than anything in the world to leave the tent and find Bryant. Maybe if she talked to him.... The noise level was such that she felt almost deafened, but just before she pushed the tent flap aside to go outside, she heard Freeland's voice, thin and piercing, "All right, good idea, and take Joanne with you.''

Hearing this, Joanne glanced around. Freeland waved for her to come back. As she reached Freeland's side, he threw an arm across her shoulders.

"Greg says he wants to hold off on making up his mind until he's seen the ridge himself, which I think is a fine idea. I'd like you to go along, and anyone else who feels undecided. One look at that ridge and you'll see what I'm talking about.''

"Great, I'd love to," she told Freeland, affirming it with a nod at Greg.

A moment later she excused herself and left the dining tent. She found Bryant not in his tent but standing toward the edge of the campsite, staring at the icy face leading up to the southeast ridge. Although she addressed him as she approached, he seemed too lost in thought to hear her. As she reached him and touched his arm, he glanced around with a startled look.

"Jim?"

"Yes, Joanne."

His voice didn't sound like the voice of a madman. His face, though taut and determined looking, did not give the appearance of craziness. "Bob's still in the tent proselytizing for all he's worth, trying to persuade everyone he's right and that if you don't change your mind, everyone should pack up and leave in the morning as a way to stop you.''

Bryant sighed deeply, then shrugged. The noisy wind whipped about them, and Joanne had had to shout in order to be heard. "That's his right," Bryant muttered, sounding more resigned than discouraged. He put his arm around her shoulder to draw her against him.

Joanne resisted the embrace as tears flooded her eyes. *And I may even follow him myself,* she thought, caught in the grip of both anger and misery. One look into Bryant's eyes had told her that there was no point in trying to reason with him. There was no way to sway him, she could tell; there had never been any way to sway him, about anything, ever. He was the most stubborn, most arrogant, most infuriating man she had ever known...and she loved him so much that moment. As she fought against his touch, his arm dropped away.

"Greg and I are going up to the ridge tomorrow to have a look for ourselves," Joanne shouted at Bryant through the wind. "Possibly others will go along, too."

Again Bryant shrugged. "Fine." He swung around, took her arm and with no further word led her back toward their tents.

FREELAND WOKE HER at four the next morning, shaking her arm. Joanne crawled out of her sleeping bag, then pulled out her sun cream, extra socks and boots. Left out overnight they would freeze, so they shared the bag with her. Freeland, Reed, and two other climbers—Claude and Charles Mandel—were in the dining tent when she entered, downing steaming hot tea. She joined them, warming her hands on her cup. Two other men soon appeared.

After a welcome breakfast of hot biscuits and fruit pies, the small group prepared to leave. Freeland was going with them. With lamps strapped to their foreheads in the predawn blackness, they gathered their equipment and

started out. First a mile hike across a gently
sloping snow bowl, then the two-thousand-foot
climb up a series of ice gullies and ribs through a
narrow gap between rocks on one side and a
hanging glacier on the other. They used jumar
handles—spring-loaded handles that slide up a
fixed rope, then hold under tension—to climb
up the rope that had been laboriously anchored
up the face. Steps had been cut into the ice in the
more difficult places. The sun rose, warming
them. Freeland climbed first, then Reed, then
Joanne. Four men followed at intervals behind
her. Joanne was pleased to be climbing but
regretful that she had not been allowed to join
in the difficult work that had preceded their
ascent. She also felt a deep dismay over the purpose of their climb. At last Freeland reached the
crest, then Reed, followed by Joanne.

As she reached the ridge, Joanne dug deeply
for breath. She instinctively sank down to where
she was straddling the crest, as Freeland and
Reed were doing. The ridge was extremely narrow. Joanne's hands, in her snow-dotted mitts,
could grip the ridge as easily as she could have a
narrow plank of wood. The south side of the
ridge, up which they had just climbed, dropped
away at a steep angle. On the far side there was
an even steeper drop of what Joanne judged to
be about twelve thousand feet. The ridge was
broken by spiked towers, cornices—overlapping
lips of snow—and frightening walls of ice. From
their base camp below it could be seen that the

ridge ran about two miles, an intimidating length, before it joined the main body of the mountain. In a rising wind, with snow whirls blown into their faces, visibility was poor, but peering down the visible length of ridge, Joanne could see no possible sight for a camp, nowhere that supplies could be stored for an assault on the summit via that ridge.

Before too long, without conversation, the group started its descent. As she rappeled her way down the rope, Joanne tried not to feel too sick at heart. Somehow, some way, someone *had* to get through to Bryant that he would have to give up his plan. Just as every other expedition had discovered, there was no way to approach the summit of Dhaulagiri via the southeast ridge. The ridge was far too narrow to support a supply camp, and without supplies no ascent was possible. Bryant would *have* to adjust to this and agree to abandon this route in favor of the northeast spur.

It was a long, wearying, discouraging day before the group hiked at last across the snow bowl to return to camp. As they reached the tents, Joanne found herself walking alongside Greg Reed. She knew she didn't have to ask, but still she voiced what was on her mind, "So what did you think, Greg?"

Reed looked at her with a rather quizzical expression. His sunburned lips curled into a small amused smile. "It's an impossible route, of course, but at the same time, after years of practicing medicine, I've learned that one should never discount the human will. In the face of the most terrible catastrophes, it's been proved to me time and time again that the old saying, 'Where there's a will, there's a way,' can't be discounted."

Joanne's pulse leapt with hope. "Then you think Jim's plan is feasible?"

"I think it's madness."

So do I, so do I, Joanne thought, her momentary hope dying away as she felt plunged once again into gloom.

By unspoken agreement, everyone ate dinner without bringing up the one subject that was on everyone's mind. After they'd finished Bryant rose to his feet. He tapped against his platter with a spoon to gain attention, and silence fell.

"Men, I'd like to attack the problem that must be resolved. My plan is this: the main body of the team will ascend via the northeast spur, setting up campsites as it goes. Ang Darje and I will split from you and tackle the southeast ridge. If all goes well, we'll join forces again either on the summit or possibly a thousand feet below the summit where the southeast ridge route joins the main body of the mountain. It's obvious that the success of this plan depends on everyone here. Darje and I cannot possibly carry sufficient supplies not only to make it to the summit but also back down. In our descent we will be dependent on supplies from the campsites set up by the team on the northeast spur. I have hopes that the plan will work and ask your cooperation. I am not asking any man here to put his life to any more risk than he assumed by the mere fact of joining up. If I am putting my own life at greater risk, that surely is my right. I ask for your support and agreement to this plan.''

Bryant stood a moment glancing idly down the table before he seated himself. As he did so, Freeland rose.

"Men, you know me. You know that Jim and I have been close friends for years. You know I would do everything within my power to support his position if I could. But the plan he's come up with is suicidal. Some of you have seen the ridge for yourselves, others have heard our reports on it. There is no place to set up a camp. We're dealing here with a narrow uneven ridge, over twenty-one thousand feet high, subjected to the most miserable, fiercest weather conditions possible on this earth—two miles of this. There is no way it can be traversed, not by you, not by me, not by Jim. If we can't make this stubborn jackass come to his senses, I ask that you back my position, pack up supplies and follow me back down the mountain. If we do this, Jim will have no alternative but to forget his madness and join us in the descent.'' Breathing hard, his eyes flashing fire, Freeland dropped down to his chair.

There was silence for only a moment, then Greg Reed spoke up. "Jim, with no way to set up a camp, how do you plan to eat and sleep?"

"We'll backpack our food." Bryant spoke slowly, clearly, with a steely edge to his voice. "I've had special lightweight, high-protein, high-fat bars made up, two thousand calories each. We can carry a month's supply for two men. I've also got a lightweight tent and two lightweight bags. If necessary we'll anchor ropes, tie ourselves to them, wrap the tent and bags around ourselves and sleep standing up. Or we'll sleep by turns, carrying each other. Or—"

"Madness," Freeland cut in, his voice high and frantic. "Absolute madness." He jumped up. "I can't bear even listening to it."

"Bob, please," Reed said. "Sit down again."

Freeland glared at Reed for a moment, then with a look of pained defeat sank down again. He began nervously drumming the table with his spoon, a noise that kept time with every word said thereafter.

"And a heat source for melting your water?" Reed asked.

"I have a small, lightweight, made-to-specifications kerosene burner that will do us just fine."

"And how heavy do you figure your packs will be?"

Bryant hesitated a moment before answering, "Fifty to sixty pounds each."

Again Freeland jumped up, obviously feeling far too agitated to stay seated. "That's a gross miscalculation. They'll be nearer a hundred pounds."

For the first time, anger visibly gripped Bryant's face. Though he stared furiously across at Freeland, his voice stayed soft. "Seventy pounds absolute maximum."

"Liar!"

"Watch it Bob, I'm warning you."

Freeland swayed momentarily, looking dizzy and sick, then he dropped back down in his chair. "Even seventy pounds is more than a man can carry at this altitude!"

Bryant rose to his feet, his eyes narrowing into blazing slits. He leaned across the table toward Freeland. "I could carry *Joanne* from here to the summit if the necessity arose, and she weighs more than the limit you're setting. As far as that goes, I could carry *you* if I had to!" he snapped across.

Silence engulfed the group for a moment, the gloom inside the tent punctuated by the howling blasts of the wind outside. Joanne glanced anxiously around, her head whirling. She felt torn in two, angry at Bryant, sympathetic toward Freeland, but above all frightened. If Bryant won.... Was there any chance at all he could go via the southeast ridge and survive to attain the summit, the first man in history to do so? No, no, that was madness; surely everyone was agreed on that. If a vote were taken, the vote would go against Bryant, she felt certain. Or would it? How would *she* vote?

Reed insisted that Ang Darje should be brought into the tent for the discussion. The sirdar had left the dining tent at the very start of the meal, joining his small band of cooks and porters in a tent nearby. Claude Mandel jumped up and left. A few minutes later he returned with the head Sherpa in tow. A renewed round of questioning began, with Reed taking the lead. Yes, Darje insisted, he understood the dangers involved. Then why was he agreeing to do it?

The sirdar's lips pulled apart in a wry smile. He shot a glance over at Bryant, who sat watching him fixedly. He had agreed to go because sahib—he pronounced the word with amusement and without a trace of subservience—because sahib Bryant had promised him a large sum of money. And for money he'd throw away his life, Freeland demanded. Money that he'd never live to enjoy?

He *would* live to enjoy it, Darje answered; he had consulted two lamas and three astrologers prior to joining the expedition, and all had told him it would be a successful and profitable climb. He was an experienced guide, having started as a young boy as a kitchen helper, working his way up from low-altitude porter, icefall porter, high-altitude porter to the position he had now held for twelve years: sirdar, head guide. Ang Darje drew himself up proudly and flashed one of his rare warm smiles. He *wanted* to go with the sahib, wanted to break new ground, to become a footnote in history.

No amount of badgering by Freeland or some of
the other men could sway him from this stand.
Even without the offer of money, he insisted at
last, he would still be willing to go. He and
Sahib Bryant were two strong men, two men
against one mountain: they would conquer her
or die.

After Darje left the controversy raged on,
though with less and less heat as everyone's
weariness grew. When repetition overwhelmed
all remaining energy, when there seemed nothing left to be said that hadn't been said a dozen
times already, Reed banged on the table for
quiet and suggested that a vote be taken.

"This is what I think we should do," Reed
said. "A one-minute summation from Jim, a
one-minute summation from Bob, then a vote.
I'll tear up this sheet of paper, pass everyone a
square, each one writes down a capital *B*, meaning he's siding with Jim, or a capital *F*, that he's
backing Bob. We'll drop all the votes into this
cap, stir them up so no one can possibly know
how anyone else has voted, then one of us will
draw them out and count them, following which
the slips will be placed here on the table so that
everyone can verify the count. Agreed?"

Mumbled agreement circled the tent, weary
heads bobbing. "Jim?" Reed said.

Bryant's eyes circled the intent faces up and
down the table, then he rose as though to be a
more open target for the eyes fastened on him.
"First, I thank all of you for the way you've

been willing to discuss this, as openly and rigorously as you have. I really have little to add to what I've already said. But please keep one thing in mind. I organized this expedition, took on the long tedious job of lining up supplies, arranging for financing, and I underwrote the climb with thousands of dollars of my own money. I'm not springing anything new on you. Most of you knew from the first what my primary objective was: to go to the summit via the southeast ridge. All I'm asking is that you honor the commitment you made when you signed up and put yourself under my leadership. You're not taking any risks that you didn't know about from the first. You'll be going via the northeast spur, setting up camps, nothing more, with a chance to be one of those who makes it all the way to the summit. If Bob proves to be right, that I'm foolish to attempt this, that it will prove too dangerous and I won't survive, that's my problem, not yours. It's my life that will be lost, not yours. It seems to me that this is my choice, my right, and all I ask is that you allow me this choice and support me in it. Someday—someday soon—someone is going to make it to the summit via this route, and I ask you—please—to give me a chance to be that one. Thank you.''

"And will you abide by the vote after it's taken?'' Freeland cried, leaping up and leaning half across the table. "If the team backs me, then you drop this idiocy and all of us go via the northeast spur?''

A muscle rippled along the side of Bryant's face, but after a moment he answered in a level voice, ''I'll abide by the vote. I can't see that I have any choice.''

Freeland sighed and seemed visibly to relax a little. His expression seemed to say that possibly he was not dealing with a complete madman after all.

''And will *you* abide by the vote,'' Bryant threw across at him, ''no matter which way it goes?''

''I'll abide by it!'' Freeland snapped. ''Of course I'll abide by it.'' His voice suggested that he had nothing to worry about; he *knew* that the vote would go his way.

Reed had suggested a one-minute summation, but Freeland talked for five minutes without anyone's breaking in to stop him. He talked excitedly of the climb they could have once this side issue was dispensed with. Instead of a push to get two or three climbers onto the summit, if the weather gave them any kind of break at all, they'd attempt to put every man there—and Joanne, too, he added with a little laugh—onto the summit en masse. That would make the history books, a sure bet. If everyone stayed reasonably healthy, if the weather didn't turn too nasty, if the White Mountain was in the mood to welcome them, they'd push up as a team and each and every one of them would stand on the summit, an unheard-of achievement.

"But a *reasonable* goal," Freeland insisted, his intent gaze moving jerkily from one face to another. "No one wants to quit and descend, but since Jim's been fair enough to agree to abide by the vote, we won't have to. In a day or two he'll come back to his senses and thank us."

Freeland choked, and it took a second or two before he could clear his throat and continue. He looked over at Bryant. "I've known Jim Bryant for almost twenty years. He's one great guy; I love the man. That's why I'm doing this, for no other reason. If you love the guy, you'll agree with me and vote to back me. Thank you."

Looking completely spent, Freeland dropped back down to his chair. Bryant gazed steadily across at him with an enigmatic little smile. In the silence that followed, Joanne could hear Greg Reed tearing a sheet of paper. A little square was pressed into her hand. One by one the men rose and walked a few feet away from the table. No one consulted anyone else. Eyes fastened first on Bryant, then on Freeland, then returned to Bryant. Joanne felt her heart beating wildly. *If you love the guy, you'll agree with me and vote to back me,* Freeland had said. Her hand trembled so she could hardly hold the pencil that someone had given her. She stared across at Bryant through tear-misted eyes. She loved him; oh, how she loved him! The thought that he might be throwing his life away—and for what? For what? For a dream, for a wild idiotic dream.

As she stared across at him, unable to decide, not knowing how she was going to vote, she saw Bryant lift his head. His eyes circled the room until they came to rest on her, then his gaze locked with hers. He looked so tired, the skin of his face, above the heavy reddish beard, resembled burned dry wood. As she gazed steadily back at him, Joanne thought she saw an earnest plea come into his eyes. *Don't stand against me, Joanne; allow me my dream. Please, my love.* Joanne dropped her eyes, no longer able to stand looking across into his. Her fingers still trembled, she felt dizzy and sick. Pressing the paper against her uplifted leg, she scrawled out a *B* as best she could. *All right, Jim, I did as you asked; oh, God help us all.* As she folded the paper up, Joanne felt a sudden heaviness. She walked forward and dropped her square into the cap.

Some had voted more quickly than she had; others stood around silently debating the issue, still undecided. As Joanne waited, she felt herself go hot and cold by turns. She wished she dared dart forward, grab out her square and change her vote. She let her eyes move over to Bryant, found him gazing steadily at her again, a slight pained smile on his lips, and as frightened as she felt, she was glad she'd voted as she had. Surely Freeland would win the vote, but her conscience would be clear. She'd be able to tell Bryant in all truth that she hadn't voted against him; she hadn't been one of those who'd snatched away his dream. She dropped her eyes, breathing heavily, trying to catch her breath.

At last everyone had voted. Neither Bryant nor Freeland had been given squares; their votes would simply have canceled each other out, as everyone knew. There were eleven votes in all, so if everyone had marked one initial or the other, no tie was possible. Surely Bob Freeland would win. Logic was on his side as well as emotion. Bryant had kept to himself as much as possible on the climb, but still it was Joanne's feeling that everyone liked him. Even more, everyone seemed to admire and respect him. No one would want to be party to his insane self-destruction. On the other hand, of course, Joanne thought, doing her best to wet her dry sunburned lips with her tongue, some climbers might easily have been swayed by what Bryant had said. This *was* his expedition; he had been the moving force, had put a great amount of time, money and effort into it. The climbers signing on had committed themselves to his leadership, and not a single man here, Joanne felt sure, lifting her eyes and glancing around, lacked the capacity to dream. To be over nineteen thousand feet in the air on a treacherous mountain, which could kill them with one white sweep, with a sudden avalanche or fierce winds or in a dozen other ways, to even be here one had to be crazy. So to crazy men was a little added touch of madness all that unthinkable? While Freeland had argued angrily, emotionally, Bryant had stayed quiet and reasonable. *Let me do this,* had been his plea. *Support me. I thank you.* Would such a low-key rational approach win for him? It was impossible to tell, Joanne thought anxiously, glancing around. Heavily bearded, dry, sunburned faces and reddened eyes weren't easy to read. The last of the votes had been dropped into the cap. Who would win?

Reed picked the cap up, lifted it above his head, and gently shook up the squares. As he lowered it again, he extended the cap toward John Naylor, who sat squatted on a chair at the table nearby. "No, you count 'em," Naylor suggested, shaking his head.

Reed glanced around the room, but each man shook his head, indicating he did not relish stepping forward to read out the votes. With a shrug of resignation, Reed set the cap down, picked up his first square of paper, smoothed it out and read the vote. "It's an F," he announced.

Freeland had three votes before Bryant picked up his first. Joanne began to relax, just a bit. If Bryant lost... did she really want him to? Another vote for Bryant, then another. A three-three tie.

Reed's hand was trembling slightly, Joanne noticed, as he picked up the next square. The tent was so quiet all you could hear was heavy labored breathing. Outside the wind had quieted. Reed read out the next vote, an *F*. Another *F*. Freeland needed only one more vote to cinch it. Joanne's eyes darted over to Bryant and again she found him looking at her. His lips were curled in a little smile, but under the smile she could sense his pain. More than four years of steady effort lost here tonight. He hadn't come here, he'd said, to ascend the White Mountain on a well-trod trail. He had come to blaze a new one, to thrust himself into mountaineering history. It was his life, his dream, but he wasn't being allowed to risk the one for the other. There was no way Joanne could rejoice in his defeat now that it seemed so certain.

Reed paused before drawing out another square. He seemed reluctant to draw out the final few votes. Five to three for Freeland. There were three votes left. All Freeland needed was one of them. It seemed a near certainty that he would get it. But as Joanne let her eyes fall on him, she saw that he sat hunched forward, his eyes frightened, his face taut, with nothing of the victor about him. Reed picked up the next square, opened it and read it. A *B*. Five to four. Another square. Another *B*. A five-five tie.

Joanne dropped her eyes, trying not to gasp too noisily for breath. Now it was down to the wire, only one vote left. The deciding vote. Reed drew it out, opened it and said, with a sigh, that it was also a *B*. Bryant had won.

"Dammit!" Freeland cried. He jumped up and stalked out of the tent, everyone moving quickly out of his path.

Bryant sat quietly staring down for a moment, then he rose to his feet, murmured, "Thank you," and followed Freeland out.

Joanne felt too unsteady to move. She held on to the back of one of the chairs for a minute, saw several of the men step forward to verify the vote. Everyone seemed rather stunned, quietly overwhelmed. "I thought Bob would take it for sure," she heard Claude Mandel remark to his brother.

"Is that how you voted?" Charles responded.

"None of your business," Claude said, smiling. The two pulled up the flap and left the tent.

When she felt steady enough, Joanne stepped up to Greg Reed. She thanked him for handling the crisis so well. As he acknowledged her thanks with a slight bow, Joanne felt a sudden urge to ask him how he'd voted. From the time this crisis had erupted, Greg Reed had seemed to her the voice of reason, but reason wisely wed to experience and imagination. If he had voted for Jim—oh, surely if he had, Jim would survive after all.

Not daring to ask outright, Joanne skirted the question. "Well, Greg, did the vote go the way you thought it would?"

Greg smiled, as though he knew perfectly well what she really wanted to know. "I thought it could very easily go either way," he said. They started walking together out of the tent.

"So you weren't terribly shocked or displeased at the way it did go?"

Greg laughed. "Few things shock me and even fewer things seriously displease me. I won't ask how you voted, nor will I tell you how I did." After accompanying her to her tent, he excused himself and walked away.

CHAPTER FOURTEEN

A FEW MINUTES LATER, as Joanne sat on her sleeping bag, about to pull off her stiff frozen boots, Bryant's voice called out, "Hello? May I come in?"

"Yes, please do." Joanne's pulse immediately sped up. On some of the lower-level camps, she had shared a tent with other climbers, but here in base camp, with ample room on the level ground the camp occupied, she had a tent of her own. Still Bryant had never come to speak to her privately before, and she hadn't expected him to. But, tonight, here he was.

He pulled the tent flap up, crouched down and came in. He squatted on his haunches before her. With a gentle push he brushed her hands aside and began pulling her boots off for her. When he got the first one off, he set it down and held her foot in his hands. Through the thick layers of cold woolen socks he massaged her foot, his eyes watching his hands as they worked, and even through the heavy cold-soaked wool of three pairs of socks, Joanne could feel the sensuous pleasure of the massage as pleasant little tingles ran up her legs and spine.

After a few minutes Bryant gently put the foot down and still without speaking pulled off her second boot. This foot, too, he then cradled in his hands and massaged, sending even more pleasant tingling through Joanne. She sat staring at his downcast face as he worked, wishing, wishing—but it was far too miserably cold for anything more than Bryant was doing.

At last he tenderly released her second foot, and his eyes rose to meet hers. A thick heavy beard covered the lower half of his face. Across his nose and cheeks he was sun- and windburned to a deep, rough-looking, reddish brown. But around his narrow red-rimmed eyes there was a ring of white, the area of skin shielded from the sun by his snow goggles, and this whiter skin gave him, Joanne thought, gazing steadily at him, a more vulnerable look than she'd ever seen on his face before. He looked terrible: dirty, unkempt, tired, so tired. And she'd never felt such a rush of love toward him, never felt such an aching need to hold him and love him. But that was impossible, she knew.

"Joanne," Bryant said, in his deep soft voice, "I could tell from your eyes just now how you voted and I came in to thank you. With the vote so close, had you voted against me I would have lost." He lifted a hand to press it gently against her cheek, his eyes brimming with love. "Thank you, sweetheart."

Tears flooded Joanne's eyes. *But when a storm blows up to blind you and you lose your footing on that narrow ridge to plummet twelve thousand feet to your death, will you thank me then?* "You're welcome," she murmured, her voice all but breaking, "I guess."

As she fought to hold back her tears, Bryant, with a warmly loving little smile, knelt before her, put his arms around her and drew her close. Her head rested on his shoulder while he leaned his head against hers. Even through her thick down jacket, Joanne could feel the warmth and strength of his body and was comforted. Bryant drew away again, smiling, then leaned forward to press his cheek against hers. He made no move to kiss her and wouldn't, Joanne knew. Her lips were swollen, sunburned and splitting, just as his were. A kiss wouldn't be pleasurable, it would hurt. Still as he drew away, smiling, he puckered his lips and blew her a kiss, from only a few inches away, and Joanne, smiling, blew a kiss back.

Bryant swung around to sit on the sleeping bag beside her. One hand rose to stroke her hair. Then Bryant's smile died away.

"I'd like to discuss something with you, sweetheart, if you're not too tired. I know how late it is and—"

"No, I'm not tired at all."

Bryant's hand dropped from her head as his face broke into a teasing grin. "That I can't believe. As strong as you've proved to be, a superwoman, you're not Wonder Woman, too, are you?''

Joanne smiled, then broke into a brief happy laugh. It was so wonderful to have Bryant here, so close. Even though they couldn't make the passionate love they had before, she felt wrapped in the wonder of how close they were, making love in a marvelous new way. When Bryant looked at her now, or touched her—the slightest touch—it was making love. His eyes, tender and warm, made love to her so powerfully she could feel it warm her from her frozen toes up. She reached out to slip her hand into one of his.

''Not too tired to talk, I mean. So shoot.''

Bryant's eyes left her face as he sighed. His fingers gave her hand a squeeze as he ran his tongue over his dry lips. After a second deep sigh, he faced her again.

''Joanne, I'd like to explain to you why I stalled so long on giving you an answer about your try for the summit. During the vote tonight, and especially right after, I found myself face to face with that, and in the very brief time since I've given it a lot of thought. From the very first I knew, of course, that if all went well I'd be taking this other route, the southeast ridge instead of the northeast spur. That meant I wouldn't be with the team during the final assault, that I wouldn't be with you, wouldn't be near enough to watch over you or protect you. That's one of the things that scared me, that made me push all thought of what you wanted out of my mind.''

Bryant paused, lifting one hand to press it hard across his brow. His narrow tired eyes came around to face her again. As his lips curled into a slight smile, he put his hand gently on her shoulder, giving her a slight squeeze, a touch that sent a fresh warm ripple of pleasure through Joanne. How open and loving his eyes were, for the very first time!

''So why did I feel so strongly that I had to be around to watch over you and protect you? Heaven knows you've proved to be tough and one heck of a good climber. But I think I know why. When I was eleven my father died. Almost the last thing he said to me, as he lay frail and gasping for breath on his hospital bed, was that I would have to become the man of the family now, take his place and watch over and take care of my mother and older sister.''

Again Bryant paused, a wry smile curling his lips. His hand dropped from Joanne's shoulder. ''I see now how absurd that was. I was eleven years old, not even in high school. My mother was a strong healthy woman. My father's long illness had cost us almost all the money we had, but my mother went right to work to support us. *She* protected and took care of *me*, not the other way around. My older sister looked after me, too, almost as though she were my mother. But in my own mind there was always the feeling that I *had* to be the man now and take care of them, that that's what being a man meant. So I always carried out the garbage—big deal!'' Bryant interrupted himself with a laugh. "And carried in the groceries and if my mother wanted the furniture moved, I was the one who moved it, things like that. To prove to myself I was protecting her, taking care of her, living up to what my father wanted.''

Bryant shook his head slowly. "So I've always had it in my mind, I guess, that if I love someone, a woman, it's up to me to watch over her and protect her." He reached for Joanne's hand to hold. "And I love you so very much, Joanne.''

His eyes expressed love, too. They gleamed with love. Joanne felt a fountain of joy splash up within her. She leaned close to press her head against his shoulder. "Oh, Jim, I love you, too, so terribly much.''

He rested his head against hers. "So again I want to thank you. Again you showed me—as my mother did years ago, as my sister did—how surprisingly strong and wonderfully loving women are. As you were making up your mind how to vote, I could see in your eyes exactly what you were going through. Loving me, you don't want me to risk my life. But loving me, you couldn't bear to hold back from me what I want so much.''

Bryant lifted his head, put his hands to Joanne's shoulder and gazed steadily into her eyes. "If you could be that strong and loving with me, then I can learn from you and be equally strong and loving with you. If you could allow me my dream, no matter how risky it is, then I can swallow my worry and allow you yours. I'll tell Bob in the morning that all restrictions are lifted, that you're to be treated just as he would treat any other team member.'' Bryant smiled. ''And under those terms, my money's on you. You'll be one of those still on your feet, still strong and healthy enough to make it all the way to the summit a few weeks from now. That's where we'll meet, on the highest peak of Dhaulagiri, on top of the world.''

Joanne's eyes filled with tears. ''Thank you, Jim. Promise me you *will* meet me there.''

''I give you my word.''

He put his arms around her and drew her close. Joanne could feel his heart beating fast and hard. In spite of the layers of clothing between them, she had never felt as close, never experienced a greater joy with him. Bryant's lips moved to her ear.

''Once this is all over, once we've left here and gone home again, will you marry me, sweetheart?''

Joanne's heart almost burst. ''Oh, yes. Yes, Jim, yes.''

His arms tightened around her and Joanne, her arms around him, held him as tightly as he held her. An eternity passed, a lifetime of loving and caring. Then, at last, Bryant slowly released his hold and drew back, his eyes seeking hers.

"Joanne, my dearest, if by any chance anything goes wrong and—"

Her pulse skipping, Joanne placed a finger against his lips. Her eyes flooded with tears. "Jim, you promised."

"I know, but—"

"No buts. You promised."

Bryant's eyes gazed intently into hers, then slowly he smiled. He leaned his head down, drew one of her hands up and pressed his lips very very lightly against the back of her hand. "You're right, I promised. Knowing that you'll be there to meet me—I love you, Joanne. God, I love you so terribly much!" Again they embraced.

This time they lowered themselves to lie on the sleeping bag as they held each other. Another eternity passed, even sweeter than the one that had gone before. Just as Bryant was saying good-night, whispering into her ear one last time that he loved her, a rough voice called in, "Hey, Jim, you in there?" It was Bob Freeland.

Bryant pulled his arms from Joanne and sat up. "Yes, Bob, come in."

The tent flap was lifted and Freeland came in. As Bryant had done earlier, he squatted on his haunches by the bag. His bearded face was grim, his eyes hard and angry. "I've been checking out some supplies. I know it's the middle of the night but I tried to sleep and couldn't, so I got up to check something out. Where is all this specially made, lightweight stuff you were talking about?''

Freeland's tone of voice, the way he spat out his words, showed clearly that he was boiling with resentment, that he had not in any way adjusted yet to the results of the vote. He was barely holding an explosive rage in check, Joanne could see.

"I've got it stacked right behind our tent," Bryant answered pleasantly. "Come on and I'll show you." His voice and manner were placating; he had won and could afford to be friendly now. He smiled a final good-night to Joanne and followed Freeland out of the tent.

Joanne had barely stuffed her sun cream, extra socks and boots down into her sleeping bag and crawled in herself, settling down for much needed sleep, when her tent flap was lifted again and a man came in. Freeland knelt by her bag. He wore a headlamp strapped to his brow and as Joanne faced him, it struck her that he looked half mad, like someone out of a horror movie: heavy matted beard, thick swollen lips, rough red skin except for the white circle around his fiery raging eyes, his skull covered by thick uncombed hair, with a light streaming out from above his eyes, half blinding her.

"Yes, Bob, what is it?" She felt a wave of fear and instinctively gasped for breath.

"Jim just told me that he's changing the rules

on me, that you're no longer restricted to base camp.''

Joanne found it even harder to breathe. Freeland looked so terribly angry, half out of his mind with rage. "Yes, I know."

Freeland glared down at her in fury, then spat out, "Well, you can just forget that, my girl. No way. I'll be in charge here once Jim leaves to kill himself, and you're not setting foot out of this camp. The damn fool can't have it both ways. He won his suicide vote by reminding everyone that we'd agreed to the rules back home, everyone knew of his plans and committed to them. So if we're abiding by the rules, then we're abiding by them, and one of the rules set down was that you weren't to go above this camp. If the rules stand, then the rules stand—he's not going to have his cake and eat it, too. I'm not going to have it on my conscience that I stood by and allowed you to risk your life just because that madman is intent on risking his. You hear me, Joanne? You're not setting foot outside of this camp.''

Joanne's heart sank. "But, Bob—"

"Don't you 'But, Bob' me!" Freeland snapped. "And if you think I can't enforce this prohibition, you're out of your mind. I'll be handing out the assignments, and if you don't abide by what I decide, I'll split up the team and take off, down the mountain I'll go, and at least three of the men will follow me, which will leave Jim stranded on the summit, if by some outside chance he lives long enough to make it. Just as he told us tonight, he needs us—needs all of us—needs the supply camps we'll be setting up—for his lunatic scheme to have any chance at all. You follow my orders or he's dead. And keep every word of this to yourself or he's dead. Good night, Joanne. Sleep tight.''

Looking possibly a bit less wild-eyed and crazy, Freeland swung around and left.

Joanne felt a sudden deep chill and fought her way deeper into her bag. All this way, all the excitement and high hopes she had had, and now—everything crashing down around her. Bryant, her love, putting his life at risk, while Freeland held her hostage in base camp. She would go crazy with worry, imprisoned here in camp, robbed of any chance to fulfill her own dreams of reaching the summit. As Joanne's eyes filled with tears, she knew it was going to be a long, long, miserable night, that the chances were she wouldn't sleep at all.

Though she lay awake for hours, she must have drifted off sometime before dawn, for she was awakened by the morning sounds and smells of the camp. She climbed out of her sleeping bag, pulled her boots on, laced them, grabbed her mittens and crawled out of her tent.

The first person she saw was Bryant, over at the far edge of the level area, strapping on a backpack. Ang Darje was beside him, his backpack already on. With a leaden weight of fear in her heart, Joanne walked over to them.

Just before she reached him, Bryant swung around. As he saw her, his eyes flashed—but with what looked far more like rage than love. Seeing his anger, Joanne felt stunned. The night before they had parted on such warm terms; he had repeatedly told her he loved her, had asked her to marry him. Yet now, a few brief hours later—

Trembling, Joanne walked up and touched his arm. "Jim, surely you weren't going to leave without even saying goodbye? Why didn't you wake me an hour ago?"

"Of course I was going to wake you," Bryant muttered between pressed lips. "I wouldn't dream of leaving without one final goodbye."

Bryant's attention returned to the straps he was buckling. Joanne watched in dismay, her heart sick. After a moment she asked, "Jim, what's the matter? You're terribly angry at me, obviously. Why?"

Bryant didn't reply. He turned to the sirdar and helped him adjust the weight of his backpack. Joanne ran her sore tongue around her dry swollen lips, trying to moisten and soften them. Minutes passed while Bryant and Darje worked on their gear, gathered additional hardware, made their final preparations to leave. A circle of climbers formed a few feet back, silently watching. Joanne felt deeply sick and terribly exposed. Bryant mustn't leave feeling like this, without even telling her what had upset him, giving her no chance to defend herself. But against what charge did she need to defend herself? It didn't make sense! They had never been closer than they'd been last night, they'd sworn their love, had agreed to marry. But now, in the cold clear light of dawn, on this frozen level of ground almost four miles high—what could possibly have happened between last night and now?

Freeland broke through the circle and came striding up. As Joanne swung quickly around to face him, she sensed at once that he was far calmer now. He looked tired and worried but no longer distraught. "How's it going, Jim?" he asked as he reached Joanne's side and stopped.

"Everything's fine, thanks." Bryant tightened one final strap and faced the circle of climbers seeing him off, smiling and waving.

Freeland held back momentarily, then stepped forward and impulsively put his arms around Bryant and embraced him. "For God's sake, man, take care," he said fiercely.

"Stop worrying, will you?"

The two men broke apart again, and Joanne felt even more panicked. Bryant was about to leave—without a soft or loving word to her. She mustn't let him; even if it meant exposing her love for him to the entire team, she *had* to find some way to stop him, to get him to talk to her before he left. She stepped forward and clasped his arm.

"Please, Jim, I've got to talk to you."

He glared down at where her hand touched

his jacket as though the touch burned him. Impatiently, he brushed her hand off. "What about?"

No matter who was within earshot, Joanne couldn't restrain herself. "You know what about! Now cut this out and talk to me."

For the first time, Bryant's eyes moved to where his gaze met hers. After a moment, with a taut shrug, he started off, away from Darje and Freeland. Joanne followed.

They came to a stop some twenty feet away. With the early-morning snow swirls and the ever-present wind, the noise level was such that they couldn't possibly be overheard. The problem would be in hearing each other.

"All right, Jim, what are you feeling angry about?" Joanne asked, the tears in her lashes threatening to freeze. She blinked rapidly.

Bryant stared intently at her for some time, then he answered, in a calm neutral voice, "Bob told me this morning that he had spoken to you last night and you've changed your mind, that you have no interest in trying for the summit after all. You'd rather stay here in base camp."

Joanne could feel herself sway. She felt suddenly so dizzy, so out of breath, it was a struggle to stay upright. "Bob told you that?"

"Bob told me that." After a pause Bryant added, "I've never known Bob to lie so I assume it's true. Is it?"

"Well—"

Bryant grabbed her arm, whether to steady

her or to shake the truth out of her, Joanne couldn't tell. "Is it, dammit? Did you tell Bob you're not going to try for the summit after all?"

"Well—" Fresh tears flooded Joanne's eyes. She felt so dizzy, so breathless, such a terrible deep-down sickness. *No, I didn't tell him that,* she wanted to cry. But she didn't quite dare. Freeland had told her to keep every word of their conversation to herself, or else.

Bryant gave her arm a hard shake, then released his hold. The fury in him seemed to drain away, giving way to despair. "All right, you've answered plainly enough. Getting your chance at the summit meant everything in the world to you—until I said okay, you had it. Now suddenly it means nothing. After Bob told me this morning, I kept thinking of your friend Scott back home. That day we worked in the warehouse together, he told me how terribly much he loves you, how much he hoped that after this climb was over, you'd return home to marry him. But once a man succumbs, once he offers his love and devotion, you have no more use for him, is that how it works? I kept thinking, too, about that night in Kathmandu, the night you had someone in your room and wouldn't allow me in, and Bob didn't come back to our room all night. Now that you've conquered me, planted your flag of conquest through my skull, is Bob Freeland next on your list? Bob isn't happy with women climbers; he fought against having you on the team. Naturally it pleases him to have you prefer to stay right here in base camp. When next I see you, will I get the happy word that you no longer care about me, that Bob is number one? Is that what awaits me?''

Bryant's eyes, steely hard now, gazed steadily into hers. His voice was cold, dispassionate, as though it didn't truly matter how she answered. Now that he'd seen behind her facade, seen her stripped of pretense, he didn't like what he saw. He felt enormous contempt for the woman he saw. Joanne felt herself shrivel and freeze under this indictment. Still she did her best to look steadily back at him, to stop her trembling, to answer him in a calm sure voice.

"No, Jim, that's not how it works. I love you—you, no one else. I've never loved anyone else, quite possibly I never will. I'm fond of Scottie; I've always been deeply fond of him, but I was never in love with him. I tried numerous times to tell him so, and while I've been away I think he's finally come to terms with it. As for Bob Freeland—'' Joanne felt a fresh wave of dizziness and her voice died away.

Bryant again grabbed her arm, his touch cold and harsh, but it steadied her. "Yes, about Bob?''

"Well, in Kathmandu that night—'' As Joanne's eyes caught again on Bryant's hard unforgiving gaze, she felt a wave of hopelessness. "Jim, there really is a very good explanation, but I don't feel free to tell you right now and in any case ı don't think you'd believe me. I like Bob, but I have absolutely no romantic interest in him nor does he have any in me. You're the only man in the world I care about romantically, and I love you so much! Last night you asked me to marry you, and one way or another I'll see that you live up to marrying me or—or—''

Bryant's lips wavered into a smile, and the first hint of softening came into his eyes. "Or?"

Struggling to answer his smile with one of her own, Joanne cried, "Or I'll haunt you forever. Oh, Jim, you promised me—you gave me your word—that you'd live through this climb and you've got to live up to that promise! You won't know a single peaceful day on the other side if you don't!''

Bryant burst into a brief laugh. He grabbed hold of her by the arms and pulled her to him for a brief intense hug. As he let go again, he pinned her under his hard gaze.

"And you agreed to meet me on the summit. I'm holding you to that. If you love me, that's where we'll meet!'' His arms released her, and he strode past her to return to where Ang Darje stood waiting.

The team stood silently watching as Bryant, after one last wave, hiked off with the sturdy sirdar a few feet behind, each of them weighted down with greater poundage than climbers at this altitude ordinarily carried. Was there any chance at all they would make it?

As Joanne stared after them, Greg Reed

stepped up to her side. He stood for a moment with her as they both watched the departing figures disappear into the swirls of snow. Reed clasped her shoulder, reassuring her with his touch.

"They're both extremely strong determined men, both physically and mentally, and the older I get the more I realize there are few words truer than these: 'Where there's a will, there's a way.'"

Joanne glanced quickly around at Reed, her heart lifting. "Then you think they actually have a chance?"

"I think they're both mad," Reed answered, "but I wouldn't rule out their chance to succeed."

CHAPTER FIFTEEN

THE ARDUOUS WORK of setting up advance camps continued.

The ascent to the summit via the northeast spur presented no great technical difficulties. The only problems were trying to live and work at altitudes so high that it was impossible to become completely acclimatized, which meant that every minor task called for more energy than it seemed possible to muster; the bone-chilling cold; the fierce ever-present wind; the constant threat of storm. The climbers—it seemed to Joanne—were like insect-size children crawling up the soft white breast of a dearly beloved mother, a mother so cold and indifferent she might, if she became aware of their presence, send them tumbling to their deaths with one annoyed puff of breath. Other climbers had made it to where they were now, above the twenty-thousand-foot mark with only seven thousand feet still to go to the summit, only to be nonchalantly driven back by treacherous storms. The White Lady did not take to all comers and with icy blasts of breath blew back those who displeased her. There was no such thing as assured success on the Mountain of Storms.

After Bryant's and the sirdar's departure, the days in base camp fell into a reasonably routine pattern. Each morning, weather permitting, a group of three or four climbers carried supplies up to Advance Camp I, which had been established on a platform cut in the snow at 21,400 feet. There was a constant shift up and back, some men staying overnight in the camp, others returning to base camp to rest and, as much as possible, recuperate. From Advance Camp I, Freeland and the two Mandel brothers climbed up a gently rising slope of two thousand feet to establish Advance Camp II at 23,500 feet, anchoring fixed ropes to aid those who followed.

In base camp, where she had little to do other than to help sort and pack supplies, Joanne was kept informed of the progress of the advance groups. During the day she did her best to stay busy, reading or writing in her journal when there was nothing else to do, so the days passed with a fair amount of ease. It was only at night, after she'd retired to her tent to try to sleep, that anxiety over Bryant and dismay over her own situation moved in to churn and anger her. If only Bryant made it safely through, she wouldn't care that her own dreams had been blasted, she told herself, but this helped very little: all it did was zero in on her deepest, most frantic worry, the ever-present fear that she would never see Jim Bryant again.

With this fear grinding more and more deeply into her, Joanne couldn't sleep; she lost her appetite; she wished she could let go and cry, but she could not and would not. A single tear would somehow be defeat, an admission that Bryant might not make it. She would *not* give in to grief because she would not allow even the possibility that grief was called for. Jim was strong, stubborn, determined, the most powerful and most willful man she had ever known. The White Lady would sense his value and with a slight imperceptible smile she would welcome him; instead of blasting him off the ridge to his death, she would wrinkle her white skin just a slight bit to cradle him, would play amused foster mother to him and keep him safe. *Oh, surely, beautiful, beautiful Lady of Storms, you will do that, won't you?*

On the fourth day after Bryant's departure, Freeland returned to base camp, accompanied by Charles Mandel, John Naylor and Courtland Mitchell. Joanne was caught by surprise by Freeland's return. The schedule he had set up had called for him to be in advance of the main body of the team from here to the summit. He was one of the few men still reasonably hale and hearty. Sore throats were endemic among the men. At least half were suffering with miserable colds. Two had come down with ear infections. Digestive upset, dizziness, lack of balance were rampant. Almost everyone complained of insomnia. Worst of all, extreme fatigue dogged everyone's steps, to where the simplest tasks seemed gigantic. These were the daily reports Joanne had grown accustomed to, and the one thing she hadn't expected was to see Freeland return to base camp.

As she watched him approach, he looked, it seemed to Joanne, like some creature from outer space in a cheaply made science-fiction film. No part of his face was visible. She knew who it was only because John Naylor had preceded him into camp and had told her Freeland was right behind. Not an inch of Freeland's face could be seen, only huge goggles and a dark snow-flecked scarf wrapped around his chin and cheeks. He carried someone on his back and was bent over almost double, struggling along. In spite of her anger at him, Joanne hurried forward to try to help.

As she reached Freeland, he stopped moving and allowed his burden to slide to the ground. It was Courtland Mitchell, Joanne saw; he seemed to be asleep or unconscious. Freeland stood with his legs apart to steady himself, swaying dizzily back and forth, gasping for breath. "Help me get him into a tent and we'll give him oxygen," Freeland gasped.

Within a few minutes, with the oxygen mask firmly in place, Mitchell revived. "He said this morning that he wasn't feeling well," Freeland explained, "so we left Camp II and headed back toward Camp I, and just before we got there he keeled over. Reed was there, gave him oxygen and checked him out, then decided it wasn't safe to leave him there overnight, so I brought him down here. In the morning we'll send him back down the mountain with a porter.'' Freeland paused a moment, looking weary and beaten. ''One more down,'' he muttered under his breath, and left the tent.

At dinner twenty minutes later Joanne saw Freeland glance her way repeatedly. As dessert was served, he rose, walked over to John Naylor, who was seated next to Joanne, and asked John if he minded changing places with him. He wished to speak to Joanne.

Naylor rose with his usual glum expression and moved to the other end of the table. Freeland's red-rimmed white-circled eyes caught on Joanne's face, and she heard him sigh.

''Listen, Joanne, I don't suppose you're going to believe this, but ever since that night in your tent I've been furious at myself for what I did.'' His dry swollen lips broke into a reasonable facsimile of his familiar crooked grin. At sight of his smile, Joanne felt much of her anger at him drain away. From the first moment of meeting until now she'd always liked this man, and in spite of everything she still did.

Freeland gulped down a mouthful of hot tea, then his eyes caught hers again. He grinned even more openly. ''Quite possibly I've been as angry at myself as you've been at me. I got carried away that night and said things I didn't mean, that I shouldn't have said. I was just so wrought up about Jim—''

Smiling, Joanne gave his arm a friendly squeeze. "Bob, I know. I understood even when it was happening. It wasn't easy for either of us, watching someone we love undertake something so risky. I knew I was only an innocent bystander getting shot down because you couldn't hit the main target.''

Freeland's crooked grin came again and he gulped down more tea. When next he faced her his grin died away. "Still I shouldn't have gunned you down just because I was so furious at Jim and the team. Then once I had—well, I didn't know how to back out of the corner I'd put myself in. Put both of us in. What I'm trying to say is that even though I didn't want you with us back home before I knew you, from the time we started up I could see that you were just what Jim said you were, a damn good climber, one of the best we've got, and somehow, some way, you're so damn healthy, too!''

His voice took on a perplexed displeased edge. "I always figured women were the weaker sex, so I just can't figure it out, but I've got men falling down all around me and you're still doing all right, as far as I can see. Is that accurate? Are you as okay as you seem?''

Joanne smiled. She felt warmed inside by Freeland's words. Again she touched his arm in friendliness. "Yes, I'm okay, but I haven't been exposed to the higher altitudes yet. A thousand feet higher up I might collapse faster than any man has. It's something I don't know as I've never been this high before.'' After a slight pause Joanne added, her pulse picking up, ''All I ever asked was the chance to try, to see what I could do. No special favors, just an equal chance. Then if I fall behind and can't make it, it's no one's fault but my own.''

Freeland sat looking at her, his face glum. He gulped down the rest of his tea, plunked his cup back onto the table and stuck out his hand. ''Okay, if you're big enough to let bygones be bygones, you've got your chance. From now on I don't even know you're a woman, you're just one of the team. I've got too many climbers ill to do anything else, so I don't suppose you'll ever believe that this is the way I really wanted it. I was just too stubborn to know how to back down on what I'd said. I had to be forced to come crawling to you, to ask your forgiveness.'' As they shook hands, Freeland grinned again. ''So all is forgiven and we're friends again?''

Joanne smiled. ''Of course.'' At last, at last, a chance at her dream!

In the morning Courtland Mitchell was somewhat improved but still weak and dizzy. He put up very little protest at the suggestion that he be escorted back down the mountain by one of the porters. Charles Mandel had so many physical problems—a miserable cough, a wretched sore throat, an infection in each ear, compounded by dizziness and an inability to hold down his food—that he stayed in base camp, as did Jack Goodson, who was also ill. Freeland suggested they descend with Mitchell and the porter, but they objected heatedly to that, so it was agreed they'd remain in base camp, helping with the movement of supplies. Right after breakfast Freeland, Naylor and Joanne loaded up and began to carry supplies up to Advance Camp I.

That evening the weather turned foul on them and for two fretful, endless days they were stuck in Advance Camp I while a snowstorm threatened to bury their tents. On the third day the weather cleared and Freeland and Joanne, accompanied by Greg Reed, began a carry to Advance Camp II. This would be the highest that Joanne had yet been, and she figuratively kept her fingers crossed that she would be able to acclimatize sufficiently to stay in the camp. The carry from I to II was slow and grim, a day-long exertion, the wind, the snow and the altitude making it miserable. The scenery was spectacular, of course, but this did little to make the carry easier. At last they straggled into Advance Camp II, frozen and exhausted.

Again the weather turned bad, the White Mountain showing her utter scorn for their presence. Freeland developed an acute case of laryngitis. Joanne suffered with a burning sore throat. Two of the three men who had been holding down the camp—Orin Thatcher and Parke Gilford—feeling ill and beaten, took advantage of the first clear morning to descend to

Camp I. For all the brave talk earlier of a mass assault on the summit with every one of the climbers taking that final step to plant his foot on the peak, it began to look as though not a single team member would be able to go any higher. With each new storm the threat of being buried alive in their tents under punishing snow became more real. The White Mountain was no lady. She was a demon in disguise, a devil draped in a lady's pure white dress.

If there was any hope of keeping their date to meet Bryant, someone had to push on up another thousand feet to establish a third advance camp at 24,500 feet, then a fourth at over 25,000 feet, from which camp an attempt on the summit could be made. When at last the weather cleared enough for the team to push on, Freeland was too ill to try; he lay in his sleeping bag burning with fever. Greg Reed gave him antibiotics, then took charge of all planning. Reed, though bothered by a cold, was still on his feet. Joanne's sore throat was slowly improving, or at least she told herself it was. John Naylor grumbled about his sluggish digestion, but apart from that he was healthy. The three of them, accompanied by two Sherpas, would make the preliminary carry to a higher elevation. They would scout out a place and establish Advance Camp III.

The morning they started out was reasonably clear. To their intense relief there was no heavy storm that day. The climb proved to be shorter and less exhausting than the earlier climb to II. The campsite they settled on, nestled among rock outcrops, was less exposed to the winds. In the late afternoon, as they began settling in, they took time to note and appreciate the incredible view. From where they stood, almost five miles up the mountain, they could see Tibet, southern Nepal and, far to the south, the plains of India. As exhausted as she was, Joanne felt a quick thrill run through her. This was something no one could ever take from her; this moment was hers forever. Then a shadow moved across her pleasure, and after another moment she turned away, ready to plunge into the debilitating task of settling in.

She did better, she had found, when she stayed busy. Too busy to think. This was not overly difficult. One of the first casualties of these high altitudes was rational thought. Joanne found this true for herself and others mentioned it, too. Her mind became as frozen as her flesh. It slowed to a crawl and then seemed to stop. No more an unending flow of thought every conscious moment. Often, at midday, Joanne would suddenly come to for a moment and realize she had no idea what she had done in the hours just past. One evening she could not remember a single thing she had done, a single thought she had had, for the entire day.

Far from making the days more difficult, this helped to make them easier. She simply did not have the mental energy to worry about Bryant, to stay in the agonized state of fear she had lived in in base camp the first few days after his departure. Whenever conscious thought returned, she would immediately think of him, wonder about him, worry about him, but then the train of thought would disappear, buried under the frozen wastes. Up in these altitudes, her body operated, insofar as it operated at all, pretty much on its own, no longer under the direction of her conscious thought. Even a normal awareness of the passage of time was lost. Hours drifted by, leaving no trace, while a given moment could come sharply into focus and seem an eternity. Waking blended into sleeping, and sleeping into waking. The line between was wavy and blurry, just as the line between reality and dream became indistinct. Those who could, Joanne among them, slugged on, wanting to make it to the top, determined to do so, yet at the same time no longer really caring. At this altitude nothing in life—even death—really mattered very much. One just kept on, for some reason or no reason, or one stopped. Either way. Because nothing rose up to stop her, Joanne kept on.

Sometimes, as she slipped into a sleeping-dreaming state, Joanne would sense Bryant's presence so acutely that she would smile in welcome. He was so close in those moments that he was *there*, she could see him, reach out to touch him. Suddenly they would be sitting together out on the back patio of his home, sipping wine, sunk in utter contentment. Or, hand in hand, they would be walking toward the bedroom eager to plunge into a world of sensual delight. In those moments, as his strong hand held hers, she knew they were married. Not only married, they had two children. She could see them. A sturdy, broad-faced little boy with reddish brown hair and freckles across his nose, a son who looked exactly like Jim, and a darling little girl who also had reddish brown hair and freckles.

As she viewed them with bursting joy, it would cross Joanne's mind that it wasn't fair: both children looked exactly like Jim while neither one resembled her. But they were so adorable and she loved them so much—and then abruptly she wasn't with Jim and the children anymore. She could no longer feel their warm young bodies in her arms, she was lying in a sleeping bag on the icy breast of a mountain, stiff and cold, miserably cold, and her lips were swollen and cracked, her skin dry and burned, her throat so sore she could hardly swallow. For a moment she would gasp in pain, trying to breathe, to orient herself, to keep her head from spinning so and her whole body from aching so dreadfully, then in time—whether minutes later or hours or an eternity—she would drift away again and Jim and the children would be back, and she'd smile in delight because it all seemed so real. Surely *that* was the reality, not the cold-ness and the pain.

Winds more ferocious than any they had yet encountered kept them imprisoned in Advance Camp III for four days. The elevation of Camp III, almost twenty-five thousand feet, marked the altitude at which oxygen was normally used full-time, but earlier expeditions had placed men on the summit without the use of oxygen, and during the planning of this expedition, it had been decided that in order to keep supplies within reasonable limits they would follow the earlier teams: there would be no full-time use of oxygen. Each camp was of course supplied with oxygen for medical use, but that was all. If others had made it to the top without oxygen, they would, too—or they wouldn't make it at all.

During their four days of captive inactivity in III, an argument broke out one morning as to what day of the week it was, and what date. Greg Reed said it was May 3. This gave them eight days before they were due to meet Bryant. Naylor said nothing for a moment, then grunted that the doctor was crazy. He'd missed a day. It was May 4.

"You're mistaken," Reed snapped irritably.

Again Naylor didn't answer at once. His response was markedly delayed, yet when he next spoke it was as though he had picked up the argument the moment Reed had dropped it. "You're the one who's crazy. I've been marking my left wrist each morning with ink. This is the fourth."

Reed shot Naylor a withering look and turned to Joanne for confirmation, but all she could do, when it finally struck her that she should respond, was to shake her head in bewilderment. She hadn't the least idea who was right, or whether either one was. Maybe they were both wrong.

Finally, on their fifth day in Advance Camp III, the morning dawned windless and warmer. The two men and Joanne, working as quickly as they could, which in other elevations would have seemed ludicrously slow, packed up their sleeping bags, tents and ropes. Pamba Tenzing, the assistant sirdar, and Sangay, their cook, loaded up the food bag, stoves and fuel, and the party began climbing up to find a site for and establish Advance Camp IV. Reed led the way, Joanne following, with Naylor and the two sherpas behind. Just after midday they reached a sheltered snow bowl flat enough to pitch their tents in comfort. Working as hard as they could push themselves, they had three tents pitched and securely weighted down before the expected afternoon storm blew up. Wheezing for breath, they gathered in one tent and in the late afternoon enjoyed the food from the high-altitude food bag. Outside the wind whipped and new snow fell.

The next day, also warm and clear in the morning, they rested and settled in more securely. At midday they found themselves greeting, with gleeful shouts, unexpected company: Bob

Freeland and Claude Mandel came staggering into camp. Though Freeland's voice was still little more than a hoarse whisper, his temperature had dropped and he claimed he felt fine. He didn't look fine, Joanne thought; he looked haggard and ill. But then, she reminded herself, so did everyone else. She knew how thin and bluish she looked, without even a beard to cover the ravages of the climb. Veins on Greg Reed's forehead stood out in a startling, frightening way. His face looked like granite about to break and crumple, and whenever he spoke his voice was snappish and angry. With each passing day he seemed to be wrapping himself more tightly in a paranoid rage. Naylor, perhaps because he'd been so glum and gloomy beforehand, looked more like himself now than anyone else did. He was still pessimistic and grumpy, but now these traits, perhaps through long familiarity, seemed appealing and endearing. When he muttered complaints about his digestion, which was even more sluggish, he said, Joanne felt moved to warm compassion. Poor John. He seemed so wretched. At the same time he was still on his feet, still one of those most able to move about and work. If any of them made the summit, John Naylor would.

The following day there was no dawn. There was only storm. The wind whipped with such force that no one dared venture outside. They were trapped in a cold, icy, violent world. The White Lady had apparently taken note of their presence, these insect-bugs crawling up her flesh, and seemed intent on slapping them away, on punishing them. The next day was the same: there was no letup. At the altitude of their camp, close to twenty-six thousand feet, there was no hope of acclimatizing. They had to move soon, either up or down, if only the White Lady would allow it!

At last came a clear quiet day. Over breakfast, with everyone speaking, moving, living at an ultraslow speed, Freeland announced he was going for the summit. Joanne said she was, too. Naylor grunted, a sound that seemed to indicate he was going along. Greg Reed said nothing. Claude Mandel, sitting cross-legged in a corner of the cramped tent, sat staring down at his cup of tea, as though looking for a leaf to read.

"Claude, are you coming?" Freeland rasped out, in his hoarse pained whisper.

Claude shook his head, as though lost in a dream. "No, not today."

When Freeland asked the doctor, Reed's eyes shot up and he glared, as though insulted by the question. "You heard what he said. Not today!" Reed repeated.

Greg's losing his mind, Joanne thought; Claude's losing his. And I'm losing mine. And Freeland's lost his. And Bryant? *Oh, Jim,* she thought and almost burst out crying. She felt light-headed, dizzy, almost as though she were falling down drunk. The southeast-ridge route, which Bryant and the sirdar had taken, joined the main body of the White Lady a thousand feet below the summit. If Bryant was still on his feet, still moving, still alive, he would have joined them here in Camp IV by now. Or would he have? She shook her head. At some point in time she'd known, but now she couldn't remember clearly what it was she'd known. He'd said he'd see her on the summit. That she remembered.

As Freeland rose to his feet, she pushed up to leave too. She and Freeland and Naylor—they were leaving to try for the peak. Onward and upward, or die.

They moved one by one out of the tent to find themselves facing a noisy gale. Freeland roped himself and started off. Joanne went next, followed by the assistant sirdar Pamba Tenzing, with Naylor bringing up the rear. During her growing-up years, her father had often told Joanne that when you climb high enough you are completely alone. No matter how many others are with you, or how close they are, you are alone. Joanne trudged along, lost in nonthought. There was only the snow, the ice, the wind and herself. Isolated. Alone. Yet not lonely. Her stiff muscles, crying out in pain, kept her company, as did her rebellious lungs, screaming for richer air. But slowly the warmth of movement quieted her pain, and her bodily rebellion died down.

The climb was easy at first, a narrow ridge leading up. As they climbed higher, they found the ridge was composed of a dizzying series of snowy spires. Freeland stopped moving and seemed confused. Where was the summit? The wind grew more violent, making their perches on the narrow ridge dangerous. After a brief stop, Freeland trudged on. Joanne followed. Where was Jim? He should have joined them in camp, or at camp, or near camp. Was this the day? She had heard a discussion earlier as to the day and date, but she couldn't recall what she'd heard. She would have worried or cried out, had she had the breath, the energy, to do so. But she didn't.

Freeland came to a stop. He had reached the summit. Before long Joanne joined him, then Pamba Tenzing, then Naylor. Each stood squinting at the others, then off at the clouds, while the wind whipped around them. Each was alone. There was no sign of Bryant. Of course not. The White Lady hadn't welcomed him or had wanted him for herself. That was it, Joanne thought. The White Lady, recognizing his value, had wanted him for herself. In her heart she cried. She had achieved her goal. She stood 26,795 feet in the air, on top of Dhaulagiri, the sixth highest mountain in the world, but her victory had proved too costly, as many victories do. She would never see Jim Bryant again, she would never see her love again. Tears filled her eyes. She watched as though from miles away as Freeland unrolled the flag he carried and planted it in the snow. He drew out his camera and began taking pictures. The process was agonizingly slow. Joanne did her best to smile, to part her swollen split lips, as Freeland swung his camera to capture her.

After snapping her picture, Freeland turned his camera on Naylor. Naylor, too managed to pull his lips into a smile. After the snap he worked his way slowly over toward Joanne, to where he could speak to her. There was a glint of wonder and triumph in his red-rimmed eyes.

"You told me that one day we'd both make it here. I thought you were crazy but you were right." He shook his head in wonderment. "I guess there's life in the old guy yet."

"Of course."

Joanne tried to smile as she said this, to share John Naylor's sense of triumph, but she didn't feel triumphant, she felt tired and heartsick. She hadn't won. The White Lady had. She had allowed Joanne to conquer her but only as a gesture of contempt: *You can have your foolish puny victory because I have your love. He is with me now where he will remain forever. Forever with me, never with you. Never, ever with you. Now that he is mine, you will never see him again.*

Tenzing, the assistant sirdar, unfurled a bright Nepalese flag, and it too, was planted and photographed. After this snap Freeland's camera broke. With a look of surprise married to indifference, he jammed the camera back into his pack. Naylor had moved several feet away from Joanne. Each climber stood gazing at the surrounding clouds again, buffeted by the fierce cold wind, each one alone, lost in his own world. Now that they were atop the White Lady, they could see little of her, and nothing beyond her. The clouds were too thick, the wind whipping the snow up to meet the clouds.

Time passed. How long? Joanne couldn't judge. She came to with the realization that Freeland was leading the descent.

She followed, glad to be moving. Once again they were traversing the narrow ridge, so knife-edged at one point that they straddled it. Suddenly Freeland stopped moving. Joanne stopped moving and stared. Her heart pounded wildly. She was hallucinating again; surely that was it. She could see two men passing Freeland, approaching her. The lead man was tall, broad, powerful—he looked just like Jim. *I'm fantasizing,* Joanne told herself. *I've seen him so often, felt his presence so often....* She stood and waited. Instead of evaporating into the fierce wind, whipped up into the clouds, the lead man kept moving toward her, becoming more and more solid in appearance. Oh, it was Jim!

Of course it's Jim, Joanne snapped at herself. *Who else have I ever fantasized about?* Her lungs screamed for air; she was too fascinated to move. The lead man continued toward her, but he was wrapped in so many clothes, his face hidden by a heavy beard, a scarf and goggles, it was impossible to know who it was. *It's Greg Reed, of course!* Joanne told herself; *Claude Mandel with him. They decided to go for the summit today after all. Of course.* At last, making sense out of what she saw, she realized she wasn't fantasizing. The lead man was only a few feet away, moving steadily forward against the wind. He reached out, put an arm around her shoulder and drew her awkwardly against him. He lifted his goggles and grinned at her. Jim.

"I'll see you back in camp," he said. "We'll be only a couple of hours behind you." What she could see of his face was gaunt and thin, his eyes were bloodshot, his voice hoarse. But, alive and moving, still alive and moving. He was the most beautiful sight Joanne had ever seen.

"It's windy up there, be careful," Joanne said, for she couldn't think of what else to say. He was alive. And well. And in two hours they would be together again in camp.

Bryant's grin broadened. His hand gave her arm a loving squeeze. He put his goggles back into place and moved on by.

With a nod of acknowledgment, Ang Darje passed her, following Jim up the ridge. Joanne turned to watch, but soon both climbers disappeared into the swirling snow. With a delighted, relieved heart, Joanne began moving again, following Freeland down.

In a little less than two hours after Joanne's group was safely back in Camp IV, Bryant and Darje joined them. As everyone sat huddled together inside the one tent, munching food from the high-altitude food bag, little was said. After the initial expressions of surprise and joy at Bryant's and Darje's safe return, no one had the energy to say much more.

Joanne sat at Bryant's right. She kept glancing around to reassure herself that he was really there, that it wasn't all just a dream. Once, when she looked up from her food to glance around at him, she found Bryant facing her. His lips broke apart in a smile. He looked tired and spent. He looked dreadful—and beautiful. His eyes said he loved her. *I love you, too,* Joanne thought, and she pressed against him a moment before lowering her eyes to continue eating. Bryant was back, was safe. Together they had conquered the White Lady, the treacherous, stormy White Lady.

IN THE MORNING the weather was surprisingly mild, as though the White Lady had not resented their climbing her, as though she was shrugging it off with a smile. The group worked silently gathering everything together, no one wasting energy on unnecessary words. Darje led the way down with Bryant and Joanne, the others following. As befitted decent guests, they tried to bury everything they couldn't take with them, leaving no debris behind. Weather permitting, they would reach base camp within a few days. There they would rest and relax for a day or two before descending the rest of the way. In Pokhara they would reclaim the clothing and other property they'd left there, fly to Kathmandu, then home.

Home.

Joanne felt again the joy of knowing Bryant was all right. Before leaving for his assault on the summit, he had proposed to her. Surely he had meant his proposal, and they would spend the rest of their lives together.

The weather stayed pleasant. As they descended the slopes, they closed up one advance camp after another, erasing all signs of human habitation. Days later, as the group trudged one by one into base camp, a whoop of joy went up from those who were occupying the camp. That night the dining tent rang with laughter and song. Joanne was one of the last to leave the festivities to go to her tent. She was delighted to hear Bryant excuse himself to follow her.

After she'd reached her tent and crawled inside, Bryant raised the flap and crawled in after her. In the flickering lamplight he crouched down beside where she sat on the sleeping bag and grinned at her. He leaned close and gingerly pressed his lips very gently against hers.

As he drew back, Joanne felt waves of love flow through her at the look in his eyes. He swung around to sit beside her on the bag and reached for her hand.

"Joanne, sweetheart, I've had a chance to talk with Bob, and I owe you the most abject apology. I should have believed you, should have trusted you." A shadow fell across his face as he squeezed her hand, his eyes searching hers. "Can you forgive me, sweetheart?"

Joanne pulled her hand free and threw her arms around him. "Oh, Jim, of course. I'm just so glad you're safe. I love you so much."

"And I love you."

His arms went around her, and they sat holding each other close, swaying slightly, loving and dreaming.

ABOUT THE AUTHOR

Jacqueline Louis knew from the time she was very young that she wanted to be a writer. She was also determined to marry and have children. Over the years this native Californian has achieved both goals. While raising her sons, she managed to find enough time to write and sell more than 200 confession stories. When her youngest son reached sixteen and obtained his driver's license, thus relieving her of chauffeuring duties, she decided it was time to try longer fictions. Since then she has published six romance novels. *Love's Stormy Heights* is her first Superromance.

Although she works at home, six days a week, Jacqueline confesses that when she's writing her characters become more real to her than her husband. He understands, though, and knows that as soon as the manuscript is in the mail, he'll become number one again.

HARLEQUIN PREMIERE AUTHOR EDITIONS

6 top Harlequin authors – 6 of their best book

1. **JANET DAILEY** Giant of Mesabi
2. **CHARLOTTE LAMB** Dark Master
3. **ROBERTA LEIGH** Heart of the Lion
4. **ANNE MATHER** Legacy of the Past
5. **ANNE WEALE** Stowaway
6. **VIOLET WINSPEAR** The Burning Sands

**Harlequin is proud to offer these 6 exciting romance novels b
6 of our most popular authors. In brand-new beautifully
designed covers, each Harlequin Premiere Author Edition
is a bestselling love story—a contemporary, compelling and
passionate read to remember!**

Available wherever paperback books are sold, *or* through
Harlequin Reader Service. Simply complete and mail the coupon below.

Yours FREE, with a home subscription to SUPERROMANCE™

Now you never have to miss reading the newest **SUPERROMANCES**... because they'll be delivered right to your door.

Start with your **FREE** LOVE BEYOND DESIRE. You'll be enthralled by this powerful love story... from the moment Robin meets the dark, handsome Carlos and finds herself involved in the jealousies, bitterness and secret passions of the Lopez family. Where her own forbidden love threatens to shatter her life.

Your **FREE** LOVE BEYOND DESIRE is only the beginning. A subscription to **SUPERROMANCE** lets you look forward to a long love affair. Month after month, you'll receive four love stories of heroic dimension. Novels that will involve you in spellbinding intrigue, forbidden love and fiery passions.

You'll begin this series of sensuous, exciting contemporary novels... written by some of the top romance novelists of the day... with four every month.

And this big value... each novel, almost 400 pages of compelling reading... is yours for only $2.50 a book. Hours of entertainment every month for so little. Far less than a first-run movie or pay-TV. Newly published novels, with beautifully illustrated covers, filled with page after page of delicious escape into a world of romantic love... delivered right to your home

Harlequin reaches
into the hearts and minds
of women across America
to bring you

Harlequin American Romance ™

YOURS FREE!

Enter a uniquely exciting
new world with

Harlequin
American Romance ™

Harlequin American Romances are the first romances to explore today's love relationships. These compelling novels reach into the hearts and minds of women across America... probing the most intimate moments of romance, love and desire.

You'll follow romantic heroines and irresistible men as they boldly face confusing choices. Career first, love later? Love without marriage? Long-distance relationships? All the experiences that make love real are captured in the tender, loving pages of **Harlequin American Romances.**

What makes American women so different when it comes to love? Find out with **Harlequin American Romance!**

Send for your introductory FREE book now!

Get this book FREE!

Mail to:

Harlequin Reader Service

In the U.S.
2504 West Southern Avenue
Tempe, AZ 85282

In Canada
649 Ontario Street
Stratford, Ontario N5A 6W2

YES! I want to be one of the first to discover
Harlequin American Romance. Send me FREE and without
obligation *Twice in a Lifetime.* If you do not hear from me after I
have examined my FREE book, please send me the 4 new
Harlequin American Romances each month as soon as they
come off the presses. I understand that I will be billed only $2.25
for each book (total $9.00). There are no shipping or handling
charges. There is no minimum number of books that I have to
purchase. In fact, I may cancel this arrangement at any time.
Twice in a Lifetime is mine to keep as a FREE gift, even if I do not
buy any additional books.

Name   (please print)

Address   Apt. no.

City   State/Prov.   Zip/Postal Code

Signature (If under 18, parent or guardian must sign.)

354-RPA-2AC3